THE WEIRD SISTERS

A JIM MALHAVEN MYSTERY: BOOK 1

HELEN WHISTBERRY

CONTENTS

OTHER WORKS BY HELEN WHISTBERRY

The Jim Malhaven Mysteries series:

The Weird Sisters

The Avenging Angel

The Ghostly Groom

Take My Hand at Midnight: A Gothic Ghost Tale

Short stories in the following collections:

Creating Cinderella

Autumn Nights: 12 Chilling Tales for Midnight

Of Cottages and Cauldrons

Villainous

Duplicitous

Ravens and Roses

Autumn Nights: 10 Sinister Stories

In Somnio

*A very heartfelt thank you to
Rebecca, Carolyn, and Maready
for their invaluable and insightful advice*

Fair is foul, and foul is fair:
Hover through the fog and filthy air.

— THE THREE WITCHES, *MACBETH*

CHAPTER ONE

I'll never forget the first time I laid eyes on her. It was late in the evening, later than I meant to be. My editor at the Crier had shot me the assignment just before lunch, but you know how it is —what with one thing and another, it was well after sunset before I rattled out to the gates of the old cemetery past the outskirts of town in my trusty Studebaker Champion.

The two-door coupe was ten years-old and nothing flashy. It had a couple of hefty dents in the body, and the once-shiny black paint had been showing its age even when I splurged out all the pay I'd managed to save from the Army on it at the used car lot in town a few years back. But it ran okay and got me where I needed to be, so I had no complaints. I'd even given it a nickname, the Champ, like it was a pal of mine. There were days when it felt like my only pal—go ahead and bust out the violins as you cry a river over me.

I winced as I hauled myself out of the car, my bad leg giving me grief again. I gave it a rubdown to ease the stabbing pain as I glanced up at the words in a fancy, hard-to-read lettering that were frowning down disapprovingly at me from above the wrought-iron gates: *Wynter's Hill Cemetery*. A heavy chain and padlock barred the way.

Rattling the gates, I yelled out, "Anyone there?" half-heartedly a few times, not really expecting there would be any warm bodies inside to answer it on such a night. It was one of those cool, damp autumn ones. The kind where it felt like the sky might open up and dump buckets of rain on you at any minute, but instead, all you got was a nasty, chilly mist that tried to steal its way down into the marrow of your bones.

I pulled the collar of my old trench coat close and sunk my hands deep in the pockets, fishing around for my cigarettes and a pack of matches and coming up empty. I'd forgotten for half a sec that I'd gifted the smokes and matches to an old bum I passed on the street earlier in the day. You'd of thought I'd handed him a century note the way his face lit up, poor sap. Maybe I felt sorry for him 'cause there's been plenty of times I felt like I wasn't far off roughing it myself so I didn't regret my generosity, but I was sure missing those cigs right about now.

That tramp reminded me that I was one of the lucky ones. At least I had a job, but the salary didn't exactly turn me into a Rockefeller. The Carsworth City Crier wasn't a bad rag as local tabloids go, but it was nothing like working at one of the big papers just an hour away in old Chicago or back east in New York City, and the pay sure didn't stretch to luxuries like a nice apartment or even a new lid for the old melon.

My brown fedora was shiny and worn along the crease where I'd grabbed it to pull it off and on more times than I could count. I'd been putting off laying out the cash for a new one. I could get a decent enough hat for not so much, but I always heard my old man's voice in my head, "Go for quality over quantity, James. That's the only way you'll get ahead in life."

Pops was the only one who ever called me James. It's always been Jim or Jimmy with anyone else, but Elliot Gardiner Malhaven was a formal kind of a guy, and he didn't let down his standards, even with his only kid. He wanted me to call him E.G. like his cronies did, so I only ever called him "Pops" in my own mind—it just seemed friendlier, somehow. More like the other boys on my block. I used to envy the way they'd joke around with their fathers. Go out in the street and toss a baseball back and forth for hours.

E.G. wouldn't have been caught dead standing in the street, much less touching a baseball. No, he wasn't what you'd call a warm and cuddly personality, but he was a sharp dresser. Even when times was tough, the wife and son could go without if E.G. needed a suit or a shiny new pair of kicks. Made me mad as blazes seeing Ma go around in an old dress she'd done over half a dozen times to try and make it look new, and me with the soles of my shoes worn through so bad that I had to squelch around in wet socks on rainy days.

But it must've rubbed off on me all the same, 'cause I never can force myself to buy cheap duds, the kind I could really afford on my wages. I find myself saving up to splurge on the top of the line, or as near the top as I'll ever get. It's funny how we pick up habits like that from our folks. I wonder sometimes if parents realize their kids are like sponges, absorbing a bunch of stuff they never meant to teach them.

Kicking myself for not making it out to the boneyard before it was all buttoned up nice and tight, I was about to give up and commence the drive back into town, thinking I'd give any amount of money right then for a smoke, when a small light beyond the gates caught my eye. It was the red glow from the tip of a cigarette, taunting me in the darkness. I couldn't see who was smoking it, just a vague shape in the gloom of the night.

"Hey," I called out. "You don't happen to have another one of those on you, do you?"

The glowing light dropped to the ground and was stamped out followed by a whole lot of nothing. I thought maybe that was gonna be the end of it, but some kinda stubbornness kept me rooted to the spot. I'd come all that way for a story, and I guess I was hoping I might still find one to take back to Morty after all. He wasn't the worst boss I ever had. Tough as nails. Fair, in his way. But I knew he wasn't gonna buy my excuses for not getting on the case earlier in the day, and it wasn't the first time I'd flubbed up either, not by a long shot. I needed that gig, so I stood my ground, staring through the gates like I could will whoever was in there to give me a break.

All that quiet in such a place at night might've rattled some guys, but I'd experienced more than a lot at that point in my life. Had experiences that turned me into a hard nut to crack, so I just propped myself up against one of the big stone posts, striking a casual pose. I was startled by a light directed at my face and had to throw a hand up to shield my eyes, but not before whoever was there got a good gawk at me.

"Not much of a looker, are you?"

The voice was sultry and low, but I could tell it was a dame, something I wasn't expecting. I could make out a bit of her outline now that she was coming closer, tall and curvy, just beyond the glare from the lantern she was holding out in front of her. It was an old-fashioned looking thing, but the light was plenty strong, nearly blinding me.

"You should see the other guy," I retorted, automatically belching out the tired old line I'd used a thousand times. When you've got a mean-looking scar taking up about half the real estate on your face, you get used to the stares and the comments. I wasn't the most handsome guy to start with, but it sure didn't help none. One of my exes, bless her heart, always tried to convince me I was ruggedly good-looking. Said she liked the combo of my dark ginger hair and light gray eyes. I guess it's not something you see every day of the year, but I never thought it was enough to turn me into any kind of movie star even before I got cut.

The shapely shadow spoke again. "Why? What does he look like? The other guy?"

I was taken aback. Most people don't have the nerve to follow up on my line, and without being able to see her face, I couldn't tell how she meant it. Serious, or just trying to give me the business.

"He resembles a corpse," I replied sourly.

"Oh, did you kill him?" she cooed.

That's right, cooed. That's the only way I can describe it. There was something downright unsettling about the way she said it. Like she found the idea of me offing a guy thrilling beyond words. I wished I could see her face to get a better read on the situation, but she kept the light between us, so I couldn't get a good look in.

"Was it in the war?" she asked.

"Nope. Made it through Pearl Harbor and then all around the Pacific right through '45 without a scratch only to get jumped a couple of years after I got back stateside by some two-bit lowlife trying to get in good with his boss by bumping off the reporter who was digging a bit too hard into their racket."

"You're a reporter? That must be exciting."

She was continuing to edge closer to the gates. I thought if I could keep her talking, maybe she'd get near enough for me to see her face. And I wanted to see her face. Badly. To see if it matched that voice.

I felt like a jolt of electricity was running through me, standing there in the dark, lobbing words back and forth with that mysterious but well-formed shadow. It'd been a long time since I felt that way. Made me remember what it was like to feel young again. Really young. Like the world is your oyster and anything is still possible kind of young.

"Reporting's usually not *that* exciting, if you want to call it that," I said. "That was more of a thrilling adventure tale than I was expecting. Nowadays, I stick to more straightforward stuff. Fluff pieces. Society doings. Gossip. You know the kind of thing. The human interest beat."

"Human interest? Is that what brings you out here so late?"

"Well, I didn't set out to be this late. Got caught up with a few things and didn't arrive before now only to find out you're all locked up snug for the night. I'll admit I was feeling a bit low until you happened along."

She was close now, like she was being drawn against her will to the stranger at the gates. Don't get me wrong. I didn't mark it down to any kind of personal magnetism on my part. Something told me she was just jaded and that any novel face was welcome, even a rough mug like mine.

One long, delicate hand with rose-tipped nails reached out through the gates toward me with an offering. A gasper and a silver lighter. I thought about grabbing the hand and pulling her close, so I could finally see her face but resisted the urge. I'd found out the hard way you had to play it soft in these situations if you want to get anywhere. Strong arm tactics only take you so far.

I took the gift and lit up. I couldn't help but notice the lighter was a fancy one, engraved all over with curly lines and some initials that were rubbed away a little and hard to make out. I thought one might be a "J," but the script was hard to read, and I didn't want to look like I was studying it too closely. I got the feeling she was skittish and that it wouldn't take much to spook her. I shut the lighter with a sharp snap that sounded extra loud in the quiet of the night and handed it back to her before taking a long drag on the cigarette, savoring that lovely bitter taste and smell.

"Thanks," I said. "There's nothing like a warm smoke on a cold night, is there?"

"No, nothing at all," she agreed.

She put the lantern down on a large rock just inside the gates and bent over to shield her own cigarette from the mist while she lit it, her long hair hiding her face from my inquisitive gaze. I remember it felt to me like there was nothing more important in the world than that I should see that face, just once. She took a quick puff and turned toward me. The lantern's light fell on both of us now, and I finally got my wish.

CHAPTER TWO

It was worth the wait. Full lips painted to match her nails.
The honey-blonde hair, long and smooth, with the ends
perfectly turned under. One of those funny little short fringes of hair
like all the smart girls were sporting crowned her forehead. Only on
her, the fringe didn't look so funny. It drew attention to those eyes. It
was too dark for me to make out their exact color, but they were big
and wide open, and I noticed she had a curious habit of not blinking, at
least not so much as most folks do. It gave you the idea she was staring
at you, trying to read your mind or look into your soul. I'm not
ashamed to admit a thrill ran down my spine.

"Is that what brings you out here?" she repeated. "Human interest?
No, don't tell me. You came to see our ghost."

I chuckled. "More like to *not* see a ghost. It's just that there's been
a lot of talk around town lately, and my editor wanted me to track
down the source of the rumors."

"Don't you believe, Mr.—?" she asked, those wide eyes looking
wider than ever.

"In some kind of phantom that haunts the gates, giving the odd
casual passerby the shock of their lives? Sorry, I'm not such a sucker
as to buy that. And the name's Malhaven. Jim Malhaven."

"Pleased to meet you, Mr. Malhaven. I'm… Victoria. Victoria Jankowski."

It was a small thing, but I was used to picking up on stuff like that and couldn't help but notice the hesitation before she gave me her name. I didn't blame her. A lone woman talking to a strange man in the dark. And at the gates of a cemetery no less. I might think twice about gifting my handle, too, if I was her.

"Call me Jim… Vicky?" I guessed.

"Victoria," she said quickly. "Vicky is so common."

"Sure. Victoria it is. So, what exactly are you doing in there, Victoria?" I asked, curiosity finally overcoming me as to just what she was doing on the other side of those locked gates. "You don't live here, do you?"

"I'm the caretaker."

I think my jaw must have dropped down to my knees in surprise.

"Well, all I can say is, there's been a new line issued in graveyard custodians since the last time I checked," I said, eyeballing the elegant silk dress and soft wool coat she was wearing over top of it. I'm not exactly an expert in women's clothes, but I know fine things when I see them, and that outfit had cost a whole lot of dimes. "Aren't you supposed to be some old geezer with a spade slung over one shoulder, chewing on a pipe, maybe with a squinty eye, though that last one probably ain't mandatory."

She laughed, a soft trill of a sound like an exotic bird.

"It's 1950, you know, Jim. Times are changing. Women did lots of things during the war." There was something about the way she said *lots of things* that made me wonder what she was thinking of when she said it.

"I guess that's right," I conceded. "So, you live on the grounds?"

"There's a cottage," she said, waving off into the dark. "It's ridiculously small." She sounded dismissive. "Hardly room enough to turn around in."

"Must be lonely out here?"

"Don't you mean boring? We never see anyone but the occasional mourner and, of course, they're not much fun. And the plots are mostly full, so we don't even get a funeral very often. At least that would break up the monotony."

It sounded callous, the way she said it. Not like she was trying to make a bad joke, but more like she was personally miffed that any visitors they had weren't livelier. The funerals not more frequent. I felt myself drawing back from her for the first time since we'd met. Something she'd said caught my attention, though.

"We?" I asked.

She looked flustered for a sec before saying, "Oh, I meant the sisters, of course. The Weird Sisters."

"Weird?"

"The Wynter sisters. Ernestine, Bernadette, and Livinia. They own the cemetery and live in the old family house at the top of the hill right in the center of it all. It's a mansion, really," she said, sounding envious.

"Why do you call them the Weird Sisters?"

"Oh, I don't know. It's just what I heard someone else call them. Something to do with some play or other."

"Macbeth? The three witches? Mr. Billy Shakespeare, I do believe."

"If you say so. I'm not very interested in things like that. But they certainly are weird, so the name suits them. But don't tell them I said that," she said, looking anxious for the first time. "I shouldn't cause any trouble."

"Your secret is safe with me," I said solemnly, drawing one finger over my heart in the sign of a cross.

"Thank you. It's getting late," she said, dropping her cigarette on the ground and grinding it into the earth with one elegant, black high-heeled pump. "I'd better get back."

"Wait," I said, coming back to earth with a bump and remembering I'd got to file some kinda piece or there'd be hell to pay with Morty. "You didn't tell me about your ghost."

"Wally? You'll probably never see him if it's true what they say. He seems to appear most often to young women, although two of the Weird sisters claim to have seen him lots of times, but I think they just don't want to be left out. I don't think they even realize how *old* they are. You should see the way they dress. In all the latest styles but about forty years too young for their age."

Her mocking tone grated on me. It seemed so at odds with her angelic looks.

"My editor'll be expecting a story from me, and I can't let him down. Not if I want to hang on to my job. Can't you tell me something about this Wally?" I pleaded. "Anything?"

"Well, they say he's a young man. Handsome. Dressed all in white. Just pants and an open-collar shirt, no suit or tie. Not even a hat. They see him before dawn or after dusk, walking back and forth through the gates, and he's clutching a bundle to his chest. It's supposed to be a baby. They say he found out his wife was cheating on him and killed her and the baby, but he regrets it, so he's doomed to bring the baby to the cemetery to visit his wife's grave forever," she finished with a dramatic flourish.

She was obviously all charged up by the story, and I was struck again at the taste for the ghoulish that she displayed, but then she did spend her days surrounded by the dead. What did I expect?

"So, you ever laid eyes on him?" I asked.

"No, not yet. But I'd love to. That's why I was hanging around out here tonight. You gave me a fright for a minute when I saw you through the gates. But then I figured out you were real."

"Not handsome enough to be Wally, huh?" I said with a grin.

She smiled back teasingly. "It's not that. I just didn't think a ghost would be trying to bum a smoke."

My investigative instincts started kicking in. "So, how'd you know what he looks like? Someone must have seen him. And does anyone know who he was when he was alive and kicking? Can't be that many guys around here that offed their wife and baby. And what about that name—Wally? Don't tell me someone had the presence of mind to ask him what his name was?"

"Oh, I don't know," she said, looking nervously over her shoulder. "I really have to get back now. It's just a story."

"Wait," I said, desperate to keep her longer, find out more about the ghost. And about her.

"I'm sorry, I really have to go, but, Jim," she said, shooting me a look. "I was wrong before. You're not so bad-looking. Not bad-looking at all. Good night."

And with that she turned and ran, graceful as a gazelle, away into the night.

CHAPTER THREE

I stood there like a chump, keeping an eye on where she vanished into the dark. Like maybe I thought she'd change her mind and come back to me. Smoked the cig to the bitter end before finally giving up and starting the drive back to town. My leg was still hurting like hell. The same galoot that marked up my face made a mess of the big muscle in my left thigh before I could wrestle the knife away from him and give him what for.

I'd ended up at the hospital on the poor side of town. Found out later the doc was a rookie. Guess they gotta practice on somebody, but he did about as good a job on the leg as he did on the face, the result being a limp and a lot of pain on my worst days. A few shots of rye usually dulled the ache, but I'll be the first to admit it had messed with the old brain pan. Not to brag, but I'd always been a handy kind of guy. Big. Strong. Able to look out for myself. I guess I took it for granted. Made it through the war when lots of guys didn't. Maybe I thought I was special. I wasn't exactly a cripple now, but I didn't feel invincible like I used to, not by a long shot.

I used the bum leg as an excuse not to join in the physical culture craze, but it crossed my mind I might should get back to the boxing training I used to do to keep in fighting shape. Carsworth City could be an uncivilized place, and you never knew when you might have to stand up for yourself against some tough, particularly when you were in a line of work like mine—sticking your nose in where it don't belong.

I shot back my cuff to read the hands on my watch as I drove, worried I'd missed my deadline, but I was in luck for a change and was back uptown at the office by midnight, trying to spin out the few facts I'd gleaned into some kind of tale that might keep Morty from blowing his top. The newsroom was full of other hacks like me, trying to make the early edition, the clickity-clack-clack of all those typewriters and the shrill ring of the telephones making quite a racket, but I was so used to it, I barely even noticed.

Yanking the second page of my meager account out of the typewriter, I handed it off to one of the copy boys to take to the boss. Watched anxiously as Morty read through it in his office, standing behind the big glass window where he liked to stare out at all of us, like we were monkeys in a zoo. What was that idea some genius had? Give a thousand monkeys each a typewriter and enough time and they'd write all the plays of Shakespeare? Well, my story wasn't Shakespeare, and I knew it.

Sure enough, Morty looked up from the pages clutched in his fist and started shooting daggers at me with his squinty eyes. I knew I was for it. He saw me inspecting him and didn't have to make any signal for me to know he wanted to see me and fast. I limped into his office, putting on a bit of a show, hoping for the sympathy angle to tone down the tongue-lashing I knew I was in for, but it didn't cut any ice with him. In no time at all, I was on my way back out his door with my tail between my legs, Morty's instructions to return to Wynter's Hill first thing in the morning, only not so polite as that, ringing in my ears. A few of the guys smirked at me but some gave me the sympathetic eye. They'd all been on the receiving end themselves one time or another.

It'd been a long day, and I headed for home, if you could call the hole in the wall I rented that. I'd spent most of my savings on the Champ, so I had to economize now wherever I could. I collapsed in what passed for my comfortable chair. Poured myself a whiskey. Thought about those rose lips and that honey-colored hair and poured a few more.

Next thing I knew, sunlight was slapping me in the face, and there I was, still sprawled in the chair, in my coat and hat, feeling like I was waiting at the train station and had woke up just in time to see the caboose roaring by. Life felt like that a lot in those days. Like it was passing me by and me without a hell of a lot to show for it.

My head was pounding and felt fuzzy all at the same time. I ran my hands over the rough stubble on my face, slapping myself a few times for good measure to try and snap out of it. Forced myself to get up and shave, change into a clean shirt, tap my hair down into some kind of order.

I picked up a copy of the Crier at the corner newsstand. *Woebegone Wally: The Wraith of Wynter's Hill!* blared out the headline. Below the fold, naturally. It'd been a long time since one of my stories deserved a prime spot at the top of the front page. Had to hand it to Morty, though. He'd punched up my skimpy facts and padded it out with promises of more thrilling details to come in the next edition. Which meant I better get busy.

I stepped into the local greasy spoon for some black coffee to clear my head and a plate heaped high with eggs and bacon for the strength to go on. Then it was back to the open road for the Champ and me and the pleasant drive out into the countryside beyond the edge of town.

The cemetery gates were standing wide open this time, so I got to stroll right on in after leaving my car parked along the edge of the road. It was kinda nice in the daylight. Lots and lots of trees. Some of them had started shedding their leaves already, but there was plenty still fired up with a riot of gold and red. It was a neat place, the grounds and markers well-cared for. I was puzzled by it, I'll admit. Must have had a big gardening crew was all I could think. The gal I'd chatted with the night before didn't look like the kind that'd ever had a minute's worth of thought about hard labor in all her life.

But when I turned the corner on one of the paths, there she was, on her hands and knees, busily digging up weeds with a hand spade along the walls of a huge, white-marbled mausoleum that towered above everything else around it. Her hair was pulled back from her forehead and partly covered by a pink scarf that looked good against its golden hue. She was wearing an old pair of dungarees and a rough work shirt with the cuffs rolled up. A heavy pair of leather gloves protected those delicate hands.

I felt an electric shock run through me again like the night before as I called out to get her attention. "Victoria! We meet again. You see, I keep turning up, just like a bad penny."

She got to her feet in one quick, graceful movement, yanking the gloves off her hands and throwing them into a basket on the ground along with the spade. As I got nearer, I noticed something I hadn't the night before. A plain silver wedding band on her left ring finger. How had I missed that?

Another thing I could see now that it was full daylight, the color of her eyes. They were a steely deep blue with the barest hint of gray, and just as wide and bright as they had been the night before.

"Oh, hello, Mr.—" she hesitated.

"Malhaven. Jim. Guess I don't have the most memorable mug, huh?" I said, running one meaty thumb down the scar on my face.

"Mr. Malhaven, of course. I have a terrible memory for names. What brings you back here?"

"Our friend Wally, naturally. My editor seems to think I missed out on the full scoop from you last night. He's promised our readers all the juicy details in the next edition, so here I am to see if you remember anything else. I dare not return without something a bit more profound this time. You never met Morty, but take it from me, I don't want to leave him hanging two days in a row, or I'll be the one that's hung out to dry."

"Was it you that wrote that story in the Crier? I wish you hadn't," she said, shooting me a distinctly unfriendly look. "Now we'll have a parade of curiosity seekers up here scouting around."

"Like me?"

"I understand you're just doing your job, Mr. Malhaven, but the residents enjoy the peace and quiet around here," she said, pointing at the row upon row of tombstones. "And so do I."

"Not too boring for you then?" I said, curious at her change of attitude. "And last night it was Jim."

"That was last night," she said coolly.

Her friendly attitude from when I first met her had vanished completely. Maybe she was regretting being too forward with a stranger in the dark now that it was the cold light of day. Or maybe she was just getting a clearer look at my mangled features than she had the night before. I didn't blame her if it was putting her off. It put me off when I caught sight of it in a mirror.

"Look, Victoria—"

She set me straight plenty quick. "I prefer Mrs. Jankowski, if you don't mind. And I don't have anything more to say about ghosts. There is no such thing, as I think you well know. Any other reporter would have picked up on the fact that I was joking last night. Any competent reporter, that is."

Cold as ice. Lucky for me I'd developed a thick layer of skin for that kind of thing. "Mrs. Jankowski, then. Maybe I could talk to Mr. Jankowski about Wally if you aren't so interested in conversing with me no more?"

"That would be a very neat trick," she said, her pale skin reddening up. "Lukasz died. In the war."

Something about the way she spit it out struck me to the heart. Like the wound was still so fresh for her that she could hardly bring herself to say the words out loud. And the way she pronounced his name in the Polish way, with that soft "w" sound at the beginning and drawing out the "s" sound at the end of his name, like it was a caress. It made me drop the wise guy routine for half a minute.

"I'm sorry to hear that," I muttered. "A lot of guys I served with didn't make it back either. That's tough."

"Life goes on," she said with a shrug, though something about the way she said *that* made me think maybe it hadn't. Not for her.

She continued, impatience dripping from that smoky voice of hers.

"The whole story's just a creepy old wives' tale that people like to share around the campfire to get a cheap thrill. There's nothing more to it than that, but if you're determined to talk to someone about it," she said, reaching out to take my arm and pull me around to face the opposite way I'd been standing. "Go up there and talk to the original old wives."

CHAPTER FOUR

She aimed me in the direction of a mansion on the top of the hill that stood right in the center of the cemetery. I'd been so taken up with the vision that was her, I hadn't paid it any mind before, but it was hard to miss—a huge, gray stone place, gloomy, like those haunted houses in the old horror films I used to sneak into the movie palace to see when I was a kid. Something about the layout of the windows and the big, double-doored entrance reminded me of a Jack-o'-lantern with an evil, grinning face. I'm not a fanciful kind of a guy usually, but it did give me the creeps, even seeing it there in the bright light of day.

"To be accurate," Victoria amended, "they aren't old wives. They're old maids, instead, but two of the Wynter sisters are true believers in the ghost, and they love telling people all about it. I'm sure they'd like nothing more than a visit from you, Mr. Malhaven."

She was making no secret of the fact that what she'd like nothing more of was to see the back of Jim Malhaven. I know how to take a hint, so I obliged her after a quick tip of the hat. It meant some uphill hiking for me, winding my way between the headstones, superstitious despite myself about walking over a grave if I could help it. The house was crowded in by rosebushes on the sides that got sun, with scraggly lawn filling in the rest of the yard. I searched in vain for a ringer to push when I reached the big front doors and finally settled for picking up and dropping one of the giant doorknockers I'd assumed was just for decoration when I first walked up.

After a few minutes, the door was pried open by a spare-looking gent in a motheaten black suit. I stated my business in my rapid-fire way. It seemed to take him a minute to catch up with me, but then he gave me the nod and let me in, indicating with the wave of a bony hand that I was to wait in one of the stiff-looking chairs in the colossal front hall. Was it weird that he never spoke a word? Not at all. Perfectly normal stuff, right?

I was still there a half an hour later—at least I'm pretty sure it was a half hour even though I only looked at my watch every thirty seconds to check, so who's to say?—when the front door creaked open and a rather meek-looking old dear wandered in. Her clothes looked pricey and new, but her silver hair was escaping from its pins and netting, giving her a wild appearance that was helped along by the stray twig that seemed to be growing straight out the top of her head.

"Why, hello! Whoever can you be?" she said as she caught sight of me. She cocked her head to one side like a curious bird and seemed to be giving me the once over with all the delight of a butterfly collector examining their latest victim spiked on a pin as she offered her hand.

Ever the gentleman, I stood and reached out my own for a friendly shake. "Jim Malhaven, ma'am. From the Carsworth City Crier."

She took my outstretched paw with both hands, holding on to it with surprising strength for such a small dame. The top of her head, twig and all, barely reached my shoulder.

"From the newspaper? How positively thrilling! Whatever brings you here?"

"Your ghost, ma'am."

"Wally? How lovely! I've tried for years to get someone to take an interest in him, but you'd be surprised how many non-believers there are in the world, young man. We've even been mentioned in the paper a few times, but it always seems to fizzle out. Come with me, come with me," she cried, dragging me in her wake. "We must find Bernie.

My sister, you know. Oh, how rude. I didn't introduce myself, did I? I'm Ernie Wynter."

"Pleased to meet—"

I didn't get a chance to complete my profound thought before she started calling out in a weak voice, all trembly with excitement, "Bernie! Bernie!"

Another old dear popped out of one of the many doors lining the grand hallway like some kind of life-size Jack-in-the-box. She was no taller than her sister and a touch plumper, but her hair was tidied up better. She seemed no less eager to meet me than the first one had been.

"Who is he, my dear?" she asked, circling and looking me up and down in a way that made me feel like that specimen in a glass case all over again.

"He's a *reporter*! From the *Crier*! I forget his name, but he's come about Wally!"

"Wonderful! And isn't it fortunate for us that Livinia is away on business today? We have him all to ourselves."

This one grabbed my other mitt, and before I knew it, I was being hauled into some kind of sitting room. It was brighter than what I'd seen of the rest of the house, done up in pale colors, with big jars of roses sitting on almost every surface giving off a perfume so strong, it made me feel queasy. They plunked me down on a miniature yellow sofa then hopped into two huge, pink velvet-covered club chairs across from me, looking like dolls in the oversized seats, their feet not even scraping an acquaintance with the crazily flowered carpet.

The one with the twig in her hair pushed a small electric buzzer on the table by her side. In what seemed like no time, like he'd been camped just outside the door, the skinny guy who'd left me cooling my heels in the hall like a chump came in and bowed slightly in the direction of the ladies.

Bernie took charge. "Oh, Cressley, there you are. Tea, please, for our guest."

I wanted to protest, tea not being my beverage of choice, but he was gone too swift. The sisters turned their attention back to me, watching me expectantly, like I was gonna pull a bunny rabbit outta my hat or something. I decided it was time to regain some control over the situation.

"Like I said, ladies, I'm from the Crier. Malhaven's the name. We ran a story about your ghost, and our readers are clamoring for more," I asserted confidently.

Ernie tilted toward her sister in excitement. "I always told you, didn't I, Bernie? That one day he'd be famous, if we were just patient. Our very own Wally."

"*Your* Wally?" I asked.

"Well, I guess he belongs to Wynter's Hill, really. But we've lived with him for so long, we've come to think of him as our very own."

"I see," I said, although I didn't one bit. "And how long have you, um… lived with him?"

"Oh, Bernie tells the story so much better than I do. You tell him, Bernie."

"Well, it all started in '21, didn't it, Ernie? Or was it '22? Anyway, it was the *Jazz Age*, you know. All that wild music. Some women got *ideas* and started playing it fast and loose, didn't they? Wally was a milkman. That's why he's dressed all in white, you see. And he came home early from his rounds one morning and walked in on his wife *with another man!*" she hissed at me, giving me a knowing look. "He killed them both, and the baby wouldn't stop crying, so he killed it, too. They executed him for his crimes. He must have been *mad*, of course, but that woman got no more than she deserved. Although we do feel *terrible* about the baby, poor little innocent."

"And where did all this happen? Does Wally have a last name?"

"Oh, I don't think I remember. Do you, Ernie?"

"I don't think it was in Carsworth City but somewhere nearby, wasn't it? Like over in Farrelburg, maybe? And I don't remember his last name, but Wally is definitely his first name."

The sisters bobbed their heads at each other and then at me in vigorous agreement.

"And then it started a year or two later, didn't it? The *sightings*, you know," said Ernie. "I was the very first to see him. I was taking the air around the cemetery. There weren't so many residents then, and it was quite a pleasant walk in the evenings. And I got to the gates, and *there he was*! Walking in and out, in and out, and with that little baby in his arms all swaddled up like a package. He was *terribly* handsome. Light hair, you know."

"No, Ernie, he has dark hair."

"Now, don't start that again with me, Bernie. I know what I saw."

"Well, I know what I saw, and he definitely has dark hair."

"So, you saw him too, ma'am?" I asked Bernie, pulling out my notebook and starting to jot down some facts with the stub of a pencil.

"Yes, many times. We both have. But we never can agree on his hair color. Isn't that odd? It's not like a ghost is going to dye his hair, is it?"

"Doesn't seem likely," I agreed. "But I don't understand. If all this happened over in some place like Farrelburg, why does he haunt the cemetery here?"

"Why, this is where his wife is buried, of course, so he comes here to visit her and try and make amends," said Ernie.

"Do you know which grave is hers?"

"Oh, there's so many, who can tell?"

"Who can tell?" I repeated, bumfuzzled at their jumps between cast-iron facts and dizzy vagueness.

"We have kept an eye out for it, of course," said Bernie. "But it would be impossible to research all of the graves. There are just too many. And then there's the paupers' section in the northwest corner, all with unmarked graves, poor things. I wouldn't be surprised at all if she ended up there. It's too bad he doesn't actually come all the way into the grounds to visit her grave, isn't it? Then we could follow him and find out which one it is. I don't like to think that such a wicked woman is buried in our cemetery. Why, we could even relocate her if we could find it."

"Oh, no, Bernie," Ernie cried in dismay. "Then he might go away and never come back!"

"Yes, you're right. I hadn't thought of that," Bernie said. "I guess we'll have to keep her after all."

"But I don't understand," I said, trying to bring them back to the problem at hand. I heard the door start to open behind me, but figured it was that Cressley guy bringing in the tea. "Where did you very first hear about Wally? Was there a story in the newspaper? Did someone tell you about the murders?"

The door slammed shut with an almighty bang, causing us all to jump, even your humble reporter, and was followed by a deep voice drenched in contempt: "Murders? There were no murders. They made the whole thing up!"

CHAPTER FIVE

The sisters nearly fell from their chairs at this sour accusation, gasping and reaching out to grab each other's hands before breathing a single word in unison: "Livinia!"

I turned around in time to see a tall, hawk-like female glaring down at us in disapproval. Like her sisters, she was dressed in expensive duds, but she wore them a whole lot better, having the shape and the height to carry it off. Her hair was black with only faint hints of silver starting to show along her temples. She seemed so unlike her sisters that she might as well have dropped in on us from the moon.

"Ernestine Wynter! What on earth is that in your hair? Go upstairs this instant and tidy yourself."

Ernie turned as white as a bowl of milk. She reached up a shaky hand and, encountering the twig on her head, beetled out, giving Livinia a wide miss on her way. Bernie stood her ground but started wringing her hands and halfway bowing before her towering sister in such a cringing way that it got me riled up somehow.

"Why, Livinia, we thought you were going to be at the lawyer's office all morning."

"My business didn't take as long as I had anticipated. I suppose this is what you and Ernestine do when you know I'll be away. Take advantage of my absence to invite strange men into the house?"

"Oh, no, Livinia," Bernie cried. "We didn't invite him. He just… he just appeared!"

"I see. Another ghostly apparition, perhaps?"

I decided it couldn't hurt to insert myself into the scene at this point. "No, ma'am. A reporter."

"A *reporter*?" She spit out the word the way me or you might say something like "cockroach," for instance. "We have nothing to say to any member of the press."

"But, Livinia," Bernie wailed. "He's going to write a story about Wally."

"I expect him to do no such thing. That's more than enough of your nonsense, Bernadette. Run along upstairs and help your sister make herself presentable."

Bernie tried out something that looked an awful lot like one of those curtsies you see ladies giving the head honcho over in England and backed out the door, coming within a cat's whisker of colliding with Cressley, who was steering one of those tea trolley things that I thought only existed in the movies, but maybe I just don't run in the right kind of circles. Old Livinia looked more put out than ever when she caught sight of him. I thought she was gonna send him away with a flea in his ear, but she gave in with what I would describe as a sigh with an awful lot of feeling behind it.

"I suppose you may as well serve, Cressley, since you went to so much trouble."

She sat herself down in one of the chairs, and I have to say, she had some style. Sat there with her legs together off to one side, hands resting on her lap, and her back ramrod straight like they teach the girls in those finishing schools. Reform schools, too, sometimes. The better ones anyway.

The guy poured out a cup for each of us and balanced some kind of silly-looking sweet on a plate, then disappeared out the door as silent as ever.

"Don't he ever say nothing?" I ventured as an ice-breaking gambit.

"Cressley is mute. An unfortunate accident," she replied shortly.

"That's too bad. Say, you're kind of a peach to give him a berth here. Not everyone would take a chance on a gimp like that."

She looked at me then as though more disillusioned than she would ever have thought it possible to be with a person, and I gotta admit, I was having a bit of fun trying to get a rise out of her. Something about those snooty types makes me want to get their goat if I can figure out a way to do it.

"Cressley is very efficient at his work. Talking is not necessary."

I detected that last bit was directed at me, but I'm not easily discouraged.

"So, what did you mean when you said they made it all up?"

"I'm afraid you're wasting your time, Mr.—" She raised one eyebrow at me in what was meant to be a terribly superior way, no doubt, but like I said, I'm not so easily discouraged.

"Malhaven is my byline," I said, all devil-may-care, like I hadn't a worry in the world. "On the ghost beat for the Crier."

"You're wasting your time, Mr. Mal-*vern*," she said, twisting up my name on purpose, I would have bet. "My sisters have lived a very cloistered life. I'm afraid it has encouraged their imaginations to run wild. They've been telling this absurd story for more years than I can count, but there are no facts whatsoever to back it up."

"Hm, that's a kicker, 'cause there's been a lot of buzz around town about it lately. What do you make of that?"

"I can only suppose it was that *girl*," she sneered.

"Girl? What's this? First I heard of it."

"Some teenager. Said she saw something at the gates one night around midnight. And what she was doing out at that time of night alone, I'm sure we can both imagine."

"Can we?"

"Coming or going to some *assignation,* one would assume," old Liv said with a sniff. I had to hand it to her. She had that whole haughty grand dame stuff down pretty good.

"This girl got a name? Maybe I can get an exclusive direct from the horse's mouth."

"I don't believe I ever heard it. If I did, I don't remember. You must take my word for it that there is absolutely nothing at all to this story and not pursue it any further. As I said, you would only be wasting your time," she repeated, rising to her feet in an invitation to scram that was impossible even for a hard case like me to ignore.

"If it's just the same to you, in my line of work we kinda like to find stuff out for ourselves, and I got plenty of time to waste. Thanks for the hot tip, though!" And with that parting shot, I was up and out the door before she had a chance to devastate me with another one of those looks. There's only so much of that a guy wants to take on any given day.

Cressley caught up with me in the hall and escorted me out. I must've been feeling kinda low about that cheap crack I'd made about him earlier, just trying to make Liv blow her top, 'cause I had an impulse to shake his hand, if nothing else, for putting up with that hell-hound of a boss. I stuck out a paw, and to my surprise, he grabbed it and gave it a hearty shake, giving me a gold-plated, A-1 wink for good measure, one gimp to another. I decided right then and there that guy was all right.

"Good man, Mr. Cressley," I said. "Good man."

I tipped my hat to him in a final salute before sailing out the door, jazzed up to finally have what might be a solid lead for a change. Chasing Wally so far had been like chasing, well, a ghost, I guess you could say.

I wandered back down the hill, surprised to find Mrs. J still weeding. It felt like years had passed to me, but I guess it'd been less than an hour all told 'cause Liv had cut my visit as short as she knew how. The weeds were all gone from three sides of the crypt now, and I had a good view of it, walking down the hill. It was fancy, that's for sure. White marble. Made to look like one of those Greek temples you see in picture books. All I could think was that someone must have thought an awful lot of themselves to build a final resting place like that. It looked nicer than my joint. Maybe I could move in.

"You survived the experience, I see," Victoria said as she stood up, arching her back like she was feeling all that bending over and taking a seat on a nearby bench.

I took up some of the real estate next to her, saying, "Yeah, you were right about what you said last night. They are kinda weird."

"They're not weird!" She stopped short. Must have seen my slack-jawed look of confusion. "That is, what I should have said is that they're a little eccentric, but harmless."

"Harmless?" I had to guffaw at that one. "You have met old Liv, haven't you?"

That made her smile. It was a nice one, genuine. "Livinia does have a stronger personality than her sisters."

"You can say that again. In spades. But it was worth the trip. She let slip a hot lead for me to follow. Can you tell me anything about this teenage girl? Claims to have seen something?"

The smile was gone now. I missed it already. In its place, a furrow of worry that I didn't like so much marred her smooth brow. "Margo Cummings? She's a nice enough girl but a bit flighty. Probably just saw a deliveryman and is trying to make a song and dance out of it to get some attention."

"Deliveries at midnight?" I said skeptically, noting down the name in my book.

"Oh, like as not you'll find she was confused about the time. She's seventeen—you know how girls that age are. They like to get themselves worked up over the least little thing. But I'm sure she'd love to talk to a real reporter. That'll be a bigger thrill than any ghost. I know her family. Here," she said, taking the pencil and notebook from my hand. "I'll write down the address for you."

I am happy to report she had excellent penmanship; I had no trouble making out the location of my star witness.

"I owe you one," I thanked her, noticing she was looking droopy and washed out. "Want any help with the gardening?" I offered, ever helpful.

"No, thank you. I'll finish it later."

"That's quite an eternal resting place someone's got," I observed, pointing out the over-the-top joint in front of us. "What kind of a swell is stowed away in there?"

"The biggest one around here. William Wallace Wynter."

CHAPTER SIX

"You're kidding with me. Any relation?"

"Their father. The rumor is he made a lot of money peddling alcohol during Prohibition. But he became more or less of a legitimate businessman later in life. He died in '41 but left his girls well-provided for, apparently. They've never had to work as far as I know."

She didn't say it bitter. Just matter of fact, like those were the breaks. Some of us poor saps had to pound the pavement all our lives to put a morsel of bread on the table while others were born with that old silver spoon in their mouths.

"You did say one of his names was 'Wallace,' didn't you? Wally's a not uncommon label for that moniker. Quite a coincidence, wouldn't you say? Liv seemed awful keen on convincing me her sisters had fixed up this whole ghost gag. Maybe they lack for imagination. Used their pop's own name."

"I don't know. They swear it's true, and there've been a few others who said they've seen him over the years. I've lived here for ten years, though, and I've never seen a thing. But like I said before, I don't believe in spirits, so maybe they don't believe in me," she said lightly. "At any rate, I doubt very much that anyone ever called Mr. Wynter

'Wally' in his life. If you think Livinia has a daunting personality, well, let's just say she takes after her father."

"You met him?"

"Yes," she admitted, kinda reluctant-like. She was getting restless on the bench now. Fidgety. Like she wasn't comfortable with my sparkling repartee, but I was determined to get more information out of her while I had her going. Besides, I liked looking at her and listening to that low, cool voice. There was something pretty special about her. Mr. Jankowski had been a very lucky man. Until he wasn't.

"Lukasz and I moved here in 1940 when he got the job as caretaker. I only spoke to Mr. Wynter a few times and that was fine by me. He was… intimidating. My husband joined the Navy after Pearl Harbor. Mr. Wynter was gone by then, but his daughters were kind enough to let me stay on."

"Kind? Liv?"

She smiled again. I liked seeing it. Wondered if I could keep coming up with the sort of patter that would keep it shining.

"Well, it was really Ernie and Bernie, I think. They're sweet. They convinced Mr. Monroe. He's the family lawyer. Lukasz was doing some odd jobs around the building where the law offices are in town. Mr. Monroe seemed to take a liking to him and offered him this job when he found out we were getting married. I guess he thought a married man would be more reliable. Anyway, Ernie and Bernie convinced Mr. Monroe, over Livinia's objections, I would imagine, to let me take Lukasz's place when he enlisted. I think it turned out just as well for them, though. So many men were called up, they would have had a hard time finding anyone reliable during the war."

"The war's over now."

"Yes," she said. "It's over now."

And the way she said it, you could tell she wasn't just thinking about the war.

"But you're still here," was my next astute observation.

"Oh, I guess they're used to me now. Three spinsters of a certain age. Maybe they feel more comfortable having another woman around the place. I have extra help, of course. It's more than I could do on my own. But for day-to-day maintenance, helping visitors, keeping an eye on the place, that kind of thing, I do all right."

"But what's in it for you? Buried out in the middle of nowhere like this."

"Not buried," she said with that trilling laugh I remembered from the night before. "Not yet."

She paused like she was choosing her next words with care, turning her head away from me so that I couldn't catch her expression.

"Lukasz and I started out our life here just after we were married. It's the only home we ever had together. For a long time, it made me feel closer to him, being here. Then the years pass, and it just becomes a habit, I guess. Hey," she said, turning back to me with a surprised look on her face. "I think I misjudged you. You're actually pretty good at your job, aren't you? Getting people to tell you things?"

She said it like it was a joke, but I knew she'd reached that point most people I talked to did sooner or later. Where they feel like they've told me way too much even if I feel like they haven't spilled nearly enough. I'd learned it was no use pushing folks once they reached their limit, though. Besides, I'd gotten more out of her than I expected.

You might be asking what it all had to do with the ghost, and I could try to spin you a line about how gathering background was fundamental for any good newspaper story. But deep down, I knew at some point I'd crossed the line from being a hard-nosed reporter to just being a guy who's sitting on a bench in the sun beside a lovely girl and who suddenly discovers he has a yearning to find out everything she's ever said or done or thought.

It was my turn to be fidgety now as she stared at me with those steely-blue eyes. I didn't seem to know what to do with my hands. I'd bought some more smokes, but I'd left the pack in the car back at the gates.

"You don't happen to have another cigarette you could lend me like you was kind enough to do last night?" I said in an attempt to hang on to her attention for just one more minute even.

"No, I don't smoke," she said before correcting herself. "Not while I'm working that is. The sisters are very old-fashioned. They don't approve of women smoking." She stood up and held out her hand, which I was more than happy to take. "I'd better let you get on with your day. Don't you need to follow up on that hot lead?"

"That's right," I said, hanging on to her delicate hand with my big one for as long as seemed polite before reluctantly letting it go. "Thanks for that address, Mrs. Jankowski. Maybe I'll be able to hang on to my job one more day if I can squeeze any more dope about this Wally character out of Margo Cummings."

"I wouldn't squeeze too hard," she said, flashing me one more of those dazzlers.

"What is she?" I said. "An overripe banana?"

"You'll see," she replied. "Contrary to the act you put on, I begin to suspect you're not a fool."

"You've seen through my disguise," I replied with a grin before remembering how it made my scar scrunch up in a way that had been known to scare babies. It was funny. I'd forgotten all about it while I was talking to her. I was usually self-conscious with dames, but she had a way about her of gazing at you, honest and straight. She never gave me not even one of those looks like most people do. Looks like, what the hell happened to you and why you got to show it off to the rest of us? Maybe she'd had time to get used to the damage the night before.

"I might have gotten a glimpse of something deeper," she agreed. "Good luck to you, Mr. Malhaven, but I think you'll find there's really nothing much to this ghost tale. I'm afraid this story doesn't have legs. Isn't that what you say in the newspaper business?"

"That's right," I said approvingly, stupidly pleased that she knew some of the lingo.

"So, I guess you probably won't need to come here again," she said. I wished I could tell if she was glad or sad at the notion. She was giving nothing away.

"Oh, I don't know. I might turn up. Those Wynter sisters were something else again. Might be a good line I could take there. That's one of my specialties. Spinning gold out of straw. Like that fella in the bedtime story."

"Rumpelstiltskin?"

"That's the one. Quite a mouthful, ain't it?"

"It is," she agreed. "But be careful. In the end, he got in quite a lot of trouble spinning his gold."

"Maybe he was a fool. I think we have just established that maybe I'm not."

"I hope not, Mr. Malhaven. I sincerely hope not."

And with that she was gone again. She had a way of slinking off, even in broad daylight, like a puff of smoke, or like she was a wraith herself. I didn't mind too much. She'd given me lots to think about as I headed over to the address she'd gifted me. I found myself turning over all the things she'd said in my mind, enjoying the memory of her voice and those prize-winning smiles.

All in all, it put more than a little kick in my step, and in no time, I found myself standing on the stoop of a brownstone in one of those sections of town where people were either on their way up or on their way down. I wondered which direction the Cummings family was going as I rang the bell.

There was the sound of a rumpus from inside the house that I put down to a herd of wild horses galloping down the hall stairs before the door was flung open by a motley crew of urchins that looked to be anywhere from seven or eight years old to the oldest one, an attractive brunette who I took to be my star witness. The brunette took one look at my mug, screamed and fainted dead away.

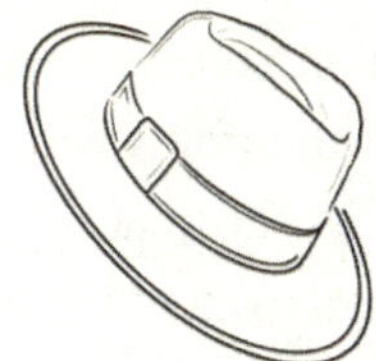

CHAPTER SEVEN

The other kids fluttered away from her like dry leaves in a gusty wind, making no attempt to catch her or even break her fall. I'll admit it was one of those rare occasions on which I found myself caught up short. I knew I wasn't about to win any beauty prizes, but I can't say I'd ever had quite that effect on another individual before, not within a half a second of meeting them anyways.

"Don't mind Margo, mister." It was one of the younger boys, tugging at my coat sleeve. He was tow-headed and fresh-faced but for a shiner darkening one of his bright blue eyes. "She's always fainting. She read about it in a book once."

"That's right," another one chimed in with corroborating evidence for the prosecution. This one was a girl, looked to be about twelve-years-old. Just the age to have lost any awe she might ever have had of a big sister. "She thinks it makes her *interesting*." Picture much eye rolling and stink face to accompany this last statement.

"I got you," I said. "Your parents at home?"

"No, they went to the movies. Margo's supposed to be watching us." This from another boy.

I took a quick head count. Seven of 'em, if you included Margo, who was still stretched out in a poetical fashion on the ground. I got to admit, she looked kinda cute, like she'd practiced it a time or two. She'd managed to fall so that her skirt flowed gracefully around her, and she had one arm draped dramatically against her forehead. Sarah Bernhardt had nothing on this kid.

"Okay," I said, flinging my topper at the boy with the busted headlight. "Hold on to this for me."

He caught it and promptly slammed my lid down on to his own gourd to the delight of his brothers and sisters who howled with glee when it swallowed up half his face, hiding the damaged peeper from view. I swallowed down a sigh. Dealing with infants was not my strong suit. I stepped into the hallway carefully to avoid treading on the prone figure of Our Lady of Tragedy and then leaned over and gathered her up in my arms. She was a lightweight, but there was a chorus of "oohs" and "aahs" from the peanut gallery, as if they had just witnessed a strong man act at the carnival.

"Which way?" I inquired.

They took off like a demented horde down the hallway and through an open door which I discovered led to a large living room filled to the brim with overstuffed sofas and chairs. Guess they needed a lot of seating for that crowd. I lay my burden down on a sofa, then took a seat in one of the chairs more or less opposite, so I could get a good view of the show. The kids spread themselves around to various points about the room where they could all get a good gawk at me. We didn't have too long to wait for the next act.

"Oh, my!" Margo rose into an artful, seated position, arranging her skirts just so and checking that her hair wasn't doing anything too terrible. "Oh, my, you must excuse me. It must have been the shock of… of seeing a stranger at the door so unexpectedly."

"Ma said we shouldn't let strangers in the house," piped up the joker who still had my hat. He was sitting near me and twirling it madly on one finger now. "They might be gonna murder us. Are you gonna murder us, mister? You look like a gangster. What happened to your face? Did somebody cut you? Is that how you got that scar? Why'd they do that to you, huh?"

I leaned over and snatched my fedora from him. "Because I asked too many questions," I said, trying to give him a friendly tip, but he was one of those remorseless types.

"What kinda questions? Something you shouldn't of? Why not? Was it a secret?"

"Michael," Margo intervened, "that is quite enough."

"Aw, come on, Margo, you know it's Mikey. Why you always got to put on airs? That's what Ma says. That you put on airs. Don't you think she's putting on airs?" he said, turning back to me, man to man, you know.

Little Margo was having none of it. "I'll tell Pa if you don't pipe down!" she screeched.

Greatly to my relief, Mikey sunk back in his chair looking surly as a bear but shutting his trap. I hadn't met Mr. Cummings yet, but I was ready to shake his hand if he could have that kind of effect on a juvenile delinquent without even being in the house.

"Please excuse my brother. He has a lot to learn about manners. We haven't been properly introduced," she added with what I guess you might call a fetching look. "I'm Margo Cummings."

"Jim Malhaven. From the Crier."

That caused a bit of a stir, but I had to hand it to Margo. She sent a quelling look around the room and everyone lay low.

"The newspaper?" she asked. "But whatever are you doing here? This isn't about my *adventure*, is it?"

I caught sight of the twelve-year-old girl as Margo was talking. Her eyes were rolling so hard, I was sure they were gonna pop right out of her head and land on the floor like a couple of marbles.

Repressing a grin, I answered Margo's inquiry. "I was told you might be able to give me an eyewitness account of this phantom up at Wynter's Hill Cemetery. Wally, they call him."

Unfortunately, that got a rise out of the spectators. A bunch of them started chanting "Woebegone Wally" at the top of their lungs, the boys jumping up to commence a kind of a war dance in the center of the room. I guessed that meant they could read at least. Must've seen the story in the morning edition. I'd have to tell Morty his moniker for the ghost had caught fire. He'd get a jolt out of that. However, for the present, all that hollering was getting on my nerves.

"SHUT IT!" I roared, rising up to my full 6'4" stretch and making as fierce a face as I knew how. And when you got a kisser like mine, that's no joke.

Silence descended, broken only by the sobbing of a slip of a girl I hadn't noticed before. She couldn't have been more than two or three years of age and was looking at me as though she had seen the Devil himself rising up through the floorboards to carry them all away. Feeling ashamed of myself for pulling the tough guy routine on a pack of innocents, I dug in my pocket and came up with a crumpled five-spot which I offered to the imp with the blackened eye. It was overly generous, but I figured I could claim it as expenses at the paper.

"Tell you what. Here's a fin for you all to share if you'll give me and your big sis a few minutes alone."

The fiver was ripped outta my hands by the twelve-year-old who I'd come to think of as the brains of the outfit. She picked up the bawling tot and started herding the others out the door, not above landing a kick here and there on one of the boys if she caught them dragging their feet. Blissful peace followed. Best money I ever spent.

I lowered myself back into my seat. Margo was staring at me warily as though a wild beast had appeared in the living room unexpectedly. I rearranged my features into as agreeable an appearance as was possible under the circumstances and attempted to smooth the waters.

"Quite a lively bunch," I said, with what I hoped was a sympathetic expression.

"They are terribly uncivilized," Margo agreed. "I complain about it to my parents all the time. I've told them I'm so ashamed to have any of my friends over here that I have to go visit them at their homes instead."

"Is that where you were? The night you saw Wally?" I asked, not sure if this would be a touchy subject, but she was obviously champing at the bit to give me the straight dope now that we had dispensed with the hecklers. She jumped in with both feet, and we were off to the races.

"Yes! I had gone to visit my friend Sally Perkins, to spend the night with her. They live on a kind of a farm outside of town, only very genteel, you know. My father dropped me off, and the arrangement was he would pick me up in the morning after breakfast. Only Sally got terribly ill sometime after we'd gone to bed. It must have been something she ate, though the rest of us were just fine. Her mother had her hands full taking care of her, so Sally's brother, Adam, offered to bring me back home. I didn't think anything of it because he'd always seemed like a perfectly nice boy. We telephoned to my parents to let them know I'd be coming home early, and my father offered to drive over and meet us at the edge of town, so Adam wouldn't have to drive all the way in."

I had a pretty good idea at this point of where we were headed so I wasn't exactly floored by her next disclosure.

"And would you believe, on the drive back, that boy got fresh with me! He pulled the car over to the side of the road and tried to kiss me. I slapped him. Hard. I jumped out of the car, and he tried to follow me, but I told him my father would give him such a beating if he didn't leave me alone, and he must have believed me because he drove off and left me all alone to walk home in the dark!" she finished wrathfully.

"That was mighty brave of you," I said admiringly. "You must have a lot of gumption."

"Well, I guess I know how to take care of myself," she said, preening a bit. "It was awfully dark, but we'd ridden a long way already, so I figured it couldn't be too much farther. I followed the road, and it was only a few minutes before I saw the cemetery up ahead. I was relieved because I knew it was only a few miles from there to where my father said he'd meet us and that didn't seem so bad."

"Things were looking up for you then?" I threw in by way of showing an interest.

"Yes, until I got closer. That's when I saw... *him*!"

CHAPTER EIGHT

At this point, she kinda collapsed back against the sofa cushions, and I thought maybe I'd lost her again, but she was too fired up with her moment of glory to waste a lot of time with that whole swooning act and quickly sat up, watching me keenly. I'm wise to what's expected in these types of conversations.

"That's something, ain't it!" I said, as though thrilled to bits by her chilling revelation. "And you all alone out there! Whatever did you do?"

I thought maybe I'd overplayed my hand, but she ate it up. "I didn't know what to do! I thought at first it was a man, a real one, you know, and after my previous experience, I didn't want to take any chances, so I ducked behind some trees across the road and watched him for a while."

"And what was he up to?"

"It was hard to see from where I was, but he looked like he was going in and out of the gates. He was carrying something clutched to his chest, and he would disappear for a while then reappear. I was worried because I knew my father would be waiting for me, but I was too scared to go past while the man was still there."

"So, what happened next?"

"I decided to start edging along the road, keeping behind the trees, when all of the sudden he looked toward me!" she said, her eyes getting wide. "And that's when I remembered that story. The one about Wally. Some of the kids I know had told me about it. And I thought, *that's him*!"

"And?" I prompted, starting to get interested.

"And… I fainted dead away."

"You fainted?" I asked, like I found it hard to believe she would do such a thing, it being so unlike her.

She nodded. "Just fainted dead away. And when I came to, he was gone."

"I see," I said, trying for a thoughtful air so as not to let on just how underwhelmed I was by this yarn. "He was… just gone?"

"Yes. I don't know how long I was unconscious, but I got to my feet and looked across to the gates and there was no one there. I waited a few minutes to make sure, then I started running toward town. I couldn't keep that up long because I had my new shoes on that I got for my birthday, and they were a little tight and rubbing at my heels, but I hurried as much as I could. I knew my father would be worried about me, and in fact, I met him along the road. He'd gotten tired of waiting and had started driving out to meet us. I looked at my watch in the headlights to see how late it was, and it was *just past midnight*!"

It must have been obvious that I did not properly grasp the importance of this fact 'cause she rushed to illuminate matters for me.

"That's the witching hour, you know. When sorcerers work their dark magic, and spirits are at liberty to rise from their graves and walk among us here on earth," she said impressively.

"I see," I said again. I went for the wise old owl effect this time though. It's always fun to see how many different ways I can say the exact same words in a conversation. You should try it sometime just for kicks.

"Father was terribly upset about what Sally's brother had done, but do you know, he didn't believe me about the ghost. Not one bit. I wanted him to drive me back to the gates, so we could see if it had come back, but he said it was far too late to be out already and that

Mother would be worried sick about us, so we came straight home instead."

What I had started realizing right about now was, there was not much meat to this tale. I felt for the girl and all, being left out on a country lane by herself in the dark by that young nogoodnik, but I must admit I'd been hoping for something a bit punchier for the next edition. I comforted myself with the notion that maybe I could uncover some startling details by expert cross-examination.

"So, can you describe him for me? Short? Tall? Hair color? How was he dressed?"

"Gosh, I was so far away, it's hard to say. He didn't have a hat on. I'm sure about that, but I don't know that I could say for sure what his hair color was. It was so dark out. His clothes weren't too dark, I don't think, or I wouldn't have been able to see him. No coat or suit jacket that I recall, but it's hard to say. I was all alone and so frightened and then fainting like that. I don't think anyone could be expected to have remembered much after that," she said, giving me a bit of the evil eye.

"Of course not," I chimed in quick, not wanting to get her riled up or accidentally trigger another collapse. "So, is there anything else you can tell me about what happened?"

"Only that Father went over to Sally's the next day and would have given her brother a lesson he wouldn't soon forget, except Sally's father calmed him down and promised to punish the boy instead," she added, sounding disappointed that vigilante justice had not prevailed.

And with that last fascinating nugget, I decided I'd have to be satisfied. I'd been noticing the buildup of sound just beyond the door and had a feeling my fiver only bought us so much time, and we might be nearing the limit. Sure enough, the door bust open, and we was overrun with Cummings of every size and description again.

Mikey made a beeline for me with a look in his one undamaged eye that boded nothing good. "Hey, mister, did Margo tell you about seeing Wally? Ain't that something? Do you believe in ghosts? I believe in ghosts. My pal Fish saw one once in his ma's room when his pop was out of town. It disappeared out the window onto the fire escape when he poked his head in the room. Ain't that something? I'd like to see one, too. Maybe you could take me out there some night. We could do a stakeout and catch Wally in the act. You could tackle him and hold him down, and I could give him what for. Whataya think?"

What I thought was, it was time to escape that joint before I got caught up in another game of Twenty Questions. I managed to wade through the pack of miniature thugs and make it out the door, but it was not such a cakewalk getting rid of little Mikey. He followed me down the sidewalk, sticking to me like a limpet on to the side of a ship and peppering me with queries all the way, until Miss Twelve-Year-Old came running up and started hauling him away bodily by one arm. I tipped my hat to her, and she tipped me the wink. That girl's got a bright future ahead of her.

I headed back to the office. There was still plenty of time before Morty would be expecting my masterpiece for the next edition, so I decided to head down to the Morgue in the basement. Don't worry, we don't have a bunch of dead bodies stacked up down there—that's just newsman jargon for where the back issues of the paper get stashed away. I was remembering what the sisters had said about previous mentions of Wally in the Crier. It seemed worth looking into since I didn't have a whole lot else to go on.

Strolling into the big, windowless room in the bowels of the building, I dinged the bell sitting on the counter a few times to see if I could summon assistance. A trim-looking, dark-skinned young man materialized from somewhere in the back. He was neatly dressed in a tie and crisply-pressed shirt with a woolen vest and a pair of black-rimmed cheaters that gave him a studious appearance.

"Can I help you?" he asked.

"I was looking for whoever's in charge down here these days," I said.

He pushed his glasses back up on his nose from where they had slipped down a ways and admitted, "That would be me."

I was bowled over. It wasn't so common in those days to see someone with his skin color in charge of anything. Not around Carsworth City anyhow. I guess I didn't do too good a job of hiding my shock 'cause he got a look on his face like this wasn't the first time he'd gotten that reaction. Not by a long shot.

"I'm Marquis Sutherland. Mr. Quigsby just hired me to organize the archives. I'm afraid they're in quite a mess."

"Morty hired you?" I replied, even more astonished because I didn't think of Morty as being the broad-minded type.

"It was at the request of Mr. Carsworth, I believe," he said, referring to the mighty publisher of our little rag not to mention that the whole city happened to be named after his family. "He sponsored me through college. My mother works for him. As a maid," he added, as though that explained everything, and in a way, I guess it did.

Carsworth was a Progressive with a capital P and was always trying to insert social reform slants into the paper. It drove Morty crazy, but the boss is the boss. I didn't mind it. I like to think of myself as a forward-thinker. The world moves on, if we're lucky, and you meet a lot of different people in my line of work. I was always ready to give everyone a fair shake unless they did something that made me change my mind.

"Pleased to make your acquaintance, Mr. Sutherland," I said, belatedly offering to cross palms with him, but better late than never, right? "I'm Malhaven. Congrats on the job and that whole college deal. Good for you. I was lucky to finish high school, and that was by the skin of my teeth. You must have some smarts. Maybe you're just the man to help me out with this problem of mine."

"It's about Woebegone Wally, isn't it, Mr. Malhaven?" he chimed in, all excited-like, as he pumped my hand. "I've always had an interest in the paranormal, so when I read the story in the paper this morning, I started doing some research. This isn't the first time there's been a write-up. Someone used to keep a pretty careful card index of all the stories the paper published. It got dropped along the way, so we'll have trouble finding anything more recent, but I stumbled across something just now and…"

He went in for the dramatic pause, but I didn't blame him none. I can appreciate the pleasure of milking a good scoop.

"I think I know who he is!"

"No kidding!" I said admiringly. "That's one up on me. You could just about fit on the head of a pin as much as I been able to find out about this character. What do you know?"

"I found a card devoted to the haunting. It mentions the first sighting was in 1923, and also that there was a theory at the time that the apparition was that of a Mr. Walter Hornschmidt."

"Wally!"

"That's right!"

"That's some good detective work there—what did you say your name was… Marcus?"

"Marquis," he replied, correcting my pronunciation with an emphasis on the second half of his handle, "but everyone calls me Q."

"Suits me, Q. I'm Jim, or Jimmy if you're feeling light-hearted. So, what can you tell me about this Hornschmidt, our man of the hour?"

"Not much, I fear. The memo on Wally's card just refers to him as 'Mr. Walter Hornschmidt, convicted murderer' with a note to see Hornschmidt's card for more information." He looked dejected. "But I haven't been able to find his card. I've looked through all the H's and even the W's, just in case."

"Huh, wonder if this is the same fella the ladies told me about."

"Ladies?"

"Pair of sisters up at the cemetery. Both claimed to have seen him, starting around '22 or '23, they said, so that matches up. Said they thought he murdered his wife and baby sometime around 1921 or 22. Any way we can check up on that?"

"Everything is in such disarray," Q said critically. "I wish I could find that card."

"That is a shame," I agreed. "Maybe there's a method to the madness, as they say, but we just don't get it."

"You may be right. I wonder…" he said. "Hang on a minute."

He disappeared for a while then came back waving a card. "You were right. There was a method and it is very close to madness. There were a number of cards filed away under 'M' for 'Murderers.' That's not a proper organizational scheme at all. By rights, everyone should be filed under their last name or at least cross-referenced. I'll have to see what I can do about that."

"I bet you get it straightened out in no time flat. That's some good thinking," I said, impressed. As a reporter, there's nothing I appreciate more than someone who has a talent for finding things out. I was beginning to think Mr. Carsworth would be getting a good return on his investment in Mr. Marquis Sutherland. "Let's see what you got there."

We bent our heads over the card and studied the scanty information written out neatly in one of those old-fashioned, fancy scripts they used to teach in the schools before the modern method came into fashion: *Mr. Walter Christopher Hornschmidt, age 32 at time of death in 1922. Married wife Renee Marie in 1918. One child, Peter Christopher. See 1922 August to September editions for story.*

"That's fine," I said. "Now we know where to look. Did Wally's card have anything else on it?"

"There's a list of sightings up until about 1943. I think that's when whoever was keeping the indexing current must have left, because I haven't found any information on any of the cards dated after that time. There are notes to which editions to look in for stories about the other sightings up until then, though."

I rubbed my hands together in satisfaction. "Well, that sounds like we're on easy street. We just have to look in those back numbers."

Q got a pained-looking expression on his face. "Come with me," he said, waving me behind the counter they had set up there to keep out the riff-raff and escorting me back to a large room off to the side.

"Jeez! What happened in here? A windstorm?" I sputtered.

There were newspapers everywhere you looked, and I mean everywhere. Packed onto shelves, piled high in corners, spread out over a couple of tables, and even strewn about on the floor so that it was hard to take a step in any direction without treading on a piece of the past.

"I couldn't believe it either," Q said in a disapproving sort of voice. "There's been no one working down here for years, and I think people came in and just took what they wanted, pushing the rest out of their way or even onto the floor. It's a disgraceful way to treat a valuable archive like this. There are issues here stretching all the way back to 1832 when the paper was founded, and just look at it," he added, gesturing around with an expression on his face like we had stumbled across a rotting corpse.

"It does look a bit of a jumble," I agreed, pushing my hat back and wiping my brow. "Any rhyme or reason to it?"

"Not that I've been able to discern so far, but I've only been here a few days, so I haven't had a chance to work on it very much."

"Well, let's see if we can't make some sense out of it," I said, pulling off my coat and rolling up my shirtsleeves.

A couple of hours later found us both hot, filthy, and frustrated. Seems like we found every year but 1922.

At least we'd found a few of the editions with the ghost sightings in them, but I was disappointed to see there wasn't much more meat to those encounters than there'd been to Margo's. There was usually the sighting from afar, some vague description, and in at least one of the articles, the one from the first report by a Miss Ernestine Wynter no less, there was passing speculation to it possibly being the ghost of "that infamous murderer, Walter Hornschmidt" without any particulars on what he'd done. This failure to elaborate made me think the murders had still been so notorious at the time that the reporter didn't even feel the need to remind readers of the details.

But if that was so, what I couldn't figure, given it had been the talk of the town, was why the Wynter sisters couldn't tell me more about it. I wouldn't have thought there was so much going on around Carsworth City back in those days that murders like that would have been a dime a dozen. You'd think it would have stuck with them more. That they might have written it down in a diary or made a scrapbook of newspaper clippings about it like an old aunt of mine used to do with anything big that happened in her corner of the world. Ernie and Bernie's vagueness about it all and Liv's attempt to squash the whole idea outright was making me more than a little curious.

I went over to fish a cigarette out of my coat pocket by way of taking a refreshing break from our hard labor when I caught a glimpse of my watch and let loose with a few not so polite utterances, realizing I was cutting it fine to get back upstairs and get my draft ready for Morty before deadline for the evening edition. Giving Q a soft punch on the shoulder by way of thanks and promising to return to help the next day, I bustled upstairs and started pounding on the typewriter keys like a pile driver.

Sure enough, Morty was standing at his window, glowering at me, but I was used to that as he spent about ninety-six percent of his time in that exact same position. There were rumors that he never went home even though we'd heard he had a wife and some tots stashed away somewhere.

I spun the bit more I'd gleaned that day into something that, if not exactly gold, wasn't straw either. At least I had a couple more concrete details to pad out the tale, and the teenage girl in jeopardy angle is always good for a few eyeballs. I also took the plunge and promised "gruesome details to come on infamous murder" in the final paragraph. It was going out on a limb if Q and I couldn't come up with those 1922 editions, but when you're in the scuttlebutt business, you always gotta throw out a hook to keep your customers coming back for more.

The copy boy passed the pages off to Morty as I watched. The boss read it through then reached his red pencil down from behind his ear and started in to decorating it. Morty always liked to put his own stamp on stories before they went to press, but I didn't mind. That meant he thought it was okay, and I wasn't one of those prima donnas like some of the guys that thought every word they wrote was as sacred as a verse of Scripture. I was just relieved I wasn't in for another scolding.

It seemed like I had done all I could for the day, so I lit out of there with the notion of grabbing a plate of grub and heading home for some shuteye. I wolfed down some pot roast and potatoes alright, but instead of cozying up at the old homestead, I found myself seated behind the wheel of the Champ and driving back out past the edge of town again. It had occurred to me that little Mikey's idea of a stakeout wasn't such a stinker, which just goes to show, if you spout off enough words, there's bound to be something that makes sense in there sooner or later, right?

The times of the sightings varied, but any time after sunset seemed fair game, and I'd spent more than one sleepless night during the war keeping watch, so I'd gotten a lot of practice at it. Maybe I'd get lucky and get another eyewitness account of Wally, this time by someone I considered a pretty reliable witness—me, myself, and I. Did the thought that I might run into *her* again figure into my strategy, you might ask. Don't you have a suspicious mind. You should really be ashamed of yourself.

I parked the car a good long way away this time so as not to tip off the ghost. The walk to the cemetery wasn't too bad. I figured the exercise was probably doing my bum leg some good. I reached the gates and was scouting out a good spot across the road where I could keep an eye peeled when I heard it.

"We have to stop meeting like this."

CHAPTER TEN

My heart might have skipped a beat or twenty at the sound of that low voice, as cool as the night air.

"Isn't that what they say?" she added with that pretty trill of a laugh.

"I told you I'd keep turning up like a bad penny," I replied after I had time to catch my breath.

"And here you are as promised."

She came right on up to the gates this time. No playing hard to get. No games with the light. She'd done up her hair in the style she'd sported the night before with the little fringe that called attention to her eyes, and she was wearing that soft wool coat again but over some camel-colored trousers this time. Cashmere, unless my eyes were fooling me. I wondered how a caretaker had the cash to fund that kind of a wardrobe, adding the question to the growing list of things I found interesting about the widow of Lukasz Jankowski.

She was wearing soft leather gloves against the chill. I noticed that when she made me another offering through the gates of a smoke and the silver lighter. After I lit up, she took the lighter back and lit up one for herself, tilting her head to blow the smoke away from my face. I was just thinking how much I enjoyed the smell of the burning tobacco out in the fresh country air before I got distracted by those eyes of hers turning back to inspect me. They seemed more intense at night than they had in the sunlight. Not unfriendly exactly, but different in some way I couldn't quite figure.

"So, what brings you back here?" she asked.

"Thought I'd like to lay eyes on this ghoul for myself. I been finding out one or two things about him. From Margo Cummings—thanks again for the tip—and the Wynter sisters, of course. But there's nothing like seeing something for yourself in the flesh, so to speak."

"Yes, though I don't suppose he has any flesh, does he?" She looked like she was giving it some serious thought.

"But you don't believe in ghosts. That's what you said this morning," I reminded her.

"Oh, of course," she said, all casual-like. "It's just intriguing to think about, isn't it? If there were such a thing. Besides, something about being out here this time of night, it doesn't seem quite so farfetched as it does during the day. Not to me, anyway," she added with a shiver, like a goose had walked over her grave as my old granny used to say.

"I'll take some convincing," says I. "But I'm one that's always willing to keep an open mind. If Wally was to come up and shake my hand, and I find out I can see right through him to the scenery on the other side, that might give me something to think about."

"I should think it would," she agreed. "You'd have to be mighty brave to offer to shake his hand. Or a mighty big fool."

"And I think we established already that I'm no fool."

"Did we? I guess I forgot."

That one hurt. As many times as I'd turned over every word of our little talks in my own head, I guess I was a dope to think they meant as much to her. I'd never been a big hit with the ladies, and the rearrangement of my facial features hadn't done much to help that.

This was right about when I told myself to get a grip. She was bored and lonely, was all. She probably would have engaged in conversation with one of the gateposts if I wasn't around. Well, I'd show her I could be a real cool customer myself.

"That's okay. As long as I don't forget I'm not a fool, I guess we'll be all right."

She rewarded my sparkling wit with a chilly smile. "What have you found out about our resident wraith? Woebegone Wally—isn't that what you named him?"

"My editor did that, to be one hundred percent truthful with you. It's his job to punch up the headlines. Gotta grab the reader's attention one way or another, you know. Guess it wouldn't hurt to give you the inside dope on tomorrow's big scoop. We found out his name in life was maybe one Walter Christopher Hornschmidt—"

I broke off as she let out a gasp like someone had punched her hard in the solar plexus and knocked all the air outta her. She took a step back away from the gate looking as white as a ghost herself and dropped her burning cigarette on the ground. All in all, the picture of someone who just got a very bad fright.

"What gives?" says I, my reporting instincts kicking into overdrive. "You heard of our Mr. Hornschmidt?"

"Wha—? No… no, of course not." She was about as convincing as a crook on the witness stand.

"You sure? You seemed a little taken aback there. Like you got a shock or something."

"No," she said, reaching down to rub one shapely calf through the soft material of her pants. "Just one of those sudden charley horses, you know. They can hurt like the devil, can't they?" she added, all nonchalant and innocent, those wide eyes looking straight into mine without a single blink.

I had to hand it to her. She had nerve. I didn't buy the excuse for a minute, but for some reason, I didn't feel equal to the challenge in those eyes, daring me to call her out as a liar.

She carefully ground out the still lit cig on the ground, looking away from me as she did it. "Who was he? This Mr.—Hornblower, did you say?"

I was game enough to play along. "Horn*schmidt*," I reminded her gently. "Turns out there was a guy who killed his wife and kid, after all. At least, we think he did. I got our best researcher," I said, with an imaginary tip of my hat to Q, "working on rounding up the details. We should have more in time for the next edition," I promised optimistically.

"A murderer. How horrible," she said quietly, kinda under her breath.

It was the first time I seen her rattled. I couldn't put it all together. She told me pretty much the same story herself with ghoulish delight on the night we first met. Why should she get so upset to have it confirmed? All I could figure was maybe passing along an old wives' tale, as she'd called it, and finding out there was real flesh-and-blood people at the heart of it is two different things.

"Yeah," I agreed. "I don't know that I'd come out here looking for him anymore, if I was you. Might not be somebody you want to run into after dark. He don't exactly sound like a Prince Charming."

"I think you're right," she said. "You can meet some dubious characters hanging around these gates." It was a fling at her old carefree flirting, but I could tell her heart wasn't in it. "I'd better go in, Mr. Malhaven. Good night," she said and stalked away into the gloom before I could think of even a bad excuse to call her back, much less a good one.

I cursed myself. Where'd I get the big idea to scare her away from visiting the gates? Now I'd have one less excuse for running into her. Not that I knew what I hoped to get out of furthering our acquaintance. Well, that's not quite true. I knew what I hoped for, but she'd made it obvious that wasn't in the cards. Better to drop the whole thing, keep my mind on the job, and try to get whatever other facts there was to find and wrap up the story. And the sooner, the better. I'd had enough heartache in my life. Only a fool would insist on chasing after more. And I think we already established I'm no fool, didn't we?

Still irritated with myself, I turned and crossed the road over to a stand of trees across from the gates. This must have been the site of Margo's big scene. I could see what she meant now. It was far enough away, particularly in the darkness, to make it hard to see the gates, although as my eyes adjusted to the gloom, I could see them okay.

There was a bit more of a moon than the night Margo would have been out there, so that helped.

I decided to settle down on a fallen log and make myself as comfortable as possible. There wasn't much traffic on that road even during the day, so I resigned myself to a boring lookout, lighting up one cigarette after another to help pass the time. Sure enough, the only thing that passed was an old jalopy full of teenagers singing one of Mr. Sammy Kaye's latest hits at the top of their lungs. Probably headed out to some Lover's Lane-type spot in the country. I wondered if their parents knew where they were and thanked my lucky stars I didn't have any responsibilities like that in my life.

Silence descended again for a space of time as I cooled my heels there on my log perch. Finally, a truck approached, rattling down the road from town. I'm kind of a car buff—maybe it comes from not being able to afford a nicer one myself—so I pegged it right off as one of those Harvester Metro Vans most of the delivery guys were using. It was kinda slick-looking, figured it must be a newer model. The van was a dark color and didn't have its headlamps lit. I thought they probably started out their route while it was still light out and hadn't thought to turn them on yet.

I stepped out into the road and tried to flag them down to tell them, like any good citizen would, but the van just sped up and raced off down the road. I guess having a six-foot-something mug with a scary face leap out of the dark at you would tend to motivate you that way. Shrugging my shoulders and hoping they didn't run into any traffic coming the other way down the narrow lane, I took up my former position, debating with myself how much longer to give to what was probably a huge waste of my precious time. I told myself I'd give it another half an hour. I was still counting down the minutes until my deadline when there was a rustling sound behind me followed by a sharp pain in my head. And then, I knew no more.

CHAPTER ELEVEN

The next thing I remember was the feel of a cool hand laid against my forehead. I cracked one eye open slightly to see two pretty slate-blue ones peering down at me in concern. As always, she looked different in the day. More open, more… honest, I guess. Maybe it was just 'cause I could see her clearer in the sunlight.

"We got to stop meeting like this," I muttered, closing my heavy eyelid with a bang.

"If you mean in the middle of the road," she said. "I wholeheartedly agree. You're lucky you weren't run over. Good thing we don't get much traffic."

I pried open both eyelids at that and tried to move my head from side to side to get a look at my situation. Huge mistake. It felt like that roomful of monkeys with the typewriters had set up shop in my brain. I groaned and decided getting run over just then wouldn't be the worst thing in the world. It would put me out of my misery at least.

She was having none of it, though, tugging with a surprising amount of muscle at my trench coat to pull me into a sitting position. I decided it was easier to go along with her than fight it and found myself first on my knees, then upstanding. I was swaying like a buoy in a hurricane, or maybe it was the world around me that was bouncing like that, but at least I was in a more or less upright position. Closing my eyes again to try and shut out the Tilt-a-whirl view, I followed her willingly enough as she took one of my arms and steered me across the road and through the gates. Afraid to open my eyes again, I stumbled along trustingly until I found myself pushed down onto a bench.

I opened an eye cautiously and was rewarded with the sight of an old-fashioned cottage, small, but neatly kept, with a fancy garden of every kind of flower I'd ever seen in front of it. The blooms were fading with the turn of the seasons, but it still looked pretty and homey, like an oasis of life in the desert of death surrounding it. My guide seemed to have abandoned me, but my head hurt too much to worry about it. I was content to sit still with my eyes closed and my face turned to the warm morning sun. Before too long, I felt a cool damp cloth being applied to the back of my head.

"That's a nasty-looking bump you have there," she reported. "Did you trip and hit your head?"

"Dunno. Can't recall exactly what happened to tell you the truth. We were jawing at the gates, weren't we? After dusk. I was telling you about our Mr. Hornschmidt."

"Mr. Horn—? Oh, yes," she said. "I suppose so. And then… I went inside?"

It was more of a question than a statement. Like *she* was asking *me* what she had done next. Even in my muddled state, that struck me. It came to me suddenly that maybe she drank at night when she was feeling lonely and missing Mr. Jankowski. Maybe she'd even turned to the hard stuff. There was plenty of smack and other dope making the rounds in Carsworth City. It wouldn't be hard even for a nice girl like her to get ahold of some, and she wouldn't be the first to go through tough times and try to comfort herself anyhow she could.

That would explain why she didn't always seem to remember things. It would also explain why she seemed so different at night. Harder. More cynical. There was plenty of people who'd been happy to report to me that I changed into a totally different guy when I drank. Only mine went the other way. I became soft, one of those maudlin, sentimental-type drunks that everyone runs a mile from in bars.

"Yeah, you went away,"—there was a little catch in my voice when I said this that was entirely coincidental— "and I went over and hid out in those trees across the road. Thought if I could catch sight of this Wally fellow myself, it would make for some thrilling reading for the general public."

"And then what?" she prompted me.

That was a puzzler, but as I sat there, bits and pieces of my mostly uneventful watch in the night drifted back to me. The teenagers, singing and laughing as their old convertible sped past. Then… then…

"A dark Metro van," I said.

"A van? At the cemetery?"

"No. That is, it was coming down the road toward the cemetery. They didn't have their headlights on, and I stepped out to warn them. Just being helpful, you know," I added, trying to sound modest about my charitable ways. "But that seemed to startle them, and they sped on past. Can't blame 'em. I'd probably run, too, if I saw me coming. That's kind of the last thing I remember."

"That seems unusual, doesn't it? Why were they driving with their lights off at that time of night?"

"I dunno. I assumed it was just by accident. The moon was pretty bright. Maybe they hadn't noticed they forgot to turn them on?"

"Maybe," she said. "But it still seems strange, especially when you consider that I found you lying face down in the middle of the road with a lump the size of a chicken egg on the back of your head. It's hard to imagine how you could have fallen and hit the back of your head and then ended up on your face, isn't it?"

"I was turned up to the sky when I come to, though," I pointed out.

"Yes, I saw you when I came out to open up the gates this morning and managed to get you turned over onto your back."

"Say, that's something," I said, full of admiration. "I ain't no lightweight."

"Neither am I. I've done a lot of manual labor the past ten years. You get used to hauling heavy loads of this and that, to and fro."

I grinned at her and surprised her into an answering smile. Then it hit me what she was saying. "That does put a different spin on it. It's sounding like someone clocked me on purpose and laid me out in the road, hoping I'd get conveniently finished off. It's just too bad for them you don't get a lot of travelers out this way. Maybe that van was up to no good, after all."

"But if they went to all that trouble," she argued. "Why didn't they just run you over themselves before they drove away? Why leave it to chance?"

"Even the dumbest crook these days knows the cops can match tire tracks. They might've been scared it would be traced back to them. Makes me wonder if they had an unusual type of tire on that van. Could make it easier to find."

"Are you going to try to find it?"

"Maybe. I'm all for the quiet life these days. This," I said, fingering the deep scar down my face, "taught me it's not worth riling up the wrong guys. Not just for a couple of columns for the daily rag anyways. But could be I'm on somebody's bad side, and they won't give up so easy. I'm not interested in running into battle, but if someone's gonna bring a war to me, they'll find out I'm no pushover. The guy that gave me this souvenir found that out the hard way," I reminded her, grimacing at the memory.

"What… what happened to him?" she asked, like she was scared to hear the answer.

"He got what he deserved. Don't you remember? I told you that the first night we met."

"Oh, yes, of course," she said, sketching me a not very convincing imitation of someone who routinely forgets when people tell them they've offed a guy. Because that's something that folks confide in her all the time, maybe.

It seemed to confirm the theory I'd just arrived at about her being under the influence when we met at night. She probably kept sober during the day while she was on the job and let loose at night. It was the only explanation for her forgetting so many details of our conversations. It made me feel sorry for her. Life must be a minefield when you have holes in the old noggin like that. I wondered if those Wynter sisters knew. They seemed like the straight-laced type. If they didn't approve of her smoking, I could only imagine what they'd do if they found out she was also drinking, or worse.

"What gets me," I continued, overlooking her memory lapse like it was no big deal, "is I'm just a guy looking into a goofball ghost yarn. It's the last story I expected to get under somebody's skin. Unless there's something more to this Wally tale then I've been led to believe so far." I looked at her questioningly.

She just looked bewildered. "I really don't know any more than I've told you, Mr. Malhaven. Like I said, I've never seen anything myself and always assumed it was just one of those legends that grow up around cemeteries. It seems like every graveyard has a ghost of some kind associated with it, doesn't it?"

"What about that name, though?" I pressed her. "Walter Christopher Hornschmidt. Are you sure it means nothing to you? I could've sworn it gave you a nasty surprise last night when I said it."

She looked me straight in the eyes with those piercing gray-blue ones of hers. "I swear it means nothing to me. I've never heard that name before in my life."

CHAPTER TWELVE

The odd thing was, I believed her. There was none of that shiftiness, the evasions of the night before. I would have sworn on my own mother's grave right then that she was telling me the complete and honest-to-God truth. The whole thing made my battered head hurt more than ever. I groaned and leant over to rest it on my hand, poking around gingerly with my other mitt to get a feel of that knob on my skull. Even though I had bigger fish to fry, that reminded me of something that seemed vitally important for some reason, probably because my poor brain was still spinning around like a top.

"My lid!"

"Your lid? Oh, you mean your hat?" she said. "Were you wearing one?"

"Of course!" I replied, all indignant.

"Not all men do these days, you know. Some of the fashion magazines say hats are going out of style."

"Guess I'm the old-fashioned type then." I made as if to get up to go look for it but had to give it a rest when the sky tilted sideways again.

"Wait here," she said, laying one hand firmly against my shoulder like she was forcing a disobedient dog into a sit.

I didn't mind. It was nice to have someone do something for me for a change. When you been alone as much as I have, it's kind of a novelty to think someone's looking out for you, even for just a few minutes. I decided to enjoy it as long as I could.

While she was gone, I half closed my eyes and concentrated. I'm a big believer in this whole mind over matter deal. I figured if I just told my brain to give it a rest with enough authority, I could get it to calm down. Sure enough, by the time she reappeared in my line of sight, I no longer felt like I was going for a ride on the seesaw at the local playground.

"No luck, I'm afraid," she said. "I looked up and down the road and all around the trees across the way, but there's no sign of it anywhere."

I sighed. Looked like I'd have to face up to laying out my hard-earned moolah on a new topper after all. I don't care much about what the ladies' journals were saying about the latest fashion trends—I just knew I felt naked without a hat. Guess I looked as down as I was feeling 'cause she held up a hand, saying, "Hold on just a minute," before disappearing into the cottage. She reappeared a few minutes later, with something hidden behind her.

She produced a dark gray fedora from behind her back with a flourish. "Ta-da!"

It looked like it had never been worn. The brim was wider than the latest styles, but like I said, fashion trends don't bother me much.

"I don't know if it will fit," she added, sounding doubtful. "You'll have to try it on."

I reached out to take it, running my hands over the soft felt. It was a quality hat. Not the kind you pick out off the rack at the corner five-and-dime.

"Was it… his?" I asked, kinda flustered, I guess you could say.

"Yes," she said softly, impatiently pulling the hat out of my hands and setting it gently on my head, trying not to hit the lump on my cranium. "Look, it's a perfect fit," she observed with a note of wonder in her voice. "What are the chances? He had it specially made for our wedding day. It's only been worn a few times."

I started to protest. "I can't take a thing like that..."

"Don't be silly," she said. "I gave away his suits and other things years ago. I only hung on to this because it seemed more personal. It gave me a funny feeling to think about giving it away to a stranger, but it's like it was meant for you. You have to admit it's a good fit."

"Like a glove," I agreed. "It's the nicest one I ever had. But it makes me feel a little funny myself..." I hesitated.

"Wearing a dead man's hat?" she suggested. "I wouldn't have pegged you as the squeamish type."

"It ain't that. I guess it's knowing it was his wedding hat. Kind of like if you had given away the dress you got married in."

"I did, as a matter of fact," she said with a smile. "At any rate, you can at least wear it until you buy a new one. Lukasz felt the same way about hats. He never went anywhere without one. I don't think he'd mind. Besides, he's left all those kinds of worries behind him now, wherever he is," she added, looking out across the monuments that littered the landscape around us. It drew my notice to the fact that the cottage sat in a remote corner of the cemetery, far from the gates.

"Guess you wouldn't have heard anything last night from here," I observed. "Kinda inconvenient, ain't it? Being so far from the entrance?"

"Yes, it is sometimes. I was surprised when we first moved here. At other cemeteries I've visited, the caretaker's office is usually up close to the gates, so they can keep an eye on the comings and goings. The sisters said their father didn't want visitors to be intimidated by it—like they had to stop and check in or anything. He wanted them to be able to come and go to visit their loved ones without bothering anyone or being bothered."

"Sounds like a real sensitive guy."

"I wouldn't have said so, but people do get peculiar ideas sometimes about the dead. Even a hard man like Mr. Wynter. Tom, one of the old gardeners who's worked here ever since the cemetery was founded, said Mr. Wynter spent a whole year planning and having his mausoleum built back in 1920. That was over twenty years before he needed it." She shivered. "Wouldn't it give you the creeps to have that thing standing there staring at you every time you passed through the gates, knowing it was just waiting to swallow you up when your time came?"

I shrugged. "I'm not an imaginative guy myself, but I will say I can think of a hundred better ways to spend that kind of cash in the here and now. Like they say, you can't take it with you. But, hey, if it gave the old guy a kick to build himself a palace for his final resting spot, it was his money to do with as he liked, wasn't it?"

"It most certainly was, young man."

Victoria and I both jumped at the sound of that icy voice. We'd been so absorbed in our chat that we didn't notice old Liv Wynter sneaking up. I turned to see her towering over us where we were sitting together on that bench. The other two, Ernie and Bernie, trailed behind her, slightly hunched over in a toadying manner that reminded me of a pair of mistreated lapdogs still slavishly following their master around in hopes of a kind word or a pat on the head.

"What is the meaning of this, Mrs. Jankowski?" said Livinia. "I thought we agreed you would not entertain gentlemen callers on cemetery grounds."

Victoria turned pink, so I jumped right to her defense. "Nothing along that line, ma'am," I demurred. "Some villain or gang of villains unknown gifted me the most godawful conk on the old noodle last evening while I was preoccupied with keeping my peepers glued to your front gates in hopes of an encore performance by our mutual apparitional acquaintance, Wally the Woebegone. Mrs. J here was just assisting me to get myself on a more even keel before I leg it back to town."

The old lady sniffed. "If I am to understand by that nearly incomprehensible statement that you are claiming to have been assaulted while spying on us, then I can only comment that sometimes we reap what we sow."

"Oh, Livinia!" exclaimed one of her sisters. I think it was Ernie, though she'd lost the twig in her hair to help me identify her, so don't hold me to that. "Really, this is quite distressing, isn't it? To think that violence has been done so close to us. And to a member of the newspaper fraternity no less. One would almost think someone was trying to muzzle the Free Press!" she added with surprising gusto.

Liv turned a baleful eye toward her wayward sister, who cowered back and lowered her gaze before the truly impressive amount of disdain that was being sent in her general direction.

"A free press, indeed," Liv scoffed. "This is more like harassment than respectable journalism. I feel compelled to warn you, Mr. Mal-*vern*—"

"Malhaven," I made bold to correct her this time, but it didn't disconcert her none.

"I am on my way now to consult with our lawyer, Mr. Harold Monroe, in town. I've just read your muckraking in the latest edition. You are bringing disgrace and notoriety to our family name and the final resting place of all these good Christian souls," she said, waving her hands at the silent crowd beneath us to help drive home her point. "And I will not stand for it. Ernestine and Bernadette, return to the house at once and await my return."

Liv swanned off without a look back. I guess it never crossed her mind that her slightest wish wouldn't be immediately obeyed by those poor ladies. The two sisters did obey, at least at first, performing a strange dance as they shuffled off toward the mansion on the hill for a bit, all the while folding themselves repeatedly into surprisingly graceful bows in our general direction, before suddenly turning and darting back toward us.

They struck out on a meandering path, ducking behind grave markers or small trees that were rather inadequately sized to hide their robust figures whenever they seemed to get the wind up that old Liv might turn back to check on them, although she never did that I could see. They finally ended up popping out from beside the cottage, gesturing us over to them with a hissing noise like an angry swan I seen once chasing a dog by a lake.

The one I had pegged as Ernie waved us over and spoke first. "Mrs. Jankowski. Mr. Malhaven. So fortunate our running into you both like this. We have an invitation we'd like to extend to you."

"An invite, huh?" I said appreciatively. "Sounds swell. What kind of a shindig did you have in mind?"

The two sisters exchanged a glance full of excitement before turning back to us to breathe out their news: "A séance!"

CHAPTER THIRTEEN

"Séance, huh?" says I, tickled at the thought. "One of those raise-the-dead type deals? Don't you need to import some special kind of help for that? What do they call those jokers? The ones that claim they can call up the dearly departed on some kind of party line to the afterlife?"

"A medium," Victoria answered quietly.

I glanced over at her, surprised to catch her looking so troubled. I figured she'd find the sisters' brainstorm as funny as I did, but she looked like she was taking it serious and was none too happy about the idea.

"Yeah, that's it—a medium," I followed up. "You got yourself one of those?"

The sisters exchanged pleased looks before Bernie chimed in. "We have something better. A wee-jee board!"

Well, it sounded like wee-jee to me then. I found out later that's not how it's spelled at all. I had never heard of such a thing, but I was in luck 'cause the ladies were eager to fill us in.

"It's a wooden board with letters and numbers on it and a special marker that we move to spell out words and so forth. Only *we* don't really move it, of course. We just sit in a circle and all put one finger lightly on it and then the spirits will move it around to answer our questions."

"Can't these spirits shift this marker thing without us touching it?" I interjected, skeptical I'll admit, though part of me hated to spit on their parade. They looked like kids let loose in a candy shop with a pocketful of change to spend.

"Oh, no, Mr. Malhaven," Ernie explained to me very seriously. "The spirits are far too weak on their own. They require our corporeal energy in order to manifest themselves in the material world. The spirit board we ordered just arrived in the mail yesterday, so we are organizing a small party to try it out tomorrow night. Don't you see? Maybe we can contact Wally and help to set his mind at ease so that he can finally find eternal peace!"

Laying aside my objection to the idea that we had any chance of making a killer feel better about murdering his own wife and kid in cold blood, I decided to raise another difficulty that had occurred to me.

"What about Miss Livinia Wynter? I wouldn't think she'd be so happy to be hosting such an event as this."

"That's why it has to be tomorrow night," Bernie said. "Once a month, Liv goes out of town on an overnight visit to one of her girlfriends from high school. And she always lets Cressley have that night off, too, so we'll be the only ones in the house. Do say you can come. If we don't do it now, we'll have to wait another whole month!"

They looked so pathetic with their big pleading eyes and wringing hands, I decided I couldn't disappoint them. Besides, it struck me just then that the goings-on at a spectral get-together like that could be spun into a scorcher for the Crier. I guess Victoria had the same notion 'cause she piped up before I could reassure the ladies about my eagerness to attend.

"No offense to Mr. Malhaven, but are you sure you want to invite him to join you? I'm afraid as a professional journalist, he'd have no choice but to write up a story for his paper, and then your sister would find out all about it anyway."

The sisters exchanged another set of looks before Bernie chimed back in. "Oh, that wouldn't matter because it would be all over by then. There would be nothing Liv could do about it," she added with what seemed to be a certain amount of understandable satisfaction at the idea of putting one over on their domineering sibling. "And we don't happen to share Liv's view that the publicity is bad for the cemetery. I think it gives us a certain distinction, wouldn't you agree? It's just too bad we don't have more open plots. I wonder if we could buy that land across the road? We're already the largest cemetery for miles around. Why shouldn't we expand? Father was a shrewd businessman, you know. I'm sure he would approve."

Ernie nodded her head in enthusiastic support of this entrepreneurial gambit, and I had to admit, there might be something to it. One thing about operating a boneyard, none of us escape that final call, so you know you can always count on more customers coming through your door sooner or later.

"Ladies, I'd be honored to take part in such a noble experiment. Like you say, maybe Wally's done his time here on earth, and we can encourage him to move along. Whataya say, Mrs. J? Shall I swing by and pick you up on my way to the party?"

Victoria shook her head. "You can count me out. I don't believe in that kind of thing. And I'm afraid I think it seems rather disrespectful to the dead to play at such games."

"Oh!" both of the sisters cried in a chorus of dismay, but to my surprise, they didn't try to change her mind. Bernie just turned back to me with instructions to arrive by eleven p.m. sharp so that we could be ready by the "witching hour" of midnight to start the board game.

"And do, please, bring a friend along, if you like," Ernie added. "To make up the numbers since Mrs. Jankowski won't be joining us."

They both simpered then trotted off toward the mansion, turning back at least a dozen times to wave like lunatics at us in a seemingly everlasting farewell.

"Sure you won't change your mind?" I asked Victoria as we stood waving at the sisters in response to their antics until they finally, blissfully, disappeared out of sight.

"No. I like to think the dead deserve our respect, perhaps even more so than the living. They can't defend themselves the way we can."

"Sounds to me like the dearly departed got themselves a first-rate champion in you. I'm sorry you won't be there," I added, disappointed to be deprived of a chance of furthering our brief acquaintance. "Won't be so much fun without you."

She smiled a bit at that. "Oh, I'm sure you'll find ways to amuse yourself. Maybe with this 'friend' you're supposed to invite?" she said, giving me a look like she expected I could conjure up another dame just as good as her out of thin air, which just goes to show how little she knew about me.

I tipped her husband's hat to her in a final salute. "I'll take care of this anyway. Just until I get a chance to find another one. I got this theory you can always judge a man by his hat, and this hat tells me Lukasz Jankowski was a good man."

Seeing those big blue eyes fill with tears, I was afraid I'd been too fresh, but she just reached out and gave my arm a friendly squeeze before disappearing into the cottage and out of my life again. A lot of the sunshine seemed to leave the sky with her as I stood there, touching my coat sleeve lightly where that delicate hand had rested all too briefly.

I was trying to get myself used to the idea that there was only so many more times I'd get to lay eyes on her anyway. I'd already milked the story nearly dry as it was. I could see spinning it out for another day or two, what with this séance gag and raking up some dirt on the Hornschmidt murder, but there just wasn't enough there and too much else happening around town every day of the week to think that Morty was gonna let me run with it much longer.

If I'd had more confidence, maybe I'd of given Victoria the old hard sell on Jim Malhaven. Tried to convince her I had something more to offer than my undying devotion, but you gotta be honest with yourself. Anyone taking a good look at my life up to that moment would have been hard-pressed to come up with any decent selling points. To win a woman like that over, you had to have something more to offer than a one-room dive and a barely-respectable job that paid for room and board and not much else. I didn't even have dashing good looks to fall back on the way some guys did.

I'd been drifting along since the war. Just ambitious enough to hold down a job and keep a roof over my head but without the drive I'd need to really make something of myself. I'd known plenty of guys at the Crier who'd gone on to better things at one of the big city papers while I kept plugging away at those two-bit local stories that Morty handed off to me because nobody else wanted to touch them with a barge pole.

It'd been different during the war. I had felt like quite the guy back then. I'd been gung-ho and full of gumption. Got promoted to Sergeant and was the kind of guy other men looked up to and would follow up those quicksand beaches they used to dump us out on in the Pacific, hurling ourselves into the whirlwind of bullets spit out by the enemy's machine guns. I was always foolishly sure I'd make it back alive, too. I wondered where along the way I'd lost that reckless bravado.

Was it when I got marked up by a no-account galoot over nothing more important than another petty racket, the kind that were a dime-a-dozen in any city? Or did it start way before that? Back in my childhood—the way Elliot Gardiner Malhaven couldn't even spare me the time of day much less a hug or a smile like any kid wants from their pop to make them feel like they matter. I wasn't usually such a deep thinker, but I'll admit, meeting Victoria had started some wheels grinding away in my head that weren't so easy to slow down. I thought about it all the way home, reaching up occasionally to run my fingers along the brim of the hat she'd given me. It made me feel close to her to think she'd held it in her own two hands.

It also made me mourn my own loss. I'd had that old fedora a long time. It felt like losing a trusty friend. Maybe I should've made a bigger effort to find it, but I believed Victoria when she said she'd made a good search. I couldn't help wondering what happened to it but decided it was just another mystery in a whole series of them that was destined to be unsolved. Turned out I was all wrong about that, the same way I turned out to be wrong about a lot of things.

CHAPTER FOURTEEN

I arrived back at the old homestead to find a brown-paper parcel all tied up neat with string sitting on my doorstep. No address or postage on it. Just the word MALHAVEN in all caps scribbled across the top of it in red grease pencil. It's not often I get a gift, and here I was getting two in one day—first, the topper from Victoria, and now this. I couldn't even remember the last time I'd gotten a present from anyone, but my birthday was months past, and besides, I had a feeling this latest one wasn't meant to be friendly even before I opened it up. Something about my name scrawled in red, like with a pen dipped in blood.

I took the package in with me and set it on the small table where I hunkered down to eat on the rare occasions when I fixed up some grub at home instead of grabbing a plate at one of the cheap joints you could find on every corner in Carsworth City. Sat myself down and stared at it for a bit.

My head was still pounding. I was feeling weary and more than a little heartsick from my longing for a gal with honey hair and piercing eyes. I'll admit, the thought crossed my mind to just throw that bundle in the trash bin and forget all about it. I had a kind of a sinking feeling. The feeling that if I opened it, I might be forced into taking some kind of action. Get involved in something that would lead to more trouble. And I'd had enough of trouble.

But nobody's ever had reason to call Jim Malhaven a milksop. If something's got to be faced up to, better to get it over with. I took out my penknife and sliced the string. Ripped the paper off and unwrapped the parcel to find a pile of brown scraps with a note on top. It only took me half a second to realize it was my old fedora cut up into at least a couple of dozen pieces.

You had to admire it really. The pieces were all about the same size and cut into squares. The squares had a funny zigzag edge, kind of like a row of pointy teeth, but it was neatly done. Someone had taken their time, someone who took pride in their work. It seemed worse to me than if someone had ripped it apart in a frenzy.

If I had to have an enemy, I'd prefer the kind of hothead who was always acting before they thought twice about what they was gonna do. It was easy to trip up a mug like that. There was a cool, methodical thinker behind that pile of brown felt squares, and those types are the worst kind of foe. They always have a plan before they make their next move, and a lot of times, they're already thinking two or three moves down the board, like those chess wizards, before you even got out of the starting gates.

I unfolded the message. It was written on a plain sheet of notepaper, folded in half. A simple communication. Two words, written in the same red pencil and block lettering as the name on the box: *FORGET WALLY*. Short and to the point. Even a lunkhead like me could follow that. I'd struck a nerve with this ghost story, and someone wanted to give me some friendly advice to leave it alone. I guess the goose egg on my head was just the exclamation point to the suggestion.

Heaving a sigh, I sat there a long time thinking as best as I could through the brutal headache that had settled in for a nice, long stay. I'd meant what I said to Victoria. I wasn't interested in fighting more battles, not just for a few inches of type in the next edition. This assignment had seemed like a joke when Morty handed it off to me, only somebody wasn't laughing. Somebody who wasn't afraid to take action to get the story spiked for good.

I stared at the ruins of my old fedora. We'd been through a lot together. Good times and bad. More bad than good, but that hat had always stuck by me when no one else had. It didn't seem right for it to come to that kind of an end. The more I looked at it, the madder I got. I think I was madder about that than about the wallop upside my skull. I was hard-headed, my cranium would heal up in time. That hat was a goner. Somewhere along the way, I realized I'd already decided what to do. I couldn't drop it. Not now.

And it wasn't just about avenging the premature demise of my bonnet, lest you get the idea I am a sentimental nut of some kind. No, it had occurred to me that whatever this story was really about, it was all tied up with that cemetery. And there was someone living there that I cared about, whether she ever returned the favor or not. I didn't like one bit the idea of Victoria being caught up, knowingly or unknowingly, in some kind of swindle. And that's what it had to come down to. No one would go to this much trouble unless there was something important at stake. And that usually boiled down to money. They say folks are willing to die for love or honor, but in my experience, money trumped everything else.

I didn't have the least clue what kind of a scheme could be centered at an old graveyard, or who might be involved, but I was a reporter. Finding out stuff like that was my stock in trade. Seemed to me like the next step was getting back to the paper and checking in with Q. Maybe he'd had a chance to locate those back issues. If we could find out more about this Hornschmidt character, I might get a bead on what to do next.

On my way to the Crier, I had a notion and stopped in at the local precinct house. I had a cop buddy there, my old pal Joey Flanagan. We'd grown up on Fifth Street together and stayed in touch. He was a detective now and threw me a good scoop whenever he could.

"Jimmy!" he yelled at me as I made my grand entrance. "How's tricks? Or should I say, how's tricks or treats? Whoo-ooo-ooo...." He made with the spooky noise, waving his arms around like he was a phantom himself.

The other guys standing around laughed. I didn't mind. At least it meant they'd been reading my stuff. That's all any reporter can ask for.

"Forget it, Flanagan. You'd have to shed a whole lot of poundage before anyone's gonna mistake you for a wraith." Joey's wife was a first-class cook, and he was sensitive about the weight he'd put on since they got married so that shut him up.

"Okay, okay," he said in surrender. "Guess you still can't take a joke. What can we do you for today?"

I pulled off my new hat and showed him the swelling at the back of my head. "Somebody's already done me for this."

"Making friends wherever you go, huh, Jimmy? That's you all over. You know who did it? Wanna press charges?"

"That's just the thing. It's all a deep, dark mystery."

I filled him in on my investigation out at the cemetery and my suspicions that there was more going on there than met the eye. Described the van as best I could. Pulled out the package with the pieces of my mutilated hat.

Joey got serious. "That's some strange doings, Jimmy, my boy. I thought this Wally fella was just a gag you dreamed up to sell some papers. Now you're making it sound like there's something behind it."

"That's what I'm thinking. Someone don't go to this kind of trouble for nothing. You know about any new scams in town, any rackets going?"

"There's always rackets going, Jimmy, you know that. There's only so much we can do. Drugs, gambling, whores. We got it all in Carsworth City just like any other burg I ever heard about. Take your pick for what's behind this. There's plenty of money in all of it and seems like as soon as we squash one cockroach, two or three more take its place."

"What about this truck I saw?"

"Dark Metro van? You know as well as I do business has been booming since the end of the war. There's plenty of those trucks around these days delivering anything and everything you can think of. And you didn't even get part of a license plate or notice anything written on the side of the truck?"

I shook my head, mad at myself.

"There's not much we can do with that," he commiserated. "I can keep my ear to the ground. Let you know if I get wind of anything out that way, but you don't have a whole lot to go on here. I'd even say it's possible someone was playing a joke on you if it weren't for the size of that lump you got. That looks like someone meant business. You sure you don't want to think twice about dropping the whole thing? You know what happened last time you got mixed up in something like this."

He gave the scar on my face a meaningful look. It was Joey, back when he was still a beat cop, who found me bleeding in the street, got me to the doc, and testified to the self-defense patter that left me a free man.

"I know, I know," I said. "But it's complicated."

"Let me guess. It's complicated like this…" Joey said, moving his hands to sketch out a shapely figure in the air. "Convince me there ain't a dame at the bottom of your interest in all this, and I'll pour some catsup over them pieces of hat you got there and eat them myself."

I just tipped him the wink and hightailed it out of there. Victoria was a lady. She deserved better than to have her name bandied about in a police station with a bunch of jokers listening in.

Trotting down to the paper, I made for the morgue, and was greeted like a long-lost brother by an excited-looking Q.

"Mr. Malhaven! I was hoping to see you today. I finally found the editions we needed. All the details on the murder! And you'll never guess—the story you were told was right in that Hornschmidt did stab his wife and son, but…" he added in thrilling tones, "the child survived!"

CHAPTER FIFTEEN

"Hey, that's good stuff, Q," I said. "Everyone seems convinced the kid met his maker, but if he survived, maybe he's still kicking around somewhere. That would be quite the interview. I can see the headline now: 'Son of Infamous Murderer Tells All to the Crier's Star Reporter.' Does it say what happened to him?"

"Sounds like there was no family to take him in. He probably was sent to the orphanage. Maybe he even got adopted. Might be hard to trace if that's the case. They usually take the new parents' surname. He might not even know who his real parents were. That would be quite a shock, wouldn't it?"

"Yeah," I agreed, sobered at the thought. "You're right there. Finding out your pa offed your ma and tried his best to do you in, too? That could be a hard pill to choke down. Let's take a look at what you got."

Q pulled out the editions for me, and I read through the articles. Some of it lined up with the story I'd heard. Hornschmidt was a milkman, but he hadn't walked in on his wife with another man. Sounded more like the kind of domestic set-to that's all too common. It was a sad fact of life that men went off on their wives all the time, and they didn't always seem to need much of an excuse to do it. But it was usually with fists, not a knife. And usually not the kids.

The kid, Peter Christopher—he was older than I'd been thinking. Almost three at the time of the murder. I wondered if he remembered anything about it. That would be a hell of a first memory to have to hang on to all your life. And what about this story of Wally carrying the baby in and out of the cemetery with him when it turned out the kid was older and had survived the whole thing?

"Look at this," I said to Q. "Hornschmidt hung himself in the city jail before he ever went to trial. That must have been a disappointment for a lot of folks. A big trial like that would have been first-class entertainment back in the day. The Wynter sisters thought he'd been executed by the State. I can't get why they don't remember more about Wally and how they got some of the details wrong. Wouldn't you think they'd remember a thing like that?"

"It may not be that unusual," Q answered. "I took a couple of psychology classes at school. They've done studies that find most people's memories aren't nearly as accurate as we'd like to believe. And the more time that passes since an event, the more inaccuracies creep into our minds. Particularly with stories like this, people tend to embellish them over time. It's like that party game where each person whispers the same message to the next person and by the time you get to the end of the line, the message is totally different from how it started."

"I ain't been to too many parties, but that sounds like good, clean fun. Most of the witness accounts mention seeing Wally clutching a bundle to his chest, though. That seemed pretty consistent. If it's not a baby, wonder what it is?"

"Yes, that does seem to be the one detail that people agree on. Do you think it's important?" Q asked.

"Let's just say it suggests a thing or three to me. But I'll need to study on it some more. Maybe we'll find out something at this séance bash the Wynter sisters are throwing."

"A séance! Really? That sounds very interesting."

"Why don't you tag along? I been told I can bring a friend, and I guess you and me are pretty friendly, ain't we?"

Q looked as pleased as punch, whether at the idea we might be friends or about this spirit shindig, I didn't know, but it did make me think I might not be the only lonely guy in Carsworth City. It also occurred to me that to be fair, I'd better give him the heads up about the trouble I'd seen.

"I got to be honest with you. There's someone don't want us investigating this whole Wally scenario." I took off my hat again and pointed out my souvenir. "Someone gave me a knock on the noggin last night to try and shut me down. I don't know how safe it would be for you to come to this party. That same someone might be keeping an eye on what I get up to next."

"I'm not afraid," Q said. "The minute we let anyone tell us what we can and can't print, we are no longer a free press and no longer acting in the best interests of the public's right to know."

I had to hand it to him. He looked like he weighed maybe one-hundred and thirty soaking wet, but I believed him when he said he had plenty of pluck. I imagined he'd been through some things already in his life. People with his skin color didn't have the easiest time around Carsworth City. He'd probably had to toughen up and quick.

"It is certainly reprehensible that someone physically attacked you," he said, all disapproving and shaking his head.

"And that ain't the worst." I pulled out the pieces of my late lamented headpiece and spread them out on the counter in front of us. "Look what they done to my hat."

Q looked thoughtful as he examined the pieces. "Talk about sending you a message. This looks like it took some effort. It's interesting that they used pinking shears to cut it up."

"Pink-o shears?" I asked, having never heard of such a thing before. "What are they? Communists?" I added with a knowing look.

"No, pink-*ing*." Q set me wise with admirable forbearance. "That's what makes this zigzag pattern. Special scissors with a crimped edge. Tailors use them for cutting cloth. It helps keep the edges from fraying while they're sewing up the garment."

"Tailors, huh? Anyone else likely to have these laying around?"

"Anyone could get hold of a pair. I imagine a lot of ladies have them if they do much sewing. My mother has a pair. She used to make all our clothes. Still does, actually," he confessed, looking embarrassed.

"That's mighty nice," I reassured him. "She obviously knows what she's doing. I'd never have known it. Sounds like they aren't too uncommon, these shears. That might not help us so much then, but it's another fact to add to what we know."

"What else do you know?" he asked.

I filled him in on all my adventures.

"Left in the middle of the road? Why, you're lucky to be alive, Mr. Malhaven! That van sounds very suspicious. The dark color and driving around that time of night with no lights like they didn't want to be noticed."

"Yeah, sure seems that way. And unfortunately for me, I noticed them and let them know I noticed them. Not my smartest move," I admitted. "So, all we got to do is find someone driving around in a dark van without their lamps lit and a pair of fancy clippers in the glove compartment, and we'll have our man!"

"Or woman," Q amended.

I was skeptical when he first said it, but I had to admit, the neat way the hat was cut up did smack of someone with a delicate touch. Could there be a woman at the back of this? And not just any woman, but *the* woman? How much did I really know about Victoria after all? I'd already seen she could be unpredictable. Sweet as a sugar cube one time I saw her and prickly as a cactus the next.

It seemed strange to me that she kept on living out at the cemetery all these years after her husband had passed away, but it would make sense if she was using her job as a front for some other business altogether. Might explain the fancy duds she sometimes wore, too. They seemed out of step with the modest salary she must get for tending to the dead.

It made me more than a little uncomfortable to think that way. No man wants to believe the woman of his dreams might have a dark side.

But I was a cynical guy at heart—realistic, I liked to think—so, it didn't seem outside the realm of things that was possible. This story had gotten a lot more serious than I'd expected. I made a vow to myself to start paying more attention to what was going on around me and stop letting myself get distracted by a soulful pair of gray-blue eyes.

I jotted down some notes on the articles Q found and took them up to the newsroom to help me type up my inches for the next day's edition. The murder was less sensational than I was hoping for, if I'm honest, but the angle of the boy who survived gave it some verve. There's nothing like a kid in jeopardy to pull at people's heartstrings. I played up the whole *where is he now?* line pretty hard. Figured that would give the readers something to chew on.

He'd be thirty-one now if I did my arithmetic right. In the prime of life. Depending on where he was and what he was doing and what he knew, it might come as an unpleasant surprise if he started putting two and two together. Part of me felt guilty at the thought I might be opening up a can of worms for the poor guy, but you learn early in my business, you can't get too caught up in the emotions and the lives of the people you report on or you'd never write another word in your life.

I headed home after Morty gave me the okay on my piece and stretched out for a couple of hours. My headache was much improved by getting some shuteye, so I spent a few hours roaming around some of the business districts in town. I found plenty of dark Metro vans, and I even started a list of them in my notebook, but it was kinda hard to know what to do with the info without something more specific to go on.

Finally, at the very tail end of my day, despite my best intentions, I found myself right back where I'd promised myself all day that I *wouldn't* go that night. Standing under the big wrought iron sign: *Wynter's Hill Cemetery*

CHAPTER SIXTEEN

This time, I didn't do any loitering around the gates on the off chance of getting the soft word, or even a hard word, from a pretty lady. Resolved to be all business, I hoofed it over to the stand of trees across the way, taking better care to find cover from any passing traffic.

Like the night before, there was little enough of it. A guy in a gray Buick passed headed back toward town, and that was the limits of the excitement until a Chevrolet truck painted an unusual green color passed me headed out into the country. It was tootling along at no great speed, so I got a good look at the operator—an old guy, white hair peeking out from under a beat-up straw hat and one of those bushy Santa beards. The fancy new truck and the weathered driver looked like they didn't match up. All I could figure was maybe he'd had a banner harvest and decided to splash out on a new ride.

After that, there was a whole lot of nothing. I hate to admit this to you, but I guess all the excitement finally caught up with me, and I fell asleep. I know I fell asleep, 'cause when I came to, I checked my watch to find it was well after midnight, and who knows what I had missed seeing by then? I found out quick there was at least one thing

I'd missed, 'cause as I started to stand up, I seen a dark van across the way, pulling away from the gates.

Rattled at being caught napping, I stumbled to my feet, trying to get a peep at the license plate or anything else that might give me a clue. I wasn't too surprised to see by the light of the tail lamps that the plate was covered up with a dark piece of cloth. Throwing caution out the door, I jumped from my hiding place, but I was too late by a mile. The van was already roaring off down the road, those red tail lights disappearing in the gloom as I stood like a chump in the road just watching.

Kicking myself twelve ways from Sunday for being such an amateur, I took a look around the gates to see if I could salvage any clues. I'd had the smarts to shove a flashlight in my pocket before I left town, so I shined it this way and that to see if anything seemed out of place and was rewarded by a couple of finds.

The first was a clear set of tire tracks in the mud just off the road in front of the gates. They looked like standard truck tires except the rear driver's side tread looked like it might have had a patch on it, like someone had fixed up a flat. There wasn't much I could do about making an impression, but I sketched out the pattern in my notebook as best I could. Maybe I could get Flanagan to send one of his boys out in the morning—even as I had the thought, I felt it. The first drop of rain. Before long, it was pouring. So much for getting a professional cast of that track, but maybe me or the cops could make the rounds of the vans in the city and see if we could find one with a patched-up tire.

The second thing I seen was a small pile of white powder at my feet. The rain was coming down too hard for me to try and dust up a sample to take with me, so I just stuck my finger in the fast disappearing pile and brought it to my mouth to give it a taste. It was bitter as anything. Gave me a hunch it was one of the hard drugs, morphine or heroin. There'd been plenty of both going around town since the end of the war. I watched in frustration as the tiny grains of evidence vanished before my eyes in a stream of mud.

I thought back to my conversations with Victoria. My suspicion that she might be under the influence some of the times I tried to talk to her. Was this part of a personal delivery just for her? And since I'd disrupted the delivery the night before, they'd stopped back by to complete their deal? She'd seemed innocence itself when asking me about the van. I didn't like to think of that open-hearted girl who'd generously gifted me her dead hubby's hat sneaking out to the gates at night to pick up her fix, but I'd been around enough addicts to know they could be awfully sly at keeping their habit under wraps.

On the other hand, maybe this was part of the scheme I'd been suspecting. Those elegant clothes I'd seen Victoria wear kept popping into my brain. Were they a clue that she was raking in serious dough under the table? If so, how'd she get involved, and what part did the cemetery play in it all? It was so isolated, it didn't make sense as a distribution center. It's not like I'd seen a steady stream of drug fiends wending their way out from town to pick up their next hit, or even dealers, come out to restock their merchandise. It was definitely a puzzle.

It was a cold night and that rain pouring down didn't help. Feeling like I'd collected what meager clues I was gonna find, I walked back down the road to where I'd left the Champ parked and started the drive back to town. I was soaked through and through and feeling shivery as a fish by the time I got home. I shed my wet clothes and climbed under all the blankets I had in the place, thinking I'd be too worked up to sleep, but I found myself drifting off right in the middle of that very thought.

I turned and tossed in a restless sleep the rest of the night. A sleep full of dreams and nightmares of a woman with honey-blonde hair. One minute, she was an angel, posed in a beam of heavenly light and smiling at me, the next, a devil, barely visible in the dark gloom of an inky night. Over and over, she changed back and forth, angel and devil, lightness and dark, good and evil. I awoke drenched in sweat at the last image of her with black, black eyes and a needle in her hand, ready to inject some of that poison into her lovely pale arm.

A brash rat-a-tat-tat on the door brought me fully awake—I don't get a lot of visitors. I shrugged on an old bathrobe and staggered to answer it only to find Izzy Schwartz, one of the Crier's copy boys, slouching on the stoop. I raised an eyebrow to convey my astonishment. Izzy always gave the impression that he had a million and one more important things to be doing at any given moment, and he sure don't believe in wasting his breath.

"The boss says ixnay on the Wally bunkum," he spouted, thrusting a crumpled piece of paper into the pocket of my robe before executing a smart about-face that would have made my old drill sergeant proud and disappearing while I was still in the middle of formulating some kind of a question for him.

Perplexed, I stumbled back inside and collapsed at the table. Pulled out the paper and spread it open, smoothing it out as I tried to bring the words into focus. "Cease and desist" were the first ones that jumped out at me. I'd have done better with it if I'd had a cup of joe first, but I finally took it to mean that Liv had carried through on her threat to get the lawyer joker involved. There was his scrawl, Harold Monroe, Esq., right at the bottom of all the legal bafflegab. I'm no expert in such things, but it seemed to boil down to cease and desist from publishing stories about the cemetery and its supposed ghost or be prepared to face some unpleasantness.

It sounded like so much hot air to me, but Izzy's message from Morty was clear enough. He was axing the story rather than risk the hassle. I couldn't blame him. From his point of view, there wasn't enough to it to justify bringing any bad hoodoo down on the paper 'cause I hadn't filled him in yet on the broader insinuations I'd been uncovering.

My first impulse was to sprint down to the paper and fill him in pronto. My second was to hold off for a bit. I didn't have enough concrete facts yet to convince him I was on to something big. It was interesting he hadn't sent another assignment for me with Izzy. I took it to mean he was granting me time to finish up any investigating I'd been doing. That if I brought him something that tested off the charts, he'd think twice about the prohibition on all things phantasmal. Like I said, Morty was an okay boss in his way.

I took a shower and drank three cups of coffee to clear my head. Swallowed a handful of aspirin to try and stop that shivery feeling that had hung around from the night before. I didn't want to come down with something, not before I got all this straightened out. If I really wanted to get it straightened out. At the back of my mind, I kept seeing a picture of Victoria, looking out at me with pleading eyes as a cage of solid steel bars shut her away from the world. Could I really face up to being the guy responsible for dumping her in the slammer?

The very idea of it sent me into another shivering fit. I decided to spend the rest of the day conserving my energy in bed. It had been a tough few days, and who knew what this spirit shindig would produce? Better to be in as good a shape as I could manage before the next act went down. I had a feeling it might be a doozy.

CHAPTER SEVENTEEN

I was feeling more chipper after I rested up. I spent some time reflecting on how helpful Victoria had been when she'd found me splashed out in the middle of the road. If she'd been in on the whole thing, would she have been so friendly? I guess you could argue she was a good actress and was trying to deflect my suspicions, but then you never looked into those clear blue eyes twinkling away in the bright morning sunlight the way I did.

Don't worry. I made myself a solemn vow to keep an open mind. Open mind and open eyes was my new motto. I couldn't afford to keep letting evidence slip through my fingers, and I didn't underrate the seriousness of my situation. I'd maybe gained the glimmer of an idea now about something that might be going on, but I was still largely stumbling around in the dark. But my mysterious opponent might not realize how in the dark I was. They might be feeling threatened simply through the completely understandable error of overestimating my investigative genius.

I hopped into the Champ to crank it up so I could collect Q at the office and escort him out to our ghostly soiree. There was a deafening silence as I tried to turn over the engine. I cranked it a few more times.

Nothing. Got out and took a gander under the hood. No question. Someone had cut some pretty important wires. Nothing I couldn't fix up with time and the right materials, but that would make me late for the séance which was maybe somebody's big idea but that didn't mean I had to go along with it.

Legging it as quick as I could over to the office, I met up with Q and told him my sad tale of the sabotage done to the Studebaker. He suggested taking the city bus out to the end of the line near the edge of town then hoofing it the rest of the way. I sighed at the thought of the walk, my bad leg giving out a twinge like it wasn't too happy about it either, but I was determined not to give whoever had tried to slow me down the satisfaction of success.

We chatted a bit as we waited for the bus. Q was all dressed to kill in a neat black suit that fit him like a glove. Made me feel pretty shabby in my baggy old gray flannel get-up. My hat was the spiffiest thing about me, and it wasn't even mine. I hadn't had a chance to replace my fedora yet, and I'll admit, I was getting attached to the one Victoria lent me. It was a perfect fit, and I enjoyed the feel of the fresh, crisp brim. It made me want to splurge on a new suit to complete the look, but that would have to wait until I had a more impressive figure written down in the balance column of my bankbook than I did at present.

"Looking sharp, Mr. Sutherland," I said to Q. "Don't tell me your ma whipped that nifty number up for you?"

"She did," he said, looking pleased at the compliment, but then what son doesn't like to hear their ma get the applause she deserves? "She's had a lot of experience."

"Say, you don't think she'd be willing to run up something like that for me, do you? That looks a lot nicer than any suit I ever bought off the rack. If I could afford her prices, that is."

"I'm sure we could work something out. She enjoys making clothes. It's more like a hobby for her than work. I'm making enough at the paper now to start buying a few things of my own, but I think she'd be disappointed if she couldn't keep making things for me and my sister."

"You got a sister, too, huh?"

"Yes. Marlene. She just finished nursing school."

"Carsworth again?" I asked, curious if our esteemed publisher was a general benefactor to the Sutherland family or just to Marquis.

"Yes, he's been very generous to us. Of course, my mother's been in service with his family since she was fourteen."

"What about your pops? Or shouldn't I ask?" I said, realizing as I said it that sounded pretty dumb since I already had.

"That's okay. I don't mind. He passed away a few years ago. He was the chauffeur for the Carsworths. It's a cliché, isn't it? The maid and the chauffeur fall in love. But they'd both worked for the family since they were in their teens, so I guess it was natural. We miss him. He was a good man."

"You're lucky. My pops wouldn't have bent over to lend me a handkerchief if he had found me lying bleeding on the sidewalk. He didn't leave us crying none when he shuffled off."

I brushed off Q's sympathy for my glum childhood as the bus pulled up and we hopped on board. I made a beeline for the back row out of habit. I get a kind of seasickness riding in big transports and had found out during my Army days that riding in the back helped out. It was only when we got ourselves settled there, and Q thanked me quietly, that it dawned on me he thought I'd done it to keep him company.

There was a definite pecking order in seating in the buses back then. It wasn't something I ever thought about but being with Q made me see it with fresh eyes. I can never get used to the strange rules people like to make for each other if they think they can get away with it.

Q was an interesting fellow, and it made the tedious ride more enjoyable having someone to jaw with. Even our walk that I had worried would be so long felt like it was over in no time. He seemed to know more about that ghost stuff than you could find out in a whole set of encyclopedias. He told me all about the history of spirit boards and even about an experiment he'd read that seemed to prove that folks were moving the marker around themselves without even knowing it, spelling out stuff they had knocking around in the dusty corners of their craniums.

If that was true, I thought we might see some interesting things spilling out from the group that was gathering. Those weird sisters probably had some pretty woolly thoughts rattling around just beneath the surface if the ones up top were any sign.

The gates were shut, but not locked, and there was no guardian lurking, so we strolled on in with me guiding Q up the path toward the mansion on the hill. You'd think it would be even spookier at night, but the windows were all lit up, making it look brighter and breezier than it did during the day. Not that I would endorse walking through a boneyard at night as a pleasant activity. I don't think Q or me minded having someone to keep us company one bit.

We were almost up to the door when we ran into another party of two. I was astounded to see it was Margo Cummings and her sister, the one I'd found to be the brainiest of the bunch back at that madhouse they called home. I finally got a name to match the face when Margo introduced her to us as Mabel. I expressed something of my amazement to see them there.

"The Wynter sisters invited me. They thought since I had a close encounter with Wally once already, that my presence might entice him to appear again," Margo said modestly. "Father took some convincing, but finally he agreed to let me come, but only if Mabel came with me. He and Mother seem to set a great deal of store by Mabel," she added, with a certain amount of ill-concealed irritation.

I tipped Mabel a wink, and she returned the favor. A girl of few words, but let me tell you, I wouldn't mind having her in my corner in any kind of a tight spot. I'd already figured out what her parents had, too—Mabel had more sense in her little finger than all the rest of those kids put together. She was the one that made bold to lift the heavy doorknocker a few times to attract some attention to us waiting on the doorstep.

It wasn't too long before one of the great doors was yanked open to reveal the sisters, Ernie and Bernie, smiling in delight as they invited us in with many a bobbing bow and sweeping arm wave. I thought I'd figured out that Bernie was the one whose hairdo was always neater than her sister's and had this confirmed for me when they introduced themselves to the newcomers.

They fussed over us, taking our coats and setting them aside on some of the big chairs there in the front hall. Margo and Mabel were dressed in their Sunday best which looked homemade by a hand not nearly as neat as Q's mother. I guess when you got that many kids, keeping them all in duds is no joke. Young Mabel was dressed in brown and had the look of someone who couldn't care less about what she was wearing but Margo had made an attempt to jazz up her pink number with a little bouquet of paper flowers pinned to the shoulder and a cheap strand of beads.

We were herded down the hallway to a large room that had been nearly emptied of furniture except for a round table, surrounded by some hard, wooden chairs. Candles were dotted along the floor around the perimeter of the room, some flickering precariously close to the filmy curtains flanking the floor to ceiling windows that lined the wall opposite the door.

The sisters indicated the tea trolley in one corner, and the Cummings girls weren't shy about digging into the tiny cakes that were piled up high on one of those fancy three-tiered china plates. The Wynter sisters then turned their attention to Q with looks of intense fascination that I immediately thought boded no good.

"How wonderful," Ernie said. "I don't believe we've ever had one of your kind in the house before, have we, Bernie?"

"No," her sister agreed. "Not that I remember. Father didn't allow it. This is quite an experience for us, Mr. Sutherland."

My stomach dropped somewhere down close to my knees. I felt like a dope for not checking whether it was okay with the sisters before hauling Q along. Black people weren't welcome everywhere in those days, not with open arms anyway, and I felt guilty I hadn't made sure of his reception before we came. I was kicking myself for opening him up to more of the kind of humiliation he'd probably suffered enough of in his life, but he was taking it all in stride, outwardly anyway. Maybe he was just glad they seemed more interested in him than offended by his presence. He'd probably had the other effect on people more than I cared to think about. Or maybe he just had way too much practice at hiding his true feelings.

If there was any lingering uncertainty in their secret heart of hearts about their unusual guest, Q put it to rest by buttering up the Wynter sisters on the swell atmosphere they had going on and fussing over the wooden board on the table with admiration. I noticed he didn't lecture them about that whole mental effect of the hidden brain. I'll say Q knew how to take the measure of his audience. That's a talent more people could stand to develop in my book.

Our hostesses insisted we all choke down a cup of tea after they dumped a couple of sugar cubes in each one before handing them to us and try the little iced cakes before we launched into the main event. Both treats were sickly sweet to my taste, but I wanted to be a gracious guest, so I didn't complain. I don't get invited out often enough to turn up my nose at any refreshments on offer. A glass of suds at the corner dive with some of the other hacks from the paper or Flanagan and some of his crew was about the extent of my social life.

Even though it was an unlikely crowd we had assembled there for our spirit get-together, I found I was enjoying myself. Guess it just goes to show how deprived I was of the ordinary human contact most people take for granted.

"So, ladies," Q finally asked. "It's nearing midnight. Shall we gather round?"

"Oh, yes," agreed Bernie. "We should get ready to start. We're just waiting for—"

The booming sound of the heavy doorknocker interrupted her announcement.

"Oh, goody," said Ernie. "Our final guest. Mr. Malhaven, maybe you wouldn't mind answering the door while the rest of us take our places?"

Always happy to oblige, I took myself off down the hallway and pulled open the hefty door, trying to guess who else the sisters might have invited.

"Well, well. We meet again."

I'd have known that sultry voice anywhere.

CHAPTER EIGHTEEN

"What are you doing here?" I asked, astounded to discover Victoria Jankowski of all people standing before me. "I thought you didn't believe in all this hocus-pocus stuff?"

"There's no law against changing one's mind, is there? We don't get that much in the way of entertainment around here—it seemed a shame to pass up a chance like this. Maybe it'll be good for a laugh, if nothing else," she said with a mocking look in her eye.

I took a sniff on the sly as she brushed past me on the way in. Thought maybe I'd smell it on her if she'd been tippling, but all I got was the sweet scent of violets. She pulled off her coat to reveal a swell-looking evening dress the color of a cloudless summer sky. It was high-necked—in deference to the feelings of the sisters, I supposed—but the fit didn't leave much to the imagination. She'd piled her hair up high and there was a string of real pearls, or some mighty convincing fakes, glistening against the soft material of her dress.

I guess I must've been goggling, because she laughed that trilling laugh at me and brushed a gloved hand against my unmarked cheek lightly before asking me to point her in the right direction. Trying to pull myself together, I offered her my arm, thrilled when she tucked her small hand in the crook of my elbow, and escorted her to the séance room.

Her entrance caused quite a stir. Margo in particular seemed over-awed by the goddess who had suddenly materialized among us. Even though she was seventeen and had pretensions of being a full-blown woman herself, she looked like a gawky child in her handmade dress standing next to Victoria in all her finery. The Wynters fussed over their employee like a movie star had landed in our midst. Only Mabel seemed unfazed, but then I figured it took a lot to shake up Mabel.

I introduced Victoria to Q.

"Oh. How do you do," she drawled in a voice so chilly it sent a shiver of ice up my own spine before she turned away, ignoring him.

It got my dander up but good. I was starting to get used to her hot and cold ways, but that was just plain rude, and Q couldn't hide this time that it stung. Surprisingly, it was Ernie and Bernie who smoothed it over by each grabbing one of Q's arms and guiding him to a place of honor between them at the table with their backs to the windows. The rest of us followed suit and chose a spot, Mabel and Margo each taking a seat beside one of the sisters which left the last two seats, opposite the large windows, to me and Victoria.

I was still steaming from her brush-off of Q, so I made a point of refraining from helping her out with her chair as punishment, but she didn't seem to notice my snub, being too busy oozing a snooty disdain for the whole deal. Prepared to find anything that happened *terribly* amusing no matter how anyone else felt about it. Her whole manner turned me right off her again, with me trying to tell myself I was glad of it. Whether she was in a good mood or a bad one, she'd made it clear I wasn't a serious contender for her affections, but it hurts a lot less to be turned down when you decide you don't want what's on offer anyhow. Call it sour grapes but that's how I was feeling.

The Wynter sisters seemed to have decided Q was the greatest authority on the afterlife in the room, so they deferred to him to get the party going.

"It's simple really," he explained, pushing his glasses back into place on his nose. "We'll all put one finger on the planchette, that's this special pointer here. Then we can ask either yes or no questions, and the pointer will point to 'yes' or 'no' here on the board. Or we can ask a more complicated question and see if we can get an answer spelled out with the letters and numbers."

"How do we start?" asked Ernie.

"Why don't we sit quietly for a moment and gather our thoughts. I think we're all supposed to concentrate on conjuring the lifeforce of the soul we wish to speak to. We should think about Wally. What we know about him. See if we can draw him to us."

Q was sure acting like he believed everything he was saying. I wondered where all that scientific talk about psychology and the unconscious mind had gotten to. Maybe he was just trying to enter into the spirit of it all, if you'll pardon the joke.

As I've said, I'm not an overly imaginative guy, but even I could appreciate the mood that was being set. The candles flickering in the gloom, everyone sitting so hushed and solemn. I glanced over at Victoria. She didn't look so amused now. In fact, I thought I detected that faint, unmistakable whiff of sweat and would have almost sworn she was afraid.

Q nodded around the table at us all, and we reached out and touched the wooden marker. The table was too big, so it was awkward, everyone having to lean over and reach in. Victoria brushed up against me, and I recoiled like I'd been prodded in the side with a hot poker, but she seemed too intent on the board to notice or care.

Q cleared his throat and spoke. "Is there anyone here with us?"

Nothing happened. Margo started to giggle nervously, but Mabel gave her a severe look that shut that down quick.

Never one to be afraid of looking the fool, I decided to give it a shot, pinching my nose with my free hand and announcing in my best old-timey operator's voice, "Calling Wally Hornschmidt. Come in, Mr. Hornschmidt. I have a party on the line for you."

This time the marker moved. I think we all gave a jump, but we kept our fingers planted as it slowly slid over to one side of the board. *Yes.*

Everyone looked to me to keep the sparkling conversation going. "We're gathered here tonight to help you out. Do you want our help?"

The marker hesitated, moving back and forth across the board between the "yes" and "no" before finally landing: *No.*

"No, you don't want our help?" I asked, making sure we understood each other.

The marker swooped around in a circle and landed back at the "no" again.

"Okay," says I, looking around at the others there at the table. "What do we do now? He don't want no help."

Victoria piped up. "Why did you do it?" she asked softly, her voice dripping with some deep feeling I couldn't read.

There was no movement for a half a minute. Then it started toward the double row of letters in the middle of the board. *P-E-T-E...* I held my breath expecting it to land on the "R" next for Peter, Wally's son. But it outsmarted me by going on down the alphabet, landing on the "Y" instead.

"Petey?" asked Q.

The marker zoomed. *Yes.*

"Nickname, maybe," I said. "That's interesting. Did anyone here know about that?"

Everyone shook their heads, but Petey's a pretty common thing to call a kid named Peter. Someone could have had that thought and be guiding the spelling without realizing it.

Bernie took over the questioning. "Petey's your little boy?" *Yes.*

"Was it something he did?" *No.*

"Was it something your wife did?" *Yes.*

"What did she do?" *H-U-R-T-P-*

"Hurt Petey?" Bernie asked impatiently.

The marker hurtled toward the "yes" again. Then, I swear to you, it zoomed right out from under our fingers and flung itself across the room. Everyone sat frozen in surprise. I was still trying to figure out how we'd managed to make that happen when Mabel jumped up to retrieve the thing. Like I said, she wasn't the easily disconcerted type.

We all lay our fingers on again once Mabel restored it to the table, and Victoria asked the next question. "How did she hurt Petey?"

No answer.

I gave it a try. "You still on the line with us, Wally?"

No answer.

I looked around the table and kind of shrugged my shoulders, like, *now what?*

Mabel suddenly made us wise to the fact that she had a voice box. "Is there anyone else here now?"

Silence, then it started to move again ever so slow. *Yes.*

"Who are you?" said Ernie, thrilled.

The pointer started moving fast. We all started chanting out the letters to try and keep up. *W-H-E-R-E-S-D-A-I-S-Y*

"Where's Daisy?" asked Margo. "What does that mean?"

She was asking the rest of us, but I guess the ghost or whoever thought she was just being dense 'cause it started spelling it out all over again: *W-H-E-R-E-S-D-A-I-S-Y*

"Seems like the better question is, who's Daisy?" says I.

For once, I wasn't trying to be a wise guy, but I don't think the spirit, if there was one, appreciated that 'cause the whole table started shimmying up and down like a bucking bronco at the rodeo. Margo and Victoria both jumped out of their chairs and backed away from it like they'd been bitten.

I still wasn't buying the whole phantom gag, so I stood up, too, to see if I couldn't work out how the table was being shifted. Before I could catch someone red-handed, though, it crashed back down to the floor with a loud BANG. That happened to coincide with one of the big windows at the back of the room shattering followed by a funny sensation like someone had blown a puff of air right through the part in my hair.

Mabel jumped up and switched on all the lights. I couldn't help but notice that I was the center of attention.

"What?" I asked.

"Your hat," Q answered, pointing a shaking finger at my head.

I reached up to snatch it off my melon. And before anyone tries to give me a refresher course in proper etiquette, I know I ought not to have been wearing it inside, especially in the presence of the ladies. My excuse is I'd been too taken up with all the goings on to remember to set it aside earlier.

I took a gander at it, and right there near the top of the fedora's crown was a pair of the neatest little holes you ever saw. I followed the line from the window to the door until I saw it. A slug, buried deep in the wood of the door frame. A bullet with my name on it.

CHAPTER NINETEEN

It won't come as any shock to you to find out that Margo let out a scream right about then and fainted dead away. It wasn't the graceful number I'd come to expect from her neither. She hit that floor like a sack of potatoes. Luckily, there was plenty of people to fuss over her 'cause I was too busy hopping it to the window to see what I could see.

The window was a mess, so I tore off my suit jacket and wrapped my hand up good so I could knock out the bigger pieces of glass before they had a chance to fall and hurt someone. Swiveled the catch on the lock and got the frame up enough so I could duck out and found myself in a thicket of those prickly rosebushes that ran all along that side of the house. Had to fight my way through, picking up more than a few scratches along the way, but by the time I got out onto the lawn, whoever had taken the shot was history.

I guess I was lucky he hadn't stuck around long enough to finish me off. If I hadn't been so fired up, I might have thought twice about chasing around in the dark after some mook with a gun and me with nothing but my fists, but that was the second piece of head gear someone had wrecked for me in as many days. There's only so much of that I was gonna put up with.

Upon trotting back to the house, I found the séance room cleared out. Of any living person, that is—I won't speak for the dead. Retrieving my ruined topper, I wandered the hall until I heard voices. Everyone had retreated to the pale-colored sitting room where I'd first visited with the sisters. Margo had been laid out on the sofa where she was being tended to by everyone but Victoria, who was standing at one of the windows, looking soulful.

I strolled over to her, putting my finger through one of the holes in the fedora, feeling like I let her down. "I'm awful sorry about that. After I promised to look after it and everything."

"What does it matter?" she said, barely glancing at it like she could hardly be bothered. "It's just a hat. Can't you get another one?"

"Well… yeah. But it was his. Lukasz. I thought it meant something to you."

"Oh, of course. I just didn't want you to feel bad about it, did I? Anyway, at least it isn't your head with the hole in it."

"That's one way of looking at it," I agreed. "Seems like someone don't like me too much."

"How is that possible when you are charm personified?"

We got distracted just then from our banter by Margo coming to on the sofa. Her minders helped her sit up as she looked over to where Mrs. J and I were posed by the window. I never seen a person go so much paler than pale before and never that fast. She raised one finger to point toward the window behind us, and then she was out again like a light when the bulb pops.

I followed her gaze in time to see a head of tousled blond hair disappear into a bush just outside. Wrenching open the window, I stuck one meaty paw out and fished around until I came up with the catch of the day which I hauled in through the window like I was reeling in a line.

"Ow!" the wriggling fish protested as it was dumped unceremoniously on the carpet.

"Mikey Cummings," Mabel announced in a voice full of doom. "Does Pa know you're out here?"

"Aw, geez. You won't tell him, Mabes, will you? I just wanted to catch some of the excitement, and boy, did I!" He turned his attention on me like a spotlight. "Hey, mister, did you know some guy took a potshot at you, huh? I was right there and I saw the whole thing. He shot right through the window, too. No way someone coulda made a shot like that, could they? Through a closed window? And it was all dark inside, too. I could hardly see what was going on. It don't make no sense, do it, mister? And the funny thing was he was aiming way too high. If I hadn't bumped his hand, he wouldn't even have come close to hitting you. Doesn't sound like he's a very good shot, does it? I don't think he knew what he was doing, do you? Huh? *Yikes*!"

That last was a response to me hoisting him high in the air so he was at my eye level. I had decided I wanted to have a talk with him, man to man.

"You bumped his hand?" I asked as clear as I could, seeing as my jaw was clenched tighter than a vise. I couldn't see my own face, naturally, but Mikey had a front row seat, and from his expression, I got the idea he wasn't enjoying the view.

"Maybe," he said so soft I could barely make it out.

"Maybe?" I repeated, just for clarification, you know.

"Just… kind of… like an accident… maybe?"

"Let me make sure I got this absolutely straight. You by accident bumped his hand so that instead of shooting harmlessly over our heads, he nearly killed me, and he spoilt my brand-new, first-class fedora? Does that sound about right?"

The room around us had gone silent. It felt to me like everyone was holding their breath, waiting for the answer.

It was hard to hear it when it came. Barely a whisper. "Kinda, I guess. I was trying to get closer to see what he was doing, and I… I tripped and I… maybe bumped his hand. Just a little."

I saw nothing but red in front of me, but I felt the tug at my elbow. I looked down to find Mabel hanging on to my arm. It was the first time I ever saw her look worried. I guess she didn't like what she saw in my face any more than Mikey did. I took a deep breath and forced myself to gently lower the prisoner to the floor. He took off running and hid behind the sofa.

Mabel reached up to give me a sympathetic pat on the shoulder. "I'm awfully sorry. Mikey's a terrible trial to us all."

I gave a nod in acknowledgement, not trusting myself to sing out just then, but the spell was broken by a trilling laugh, unnaturally loud in the quiet. We all turned to look at Victoria who'd made her way to the sitting room door.

"This is the most fun I've had in a dog's age," she said with a grin. "Quite the farce all around. It's getting late, though, and I need my beauty sleep. Don't worry. I'll see myself out."

True to her word, she slipped out the door before anyone could say a word. We could hear her high heels echoing down the long hallway until she reached the front door.

"Well!" said Bernie. "I must say, Mrs. Jankowski behaved rather oddly tonight. Don't you think so, Ernie?"

"It has been a very odd night, Bernie," her sister replied. "I don't think we can hold *anyone* responsible for how they've behaved," she added, giving me the evil eye.

I got the idea she didn't exactly approve of me manhandling a child, but then she hadn't yet learned that Mikey was one of the Devil's own imps in human form. When I thought of what had almost happened. And all because Mikey couldn't mind his own business.

I tried to cool down and think it all over carefully. If the little terror was right and the guy was aiming up, that meant he was just trying to give me or someone else there a scare, like a warning shot. He was probably as startled as anyone that he'd almost done for me. That would explain why he took off and didn't hang around to finish the job.

Margo came to again and tried to give Mikey a good box on the ears for scaring her, but he was far too quick on his feet to stand for that. Turns out, the Wynter sisters had already arranged with Mr. Cummings to keep Margo and Mabel overnight, so a phone call was made to let their parents know another member of their extensive brood had been added to the sleepover. Then Ernie bundled all three of them upstairs to bed before I got a chance to pump Mikey for more info on the mug with the gun, but I figured there'd be plenty of time for that in the morning when my feelings had settled down a touch.

"It's getting terribly late, Mr. Malhaven. Wouldn't you and Mr. Sutherland care to spend the night?" Bernie offered. "There's a room in the servants' quarters. It's not much, but the beds are comfortable enough, I believe."

Q and I exchanged a look. A long walk in the cold and the dark after all our excitement held no appeal for either of us. We decided to take her up on the proposition. The room was dusty and stuffy from being unused, with just a couple of narrow beds and some thin blankets for comfort, but I didn't care. Somewhere along the way, my headache had come back about a hundred times as strong, and I was feeling as shaky as a newborn calf. As soon as I lay my head down on the pillow, it was lights out for me.

I awoke to find Q looming over me, tapping my shoulder to get my attention.

"What's up?" I mumbled.

"I have to get going, Mr. Malhaven. I don't want to be late for work."

"Is it that time already?" I said, squinting groggily at my timepiece. "I'll come with you. I want to check in with Morty about his notion of killing this Wally line of inquiry. Maybe I can change his mind when I tell him about the latest developments," I added, getting to my feet.

I couldn't tell you what happened next, but according to Q, I took a page out of Margo's playbook. That's right. I passed out and collapsed to the floor. Like a sack of potatoes.

CHAPTER TWENTY

The rest of that day is a blur to me. I thought at one point I spied the gimlet eyes of old Livinia Wynter glaring in at me, but that's about all I knew until what must have been some time that evening. The first thing I really remember for sure was thinking I wasn't feeling quite up to the mark. My head was raging, and I felt hot all over. The next thing was a blissfully cool cloth, gently wiping down my burning face.

I cracked open my eyes to see who was at the other end of that frosty relief. Why wasn't I surprised to find a pair of steely blue ones gazing back at me? I waited for her to say something, curious to know which Victoria I was gonna get. The hard-hearted Hannah of the night before? Or the ministering angel who gave away a dead man's hat to save a fella from having to go around in public bareheaded for more than a minute?

"Mr. Malhaven? Are you awake?"

She sounded like she cared. I decided she must be in a lighter mood.

"Am I?" I said. "Or have I died and gone to heaven?"

That made her smile. The smile that I liked to see. Genuine, without that crust of cynicism hardened over top of it.

"Hardly heaven. I'm afraid you aren't very well. You've been running a high temperature. The doctor's been to see you. I'm supposed to see if you can take some of these," she said, holding out a couple of white pills, "as soon as you wake up."

"Guess that's now," I said, trying to leverage myself up on the bed. Realized I'd been stripped down to my skivvies, and I felt about as weak as a baby. All in all, kind of humbling for a big, strong, self-reliant guy like me.

She helped hoist me up enough to swallow the pills and a mouthful of water. I collapsed back down on the bed, stupidly exhausted by that small effort.

"I think I seen better days," I commented.

"And you will again," she said, pushing the hair back from my forehead in a soothing way and giving it another go with the cloth across my brow. It reminded me of the way Ma used to take care of me back when I was a kid. She even started humming a tune, like a lullaby, but familiar.

"What's that song?" I asked. "I know it, but I can't put a name to it."

She blushed. "Oh! It's just something Lukasz used to sing to me. A kind of a joke between us. *Daisy, Daisy, give me your answer do…*" she sang shyly in a crystal-clear alto.

"*I'm half crazy, all for the love of you,*" I offered back in a creaky baritone before starting to drift off again. I guess whatever was in those pills was potent, 'cause I couldn't keep my eyes open even though it seemed like there was something important I needed to say.

I must have mumbled something, 'cause she leaned in close enough to me that I could smell that violet scent again.

"What did you say? Mr. Malhaven? Jim?"

I managed to spit it out just before I nodded off again: "Who's Daisy?"

The next time I woke up, she was gone. In her place was another pretty lady, this one with deep brown skin and a crisp white nurse's uniform and cap. She'd been sitting in a chair, reading a magazine, but she must have some kind of sixth sense, 'cause she looked up and come over to check on me right away.

"Hello, Mr. Malhaven. I'm Marlene Sutherland, Q's sister. I'm keeping an eye on you tonight while Mrs. Jankowski gets some rest. She stayed here with you all day, you know."

"Did she?" I croaked, trying to clear my throat.

That earned me a cool sip of water. Marlene had to help me up so I could drink it, but she was stronger than she looked, and you could tell she had that whole nursing thing down pat. She even had a napkin ready to wipe the dribble of water that got away from me down my chin. She fluffed up some pillows behind me, making everything comfy before I lay my heavy head back down.

"It's swell of you to come help me out like this," I said.

"Any friend of my brother's is a friend of mine. Besides, I just graduated a few weeks ago, so it's good practice for me. I've applied for a few jobs, but nothing's come through yet, so I have plenty of time on my hands," she said, looking downcast.

"Is it tough going? You know? Finding a job for…" I fumbled, not sure exactly how to put it.

"For someone like me?" She rescued me from my predicament, taking pity on my discomfort. "It can be. Some people are old-fashioned. They don't want to be taken care of by someone from a different race."

"Well, we're all in the human race, ain't we?" I observed sagely. "Anyway, I appreciate it. Q's good people. I can see you are, too."

"You don't know me very well yet, do you?" she said with a laugh.

I couldn't help but chuckle at that myself before asking for an update on my situation. "What's the story with me? Can I get up and go home now?"

"Oh, no, Mr. Malhaven," she said, looking shocked. "You've had a dangerously high fever. We're not sure even now that it's gone for good, although you are looking better than when I first arrived." She pulled out a miniature pocket watch and took ahold of my wrist to count my pulse. "Your heart rate is better, too. The doctor is supposed to come in to check on you in the morning. Are you feeling hungry at all? I can warm some beef broth for you."

"That don't sound too appetizing," I said, just being honest.

"I know," she said with a sympathetic smile. "But it's very nourishing. You want to get better so you can get out of here, don't you?"

I had to acknowledge the truth of that, so she jumped up, disappearing while I took another doze. I woke up just long enough to take a few sips of a nasty-tasting liquid before it was off to Dreamland again for me.

Next time I come around, I had an altogether different type of nurse—Cressley, the mute butler. He gave me the nod and made a couple of signs that was easy enough to interpret. He was there to escort me to the necessaries. I welcomed not having to try that out in front of one of the ladies. I guess they might have took it in stride, but I sure wouldn't.

My legs felt like someone replaced all the bones with rubber, but we managed to trip down the hallway and back without calamity. I was happy to make it back to my bed, though not so much when Cressley poured a foul-smelling cup of steaming hot liquid from a flask and passed it over to me. I made a face, but he just shrugged his shoulders as much to say, *what can you do*? I guess there's times when you just gotta take your medicine, so I pinched my nose shut and did my best to gag some of it down.

I gave Cressley the eye while I chugged. There'd been a lot of strange goings-on centered around the Wynter property, and Cressley had been with the family a long time. It made me wonder if he might not be a valuable source of some inside dope if I could find a way to communicate with him. I'd been worrying about Victoria being the brains behind a crime syndicate, but it occurred to me there was another good candidate.

If Livinia took after her old man like Victoria said, maybe she'd picked up some of his business savvy, too. William Wallace Wynter had reportedly been a power to be reckoned with during Prohibition days, and Liv was certainly no slouch when it came to the forceful personality department. Could it be that she had grabbed the baton from her father, only she was running drugs instead of booze? It seemed like a crazy idea when I thought of old Liv's holier-than-thou, ladylike deportment. But then again, that would be pretty good cover for a crime boss, wouldn't it? Who was gonna suspect a God-fearing pillar of the community, and a spinster of a certain age to boot? What if she was using that to her advantage?

I was just pondering whether to ask Cressley to fetch my notebook from my coat pocket to see whether we couldn't start a written dialogue when the door opened to admit the very person I'd been longing to see again despite knowing that for my own peace of mind, I really ought to try and forget all about her.

"There she is, my own Florence Night—" I started to call out, before realizing Victoria was not alone. Miss Livinia Wynter was following close on her heels, and she did not look pleased to see me. Not pleased at all.

CHAPTER TWENTY-ONE

*L*iv's raven-like eyes narrowed at my seemingly jovial state of mind, like I was just the type of unreliable character capable of faking the whole boiling temperature, passed out in bed routine as simply another ruse to make time with a beautiful gal.

"It seems you have recovered, Mr. Mal-*vern*," she spouted, mangling my moniker yet again. I decided to be the bigger party and let it pass. "I assume that means you'll be returning home now. We all have much more valuable things to do than babysit an unwelcome guest."

"Oh, Miss Wynter," Victoria protested. "I'm not sure the doctor would approve of us trying to move Mr. Malhaven in his condition. He's really been very ill."

"So I was told," she sniffed. "Although he seems quite... *lively* at the moment. But if you're that concerned, I suppose I could have Cressley drive him into the city." Like she was making a big concession to my convenience, much against her better judgment, you know.

"That's mighty neighborly of you," I spliced in. She just glared at me in reply. Maybe she didn't think I was being sincere.

"I really think we should wait and see what the doctor says,"

Victoria insisted, sticking up for me like a trooper. "He promised to return by lunchtime at the latest."

Liv sniffed again but inclined her head a bare inch or so in recognition of the possible necessity of me loitering under her roof for at least a few more hours, before turning on her heel and sweeping out the door.

Victoria gave me a sympathetic look that was worth enduring any amount of Liv's scorn. "I'm so sorry. She found out all about the séance when she got back home. I'm afraid Ernie and Bernie couldn't dream up a good excuse for why the window was broken and there was a bullet lodged in the door, so they ended up spilling the beans, and as you might imagine, Livinia is none too pleased about it. How are you feeling?"

"I'm a pretty tough nut. I could probably move myself along as it seems I've worn out my welcome." I started to rise then plunked back down again when the room took an unexpected turn. "Maybe you could just hand me my duds. Might as well get dressed while we wait for the doc."

She not only handed them to me but did the lion's share of the work of getting me all fixed up. I thought I caught her blushing once or twice, but since I turned as red as a beet the minute she first touched me, I didn't blame her none. She was even a fair hand at tying a tie. We both looked ruefully at those neat punctures in the fedora.

"Leave it with me," she suggested. "I can take it to the haberdashery shop that made it for Lukasz. I have an idea they can match this felt and patch it up. I've seen it done before for moth holes, and you couldn't even tell there was ever any damage."

"That's funny. After the séance, your big idea was for me to chuck it out and start over again."

"Oh? Well, I was probably still in shock. It's not an everyday thing to be standing that close to a speeding bullet, is it? It was a big mistake to go. I should have listened to my first instinct. What did you make of it all? Who do you think is behind it?" she asked, those eyes as wide and innocent-looking as I'd ever seen them.

"Your guess is as good as mine," I said, trying to figure if this was a gag of hers to trick me into laying my cards on the table. "Wally seems to be getting somebody's goat, that's for sure. What did Liv make of it?" I asked, curious to find out if there was anything to my other theory about Livinia being involved.

"She seemed to think it was a burglary attempt. Started raving about the family silver and had anyone checked the safe."

"Safe, huh?"

"Yes, the rumor is Mr. Wynter started keeping a cache of money in the house after the Crash in '29. He lost faith in the banks and liked to keep his wealth close to him. There's even been talk of gold stashed in his tomb. I get the impression Livinia has kept up the practice of keeping at least some funds in the house though it really would be safer to keep it in the bank, wouldn't it? Banks are perfectly sound these days."

"I suppose so. I never had enough in one yet to make it worthwhile worrying about losing it. I guess the two younger ones go along with whatever big sis wants?"

"Oh, Livinia isn't the eldest. She's the baby of the family, by quite a few years actually."

"You're kidding!"

"No. It's a natural mistake. She obviously has the more dominant personality."

"I should say. I feel for those two. And for Cressley. Seems like he puts up with a lot from her."

Victoria looked taken aback, shifty even. "Oh, I don't know. She's been very kind to let him keep his job. I shouldn't think it would be easy to find another one with him not being able to speak."

"I was wondering about that. Do you think he reads and writes any? I had an idea of asking him a few questions."

"Of course. He's very intelligent. He does all the shopping and running of the household. Livinia often sends him out to give me instructions. He keeps a pad in his pocket to write out what he wants to say. We've had some very interesting conversations that way," she reminisced with a smile as she opened the curtains in the tiny room, letting in some light.

She looked so much softer and more appealing standing there in the bright morning sun like that, wearing a simple house dress that looked like it had been through a lot of washings, than she ever had the night before in all her fancy dress. I felt like I never would figure her out.

First, she said I should just forget about the hubby's hat and find myself another one. Now, she was gonna go to a lot of trouble to get it all fixed up for me. Last night, she'd seemed like she thought she was miles above Q, or any of the rest of the company for that matter. This morning, she was enthusing about how much she enjoyed passing the time of day with the family's mute butler.

I guess if there was one thing you could say about life with Victoria, it was that you'd never get bored. She was always full of surprises. And I was about to find out that wasn't the last one of the day.

The doc came and gave me the all clear to relocate so long as I pledged to climb right back in bed once I got home. Liv made good on the promise of a ride, and Victoria escorted me out to a shiny black Cadillac idling on the driveway. Cressley opened the back door for me with a flourish. I decided to play along, get the full treatment. It wasn't every day, or any day, that I got chauffeured around like that. I was settling in when Victoria knocked on my window. I rolled it down.

She leaned close to talk to me. "I almost forgot to ask you. Why did you say that last night?"

"What?" I said, not catching her drift.

"I thought you said, 'Who's Daisy?'"

"Hey, that's right. I guess it was that song that reminded me. You remember, it's what the ghost asked us during the séance. Except it wasn't that exactly. It wanted to know *where* Daisy was. It was me that wanted to know *who* Daisy was."

"Oh!" she said, looking startled.

"What?" I asked, as Cressley revved the engine and threw it into gear.

She looked very pale and sad standing there alone on the driveway.

"It's me. I'm Daisy."

CHAPTER TWENTY-TWO

I tried to get that dope Cressley to stop so I could ask Victoria what in the blazes she meant, but I guess he was under strict orders from Livinia to get me the heck out of there. I had spied old Liv standing at the top of the steps shooting us deadly looks like that Greek lady with the snakes in her hair, so I couldn't blame him none. And I sure didn't want to get Victoria into trouble with her boss, but it was kinda inconvenient not to be able to ask her what in the world she was talking about.

What did she mean she was Daisy, and how did it all tie up with our phantom telephone experiment? I was starting to feel like the more I found out, the less I understood about what was going on. If I hadn't been feeling as limp as an earthworm, I might've used more forcible persuasion tactics on my driver. As it was, I made up my mind to sneak back out and see if I couldn't have another heart-to-heart with Victoria when Liv wasn't on the beat.

Cressley was a competent driver, and it was a smooth ride back into the city. I didn't get too many opportunities to ride around in comfort like that, so I decided to forget my troubles and just sit back and enjoy the view. All too soon, we pulled up to a spot right in front of my building. Cressley kindly helped me inside before scramming. I was feeling shakier than I liked to admit, so I crashed on to the bed and was out within less than a minute. Didn't even stop to take off my coat.

I awoke to the noise of somebody bustling around the place. Recalling the bullet episode and the knock on the head, I had a bad moment thinking some joker had broken in to finish me off, but instead of that, I got a motherly-looking woman with warm brown skin and a quiet smile that didn't show off her teeth none but managed to convey the idea of friendliness just the same. The likeness to her pretty daughter was striking, so I wasn't surprised when she introduced herself as Dorothea Sutherland.

"Pleased to meet you, Mrs. Sutherland," I said. "Forgive me for being nosy, but how did you get in here, and what are you up to?"

"Your building superintendent let me in. I told him I had looked after you when you were little, and I was here for a visit. A small fib, I'm afraid, but Marquis was worried about you. I promised him I'd come check on you, and it's just as well I did," she added, clucking her tongue at the state of me.

Before I could protest, she had wrestled away about half my clothes and tucked me up under the covers in that way only mothers seem to know how to do. She brought me a steaming bowl of chicken noodle soup that was quite the step up from that drool they'd tried to force down me at the Wynter joint and settled herself in my only comfortable chair, pulling out some knitting. The soft tap-tap-tap of the needles clicking against each other was soothing, and I drifted away again.

By nightfall, I was starting to feel more like my old self. This was helped along by the inch-thick steak and pile of steaming potatoes Mrs. S dished up for me. A guy could get used to that kind of treatment, but I was starting to feel like a fraud for taking advantage of her, so I had to kick her out, as kindly as possible, of course. Not before she pulled a tape measure out of her purse and insisted on taking all my measurements though.

"What for?" says I.

"Marquis said you wanted a new suit. I've never made one for someone of your height before," she added, as she danced around me jotting down numbers on a piece of paper. "It will be quite an interesting challenge. And won't you fill out a suit nice—such broad shoulders!"

"But I don't know if I can afford it," I protested, blushing as she stooped down to calculate my inseams. "I gotta warn you, I don't exactly got a wad of extra bills burning a hole through my pocket."

"Don't worry," she reassured me. "My cousin works in the garment district, and he gets me good deals on cloth—I'm thinking a nice gray to bring out the color of your eyes. It won't cost much. Just the cloth and some of my time."

"Can't be anything more valuable than that," I said as she picked up her purse to skedaddle. I surprised her, and myself, by giving her a quick peck on the cheek. "You been swell. It was like having my own ma back again."

She got all teary-eyed at that the way ladies do, which almost set me to bawling. All in all, we parted on the best of terms with promises to keep in touch.

Goodness only knew what Morty thought I was up to after the way I'd dropped out of sight. He might be pulling out what little hair he had left if I didn't check in soon, but I decided to get one more good night's rest before reporting in for duty. Mrs. S had gone a long way toward fixing me up, but it had been a rough couple of days that had left me worn down.

After a solid eight hours, I felt like a new man and spent the better part of another hour setting the Champ to rights before driving over to the office. I thought about stopping along the way to pick up a new hat, but I wanted to give Victoria a chance to fix up the one she wanted me to have. It felt like a connection between us, and I didn't want to sully it by buying a cheap stand-in. It didn't feel right showing myself in public without a lid on, but I figured it was character building.

I popped up to the newsroom only to look into Morty's office to find the boss in conference with a swell who was all puffed up in an expensive suit and sporting slicked-back silver hair. To my surprise, Morty waved me over to his cave and introduced me.

"Monroe, ambulance-chaser," he informed me, before waving a

half-chewed cigar in my general direction and identifying me as "Mal-haven, hack" to the gent. Morty was a big believer in saving his breath whenever he could.

"I am Harold Monroe, lawyer for the Wynter family for many, many years." The swell amplified a bit on Morty's description, with a dirty look in his general direction that bounced right off the boss, no problem. "You are Mr. James Malhaven, I take it."

"Jimmy," I said, sticking out a hand. I try to get off on the right foot with folks whenever I can. Unfortunately, my paw was left hanging in the air. Monroe was having none of that.

"Mr. Malhaven, I have had to take the unfortunate step of coming down here in person to see if you can explain to me any possible reason why you have persisted in ignoring our entirely reasonable request that you put aside whatever journalistic ambitions you have about this Wally nonsense and leave my clients in peace."

"What's the big deal?" I asked, lighting up a cigarette. "At least two-thirds of the sisters seem to be getting quite a kick out of it."

"Miss Ernestine and Miss Bernadette Wynter do not always display the excellent common sense of Miss Livinia Wynter. That is why Mr. Wynter left the estate to her care. She has legal authority over the cemetery and her sisters' well-being and will do what she feels is best to preserve the family's good name and business interests."

"Good for her," Morty growled. As was not uncommon with the boss, the exact meaning behind this remark could only be guessed at.

It disconcerted the mouthpiece anyway, 'cause he gave Morty a doubtful glance before launching in again on me. "Am I to understand, Mr. Malhaven, that you actually came to the house and attempted to contact this alleged spirit even after you had been served with our cease and desist warning?"

"Hey, now," I protested. "I was invited there by the ladies. They asked me in person. What, did you want me to hurt their feelings by turning them down flat to their faces? That ain't what I'd call polite. My ma raised me up better than that," I added with a cock of the eyebrow intended to convey some question about his own mother's etiquette instructions.

"You know precisely what I mean," he sputtered. "You are encouraging these susceptible ladies in their folly for your own purpose."

"Which is?" I prompted, curious to know what it was I was up to.

"Publicity, of course. To sell more *papers*," he sneered, like we were serving up some kind of tabloid junk instead of the high-quality journalistic endeavors we took so much pride in. "It wouldn't surprise me at all to find out you had arranged for this alleged assailant to fire into the house while you were there so that you could titillate your readers."

"Say, that ain't a bad thought," I said, affecting to be much struck at the notion as I ground out my cigarette in the ashtray on Morty's desk. "Whataya think, Morty? I think Monroe is onto something. Here we've been running ourselves ragged trying to chase down stories when we could've just been arranging them at our own convenience the whole time."

Morty let out with a hearty, "Hah!" From him, that's as good as anyone else rolling in the aisles.

"I am glad you both find this so very amusing," Monroe said. "Maybe I'll be the one laughing when we file suit against the paper. What will your publisher, Mr. Louis A. Carsworth, think about that, hmm?"

Morty pondered that a bit before proffering the following monologue: "Carsworth is an OK guy."

Our distinguished visitor threw his hands in the air to imply a certain amount of disgust with us and stormed off. I started trying to fill in Morty on the thrilling details of my doings and my brilliant theories, but he just waved his cigar in front of my face, saying, "Shysters like that give me a swift pain. Go knock yourself out."

Carsworth's not the only guy at the paper who's A-OK.

CHAPTER TWENTY-THREE

Now that I had the go-ahead from the boss to keep up my inquiries, I was raring to go. My only problem was what to tackle next. I decided to go bounce some ideas around with Q.

"Hello, Mr. Malhaven!" he said as I breezed in. "It certainly is good to see you up and about again."

"Much thanks to those two lovely ladies of yours," I said. "That was mighty friendly of you to recruit some help for me like that."

"My mother enjoys looking after people, and Marlene appreciated having a chance to do some nursing. She worked so hard at school, but it hasn't been as easy for her to find a job as we had hoped."

"She's only been at it a week or two. These things take time," I said, trying for the encouraging word.

"I suppose so," he agreed.

To cheer him up, I filled him in on my meeting with Morty and the Wynter mouthpiece. "Now, I just got to figure out what's next."

"It's all quite a puzzle, isn't it?" Q observed. "What did you make of what we found out from the spirit board?"

"All that stuff about Petey? The way the ghost was trying to shift the blame off onto his poor wife?" I asked. "Makes me think that someone knows more than they're telling. Maybe those Wynter sisters.

It always struck me as unlikely they don't remember more about the murder. It must have been the talk of the town when it happened. Maybe they heard some rumor at the time about the wife hurting the child, and it came back to them. If not knowingly, then, like you said, from deep down in what little brains they seem to possess."

"Maybe so. But didn't it feel uncanny the way the planchette went flying off the table like that? I keep thinking about it, and I can't understand how anyone could have made that happen without our seeing it. We were all staring at the board when it happened."

"And how'd they make that table do the jitterbug?" I reminded him. "You're starting to sound like you wanna believe we called up a ghoul after all, but I just don't buy it. There must have been some trick to it. I was just gonna take a closer look at that table before we had all the excitement with the mysterious stranger at the window."

"That was a close call!" he said. "I suppose, since they were apparently aiming over our heads before the Cummings boy interfered, that it was meant to be another warning, like cutting up your hat and disabling your automobile. Who do you think it was? The same person who attacked you outside the gates?"

"Seems like a good bet unless I somehow managed to get a whole bunch of random guys riled up and chasing me around town for their own amusement. It must all tie into this Wally caper or the cemetery some way. I guess I better check in with our friend Mikey and see if he can tell us anything about the mook he saw with the gun." I sighed, not looking forward to another go-round with that chatterbox.

"I wonder if you should also consider visiting the orphanage?" Q suggested. "I've been doing some more digging and managed to find a small story, just a paragraph, in one of the later editions saying the boy had been released from the hospital to the care of the Sisters of Mercy."

"Sisters of Mercy, huh? That's that creepy-looking museum over on the corner of Fenton and Main, ain't it?"

"That's right. It might not be easy getting any information from them—I believe they're usually pretty close-mouthed about adoptions —but it could be worth a try. If we could track down Peter, it's just possible, even as young as he was, that he remembers something about what happened."

"I guess I can give it a whirl. Normally I'd say I could charm it out of them, but those birds always look pretty grim when I pass by that place. All dressed in black from head to toe like a gang of crows," I added with a shudder. To let you in on a secret, I'd always been kind of afraid of nuns, the way some people are of spiders or clowns. "All right. I'll do those two things next. Mikey and the nuns. What a morning!"

"And don't forget about Daisy. That was the last communication, wasn't it? *Where is Daisy?* What do you think that meant? We haven't seen anything yet that would connect a Daisy to our ghost. Do you think it was something unrelated? And if that was somebody's subconscious talking, who do you think it was?"

"Oh, I might have a lead on that," I said cagily, reluctant to drag Victoria's name into it until I found out more about the connection myself. "But I'll have to do more legwork first. Thanks for the reminder, Q."

"No problem, Mr. Malhaven."

"I wish you'd call me Jim or Jimmy."

"I'm sorry. It just doesn't feel right."

"Because we got different color skin?"

"It's not that," he said, clearing his throat and looking embarrassed. "It's because you're so much older than me. My parents always taught me to respect my elders."

I had to laugh at that one. "I can't have more than a decade on you, buddy, but you don't gotta rub it in just the same."

He smiled. "But do let me know if there's anything else I could do for you."

"Just keep mulling it over. You got a good brain. Maybe you'll see some connection I'm not making. Not yet, anyway. I'm kind of the slow but sure type."

"Inexorable? Relentless? Unyielding?" Q suggested, like he was a walking, talking dictionary.

"All them things," I agreed. "Don't worry. We'll get to the bottom of this sooner or later. I'll check back with you. Let you know what I find out."

I tried to play it off with Q like I was full of confidence, but I didn't really have that much enthusiasm, or optimism, about the morning's missions. For one thing, it wasn't until I was parking the Champ about a block away from the Cummings residence that it even occurred to me that it was a school day and the kids would all be tucked away safely in class.

Kicking myself for a wasted drive, I was about to pull out to head downtown to visit the orphans instead when I caught sight of the back of a tow-headed midget ducking behind a trash bin across the street. I got out of the car and casually crossed the road and made as if to stroll on past before taking a dive down the alley in time to catch one sneakered foot as it tried to take a powder.

"Ow! Hey!" the miserable-looking heap on the ground protested at me.

"Look what we got here."

Mikey glared up at me with a baleful eye. "Geez, mister, whataya trying to do? Kill a guy? I was just minding my own business, and you come and upend me for no reason. Whataya want to do a thing like that for? You know what I could do? I could yell for a cop right now. You ain't allowed to beat up a little kid for no reason, ya know. All I gotta do is scream murder and you'd be in big trouble, wouldn't you, mister? How'd you like it if I did that, huh?"

"Go right ahead."

"Huh?"

"Yell for one of our boys in blue."

"You *want* me to call a cop?"

"I don't mind. Of course," I said, like it had just struck me, "then they would have to figure out how you come to be wandering around the streets of the city all by your lonesome instead of being shut up in school like all the good kids are right now. And they'd have to tell your parents where they found you. It might even get your ma and pa in trouble for not keeping an eye peeled on you like they should. I wouldn't be surprised if you was all called up before a judge at the family court. Might decide you'd be better off living at the orphanage with all them nuns to look after you. Nuns are real strict, you know. Wouldn't be much fun for you, but I bet your parents wouldn't mind. Probably save them a world of trouble and heartache."

I'd gotten carried away with my own idea, looking away into the distance as I painted a satisfying picture in my mind of the perpetual troublemaker being slapped over the knuckles with a ruler by one of those black crows, so I was thrown to hear a loud sniff.

Looking down, I seen a sight I would never have expected in a thousand years—that hard-headed reprobate bawling like a babe in arms. Ain't that something?

CHAPTER TWENTY-FOUR

Guess little Mikey wasn't quite the hard case I had pegged him to be.

"Hey," I said to him, feeling like a brute for taking my patter too far. "Don't pay no attention to me. I'm just ragging on you. C'mon."

I scooped him up and carried him a few blocks over to the soda fountain at a drugstore I knew about. He didn't fight me none, just locked his arms around my neck and buried his face in my shoulder, which just shows how much I'd shook him up. I'm a big guy and he was skinny for his age, but he was still no lightweight, so I was more than happy when I could plunk him down on a stool at the counter. I told him to order anything on the menu he liked. He hiccupped a few times before admitting a banana split might go some way toward soothing his ruffled feelings.

The soda jerk gave us the eye, like, why wasn't this kid in school and what was I doing to him to make him cry, so I muttered, "My nephew. His poor little dog got run over this morning. I'm trying to cheer him up."

That almost made the guy bawl himself. He must've had a soft spot for kids, or for pups, or both, 'cause he put as much extra topping on that sundae as he could fit. It was something to see how fast Mikey demolished the lot—I didn't have time to smoke more than a couple of cigarettes while I was waiting, but at least it seemed an efficient method for restoring his natural high spirits before we left the joint. I grabbed for his hand just in case he had big ideas of escaping now that he'd gotten something outta me, but he seemed happy to hop along down the sidewalk next to me like I was his best friend in the world.

"So, Mikey," I said. "I'm real glad I happened to run into you. It'd be a big help if you could describe that palooka with the gun. You think you'd recognize him again if you saw him?"

"Naw!" Mikey said, dismissing such a silly notion with a titter.

"Naw?" I inquired, hoping to prod him into his normally overpowering chattiness. "Why not?"

"'Cause he had a mask on, didn't he? Like a hood. It covered up his whole mug."

"Is that right?" I said, trying to draw on some inner well of patience as Mikey again failed to elaborate.

"Sure. Crooks like that always wear a mask when they're doing dirty work. Didn't you know that?" He looked mightily disillusioned with my ignorance of the criminal's playbook.

"Well, sure, if they're smart. So, there's no way you would recognize him then? Wasn't there anything about him that stood out to you at all?"

"I dunno. It was kinda dark out. And then I seen he had a gun, so I was mostly looking at that 'cause I never seen a gun up close like that before. Only in the picture show. I wanted to see what kind it was only I couldn't get a good look at it 'cause his hand was shaking so bad, he was having a hard time keeping it still. Could be he would have hit you if I hadn't bumped his hand like that. Could be maybe I even saved your life," he ventured, eyeballing me to see how I would take this new angle. It was obviously still weighing on him that I hadn't shown the proper appreciation for his meddling on the night of the séance.

"Maybe," I conceded through gritted teeth, not wanting him to dry up in case there was something I could use still locked away inside that gadfly brain. "Is there anything else you can remember?"

"Not really. Just his hair, I guess."

Finally, a development. "What about it?"

"It was sticking out at the back where he hadn't pulled the hood all the way down good. His hair was white, so it must have been a real old guy. Maybe that's why he was shaking so bad. You ever seen an old guy all shaky like that? What makes old guys that way, huh? Ma says it's from the drink. There's an old guy that hangs out on the street corner near our house. He's always got a bottle of booze in his hand, and he shakes all over like a bowl of Jell-O. Ma says that's why Pops shouldn't drink none, but he says he needs a whiskey and soda to drown out the noise in his head when he's at home. Why do you think Pops has noise in his head? I thought only people who were crazy heard stuff in their heads. Do you think he's going crazy, huh, mister, huh?"

I wouldn't be a bit surprised, I thought to myself, before turning to him with as big a grin as I could muster. "Say, that's some real detective work, kid. That bit about the hair might help narrow down our suspects."

"You think so?" he said, looking as pleased as pleased could be with himself. "See, I told you we should double up. I could come on all your stakeouts, and you could hold down the bad guys while I give them the third degree. Wouldn't that be something?"

His enthusiasm for violence was starting to alarm me. "It would, indeed, but for now, you really oughta be in school. We all gotta do our time before they let us loose on the world, you know."

"That's what Ma always says, but I never learn nothing in school."

I could believe that. If I'd been the religious kind, I'd have sent a prayer heavenward just then for the poor saps at that school who had the thankless task of trying to stuff Mikey's head with some kind of facts. It must be like pouring water into a sieve.

"Besides, look what happens when I skip out," he argued. "Oh boy, will everyone be green when I tell them I got to eat a whole banana split all by myself while they was stuck in class."

In spite of my earlier bravado, visions of being called before a judge for contributing to the delinquency of a minor started dancing in my own head.

"You know, Mikey, if you wanna be partners one day, you're gonna have to learn to play it close to the vest when we're on a case. You can't go blabbing about everything we do to everyone you meet. You might should start practicing that now."

"Oh, right," he said, giving me a squinty eye that I guess was meant as a wink. "I gotcha. Like in them spy movies. You don't have to worry about me. I'd just like to see someone try and make me talk. They could pull out my fingernails, burn me with a hot poker, hang me upside down, and I wouldn't say a thing. I don't talk that much anyways as a rule. You don't have to worry about me none, mister. I'll be as quiet as a mouse."

For some reason, I didn't find this statement or even the finger he lay ever so solemn across his lips reassuring, but I was saved from reply by him suddenly yanking his hand out of mine.

"It's Ma!" he hissed. "I gotta cheese it!"

I watched with a feeling of doom as he legged it over a nearby fence like a jackrabbit fleeing for its life. I wasn't so confident he wouldn't rat me out, but I decided there was nothing I could do about it. Mikey was like a charging bull. You just had to hope he got distracted by something colorful enough to catch his eye right before he hit you. Given the way his mind worked, seemed like there was at least a 50-50 chance of his forgetting all about our outing if luck was on my side.

A tired-looking woman approached me on the sidewalk, and I automatically reached up to tip my hat to her before remembering I didn't have one to tip. I gave with the polite nod instead. My heart bled for her, but maybe the marvelous Mabel made up for the disappointment that was Mikey. When you turn out that many kids, there's bound to be at least one dud in the bunch.

Disappointed by the tiny amount of useful info I'd managed to squeeze outta Mikey, I decided to see if I could fare any better with the nuns. I drove downtown to the Sisters of Mercy, a grim and gray three-story building that loomed over its corner of the street. There was two angels carved over the big front doors with their arms stretched out to each other. I guess the idea was supposed to be they was watching over the kiddies within, but it looked more like they was reaching out to comfort each other. Of course, that might have just been my imagination running riot.

I took a deep breath and scooted inside. There was a civilian at the front desk, a young man with a pencil stuck behind one ear, a lock of unruly brown hair trying to sneak down his forehead, and a stack of ledgers in front of him. He looked like he was doing some hard figuring, reaching out with one hand to work the buttons of an adding machine at his side. His fingers moved like lightning. He had an intense look of concentration on his face, so I gave it a minute until he seemed to reach a conclusion which he jotted down with the pencil he fished out from behind the ear.

He looked up then and caught sight of me, standing up to welcome me while tucking his pencil away and sweeping his hair back into some kind of order. "Oh, hello. I hope you haven't been waiting long. Our usual receptionist is out sick today, so I'm doing double duty as accountant and official greeter. What can we do for you?"

"I'm Jim Malhaven from the Crier. I was wondering if I could talk to someone around here who's in the know."

"A reporter?" he said, looking taken aback. "I guess you'd better speak to Sister Honoria then. I'll go see if I can find her."

Sister Honoria. I didn't like the sound of that. I could picture her already. A mean old bird with a hooked nose and hands like claws. I skulked around the lobby nervously, debating if I should turn tail and run outta there while I still had a chance, but it already was too late. I heard their footsteps coming down the hallway and turned, pushing down my feeling of trepidation and pasting a smile on my face.

Standing before me was the most beautiful woman I ever seen in my life.

CHAPTER TWENTY-FIVE

"Mr. Malhaven, is it? I'm Sister Honoria."

I thought Victoria was a looker, but this one had even her beat. She had to be young—her face was unlined and as sweet as the day was long. Her hair was all covered up with that veil thing nuns wear, of course, but she had big green eyes and all her features were in the right place. I gave myself a quick mental lecture. Like I said, I'm not religious as a rule, but even I know there's certain thoughts you don't have about a nun.

She looked tickled to death to see me. I wondered for a minute if she'd mistaken me for somebody else, but she set my mind at rest. "You're that reporter from the Crier—I've seen your byline, I think. Isn't that what you call it?"

"That's the lingo," I said, still in a state of shock at the picture standing in front of me compared to what I'd been expecting.

"Did Mr. Carsworth send you?"

"Carsworth? Not particularly. Why?"

"Oh, I thought he might have sent you to do a story on the orphans. He's one of our biggest benefactors, but you probably know that."

"No, I didn't. Guess he keeps it under wraps, but that's not a bad idea—doing a piece on the kiddies. Pulls at the heartstrings that kind of stuff. Maybe we could get you some free publicity. Are you hard up for cash?"

"Always," she said with a smile. "Mr. Leonard here could tell you more about that than I can, of course. He has to work quite a lot of magic some months to keep his ledgers in the black."

The young fella hastened to explain lest I get the wrong idea. "Sister Honoria! You make it sound like I cook the books. She just means we have to economize more some months than others. Buy cheaper cuts of meat for the children than we'd like. Not take them on any special outings. That kind of thing. We could always use new patrons. A story in the paper might go a long way toward refilling our coffers."

I got a glimmer of how I might be able to turn their shortfalls to my advantage. "I could see doing something along that line. It might help if we had a real human-interest angle we could zero in on. Maybe you got some famous graduates from here?"

Sister Honoria frowned. "Well, of course, many of our children have gone on to lead very successful lives. Starting out life in an orphanage by no means dooms you to a lifetime of failure, but I'm not sure exactly what you're getting at."

"Here's an example," I said. "This story I'm working on right now —maybe you been reading it? Wally, the Wraith of Wynter's Hill?"

"Yes, I have seen those," she agreed, that sweet face looking troubled. "Your last story connected the sightings with a real-life murder, didn't it?"

"That's right. And we have reason to think the child who survived it may have ended up here under your care. What if he went on to bigger and better things? That would be very inspirational to our readers, wouldn't it? To think you ladies had helped that poor little mite go from tragedy to triumph. People eat that stuff up. I can hear the chaching of the cash register already."

Sister Honoria looked more than a bit disappointed in me. I guess in my excitement to find out what happened to young Peter Hornschmidt, I had neglected to take the temperature of the room. Strictly amateur hour on my part.

"Mr. Malhaven, we couldn't possibly exploit one of our charges in that way. For one thing, we take the privacy of our children very seriously. And secondly, to take advantage of a horrific tragedy simply to further our own ends would be very wrong as I'm sure you must agree," she pointed out sternly. She might have looked like an angel, but there was no mistaking the core of pure steel under all that.

Properly humbled, I jumped in to smooth over my slip-up, thinking it was better to stay on her good side just in case I could wind up another pitch on the Petey front that might land better. "Of course, Sister. I lost sight of the proper side of things for a second there in my enthusiasm to punch up a story. One of the hazards of my job, I'm afraid—my editor's always on my back to jazz things up," I said, with a mental apology to Morty, "but that don't mean we can't still work up a column or two on the good works you do here. Maybe you want to show me around? Give me some background I can run with?"

"I suppose so. As long as we're clear about what is out of bounds."

"Absolutely. You don't gotta worry. You tell me Mr. Carsworth is a big fan of yours, and he's the final word at the paper. We never run anything he wouldn't approve of."

She looked more relaxed at that line of reasoning, and I did my best to win her back over with my appreciation for their operation during our circuit around the joint. I didn't even have to work that hard at appearing impressed. It actually was something what they had accomplished there with so little money. Nothing like as grim as I'd been imagining.

We ended up out on the playgrounds at the back of the building watching the kids let off steam. There was a ton of laughing and screaming, just like any playground, and the inmates looked well-fed and happy enough. The nuns seemed pretty happy, too—smiling and doling out equal parts friendliness and firmness as their charges required. And there wasn't a ruler in sight.

One of the smaller tots stumbled and fell near us, skinning her knee. Sister Honoria picked her up to comfort her, holding a handkerchief to stop the bleeding as best she could.

"Ah, Samuel," she said to young Mr. Leonard, who'd been following us around like a guard dog, "if only we had our nurse."

"I know, I know, Sister. I've interviewed three this week, but not one of them was willing to work for the salary we can offer."

"What's this?" says I. "Are you hard up for someone in the medical line?"

"Yes," Sister Honoria informed me. "Our last nurse resigned when she got married, and we've been having quite a time finding another qualified candidate. Why do you ask?"

"It just so happens, I might know of someone. Only—"

"Yes?"

"Well… how much would the color of her skin matter to you?"

"Not at all, of course. Look around you, Mr. Malhaven," she said, indicating the horde of munchkins before us. "You'll see we have every color you can imagine here, and God watches over all of them equally."

I could see what she meant. They had every kind of kid there, and the way they was all playing and laughing with each other, kinda gave me hope that their future might be different than our past. At least, I liked to think they might have a chance.

"I'll put her in touch with your Mr. Leonard then, shall I? Her name's Marlene Sutherland, and she's a peach."

"If by that," said Mr. Leonard, "you mean that she is a competent and caring nurse, I'll look forward to talking to her."

I gave him a friendly tap on the shoulder. "You won't regret it."

We parted on better terms than we started at, and I had to be satisfied with that for the present. I'd have to mull over this whole Petey deal—maybe there was another way to play it. And it wouldn't hurt to have an inside man, so to speak, if Marlene got the job. Not that I'd want to get her into any trouble, but at least it opened up some possibilities, like Q or me showing up to visit with her, and who knew what that might lead to?

I stopped in at a hole-in-the-wall to demolish a hamburger piled high with grilled onions while thinking over my next step. Decided to head back out to my old stomping grounds, Wynter's Hill. That Daisy mystery was gnawing at me, and I was anxious to catch up with Victoria and find out what it was all about.

It being early afternoon, the gates were standing wide open. I didn't see anyone hanging around, so I set out on a casual stroll, keeping tabs on the goings-on. First thing I noted was a Chevy truck painted a distinctive mossy green color parked along the drive. There weren't so many of those around, not that color. It seemed likely it belonged to that farmer-looking fella with the Santa beard I'd observed on one of my vigils in the night. I wondered which of his dearly departed he was visiting.

The next thing I seen was Victoria. Wanting to be friendly, I started to sing out to her, but there was something about the way she was creeping and peering around like she wasn't so anxious to see or be seen that kinda discouraged me. Instead, I ducked down behind an oversized pillar marking one of the boneyard's more important citizens and kept an eye on her.

She went down on her knees in a shady corner and started digging in the dirt. The way she kept craning her neck around as she worked raised my suspicions about her all over again. She sure didn't look like the picture of a person with nothing to hide. I cooled my heels where I was until she finally got to her feet and walked away. Waiting until she was out of sight, I legged it over to where she'd been kneeling.

I wasn't sure what I expected to see, but it wasn't this. A grave marker. One of those miniature ones for poor, innocent little children with the lamb lying across the top. I knelt down to get a closer look. The writing on it was clear as could be:

Karolina Magda Jankowski
Beloved Daughter
November 18, 1944 - January 2, 1945
We'll Meet Again

CHAPTER TWENTY-SIX

"Are you spying on me?"

I jumped to my feet at the sound of that voice, feeling like I'd been struck a blow, even though when I turned around to face her, she looked more sad than angry. Somehow, that made it worse.

"I'm sorry," I offered humbly. "Guess I can't help it. It's what I do. Find out things."

"At least now, maybe you'll understand why I stay on here."

"To be close to her. Your daughter."

"Yes. She was born a few days after I got the telegram about Lukasz. She struggled from the first, like she wasn't meant to be of this earth, but I had a short time with her, at least," Victoria said, reaching over and touching the tiny lamb on the stone. "I tried to find comfort in thinking that she'd gone ahead to join her father. That neither of them would be alone."

"But you were."

"Yes," she said.

"So, you plan to live the rest of your life hidden away here? For her?"

"I don't know. I don't know that I have a plan. It seems easier to just drift along, doesn't it, then to have to make a decision. Take that next step."

"Haven't you ever thought about going somewhere else? Starting fresh?"

"Sometimes. But I found I couldn't bring myself to leave her. Maybe it's because I was abandoned as a baby. I never want her to feel unloved or unwanted the way I did."

"Whataya mean? Like an orphan?"

"Yes, it can happen to even the best of us," she said with just a hint of a smile. "They found me on the doorstep one night. At the Sisters of Mercy."

"Are you kidding? I mean, of course you wouldn't kid about a thing like that. It's just that I was there on a visit only this morning."

"You were?" she asked, surprise written large across her face. "Whatever for?"

"I had a scheme about tracking down that Hornschmidt kid. We found a blurb in one of the back numbers that the nuns took him in after he got out of the hospital, but Sister Honoria wasn't buying the line I was trying to sell her. She's stricter than she looks."

"Sister Honoria is very pretty, isn't she? But don't let that fool you. She's as tough as they come."

"Yeah, I found that out quick. I guess I should've known she wasn't likely to blab about one of their charges, especially not to a member of the press, but it seemed worth taking a shot. You sound like you know her?"

"She was just starting out as a teacher during my last year there. We were close in age and became friends, and we've always stayed in touch."

"How long were you there?"

"Until I was eighteen. For whatever reason, I was never adopted. Most of the kids aren't. There are always more children who need homes than there are parents willing to take them in."

She smiled at the dismay written all over my ugly mug. "Don't worry, you needn't feel sorry for me. The nuns were really kind. It was like having a whole troop of mothers, or lovely aunts. I was actually considering taking the veil and staying on there myself when I... well, I met Lukasz one day when one of the other girls and I went to the movie house together, and that was that," she said, with a look on her face that, I'll admit, made me feel jealous. I couldn't help but wish I had the goods to inspire such a look as that.

"It's funny, though, now that you mention it," she continued. "I remember playing with one of the boys there when I was very young. He was a few years older than me. It always seemed to me like the nuns made a special fuss over him, like they were trying to make it up to him for some unusual hardship he'd been through."

My ears perked up at this. "Do you remember anything about him?"

"Only that he seemed sad, and that his name was Kit."

"Kit? That could be short for Christopher. That was Peter's middle name. Do you remember what happened to him?"

"Yes, I do. He was adopted when I was, oh, I must have been around five or six. That was always big excitement when someone found a home. We used to peek over the banisters in the hallway to try and get a glimpse of the family. I remember the woman had a lovely fur coat, and the man was beautifully dressed as well."

"Sounds like they had money?"

"I think so. They gave me that impression anyway, even as young as I was. You learn to gauge things like that early when you don't own anything yourself," she said matter-of-factly. "Don't get me wrong— we never went hungry, or lacked for warm clothes, but we never had money of our own to spend on extras. We used to keep an eye out whenever we went for walks for any loose change that might have been dropped on the ground. Finding even a penny that we could spend on sweets was a big thing for us back then. It's a habit I've had ever since."

She looked up at me shyly. "That's what I was doing just now, in case you were wondering."

"What?"

"Burying a penny. Whenever I find one, I bring it to Karolina. So that she'll never lack for sweets. It's silly, isn't it? I'm always afraid someone will catch me doing it, so I try to sneak over here when no one's around. Now you've discovered my deepest, darkest secret," she teased me.

She was trying for the light touch today, but now that I knew how much of hardship she'd seen, it made it easier to forgive her for being so hard sometimes. A childhood like that, even if the nuns had been good to her, then losing her husband and baby within the space of a couple of months, that had to leave a mark. I guess I'd have been surprised if she *didn't* do something like take to the drink to try and forget now and again.

"Don't sound silly to me. I bet you were a real good ma to that little girl. You still are."

She got teary-eyed at that, and I wasn't too far off it myself, so I thought I better get into the meat of my visit before we both started howling.

"I got a feeling that ain't your only secret," I said. "What about this Daisy gag? That's really what I come back for today to ask you. What's Daisy to do with you?"

"I'm afraid it's my middle name. At least, the one they gave me at the orphanage. They used to keep a supply of girls' names and boys' names written on slips of paper. Whenever a child arrived who didn't already have a name of their own, they'd pick two names, a first and a middle. I was certainly glad they picked Victoria first and Daisy second. I was always embarrassed by the Daisy. That's why Lukasz used to tease me with that song, after he found out. It became a joke between us, a private nickname."

"That's kinda interesting. Why do you think that question showed up on the spirit board? *Where's Daisy*? If it was meant for you, you was right there, after all."

She looked awful uncomfortable at that. "If you're trying to suggest Lukasz was attempting to contact me from the great beyond, I've already told you I don't believe in that sort of thing."

"Q says instead of a specter, it's the guests themselves moving that marker around and answering the questions. If it wasn't you, was there anyone else there who knew about that name?"

"The Wynters do. I know they heard Lukasz use it because they asked me once what it meant. But if you think one of them did it, that's a very cruel sort of joke to play on a widow when they know that it was a private thing between my husband and me. It doesn't seem like the kind of thing Ernie or Bernie would do. They're really very sweet, as I'm sure you've discovered."

"Maybe they didn't do it on purpose. Q tried to explain it to me, something about the junk we all got rattling around the back of our brain pans. Hey," I said, my scientific explanation interrupted by a guy who'd appeared on the scene not far from us, "do you know who that gent is over there? The geezer with the beard?"

Victoria followed my gaze. "Why, that's just Tom. Tom Hooper. I think I mentioned him to you before. He's worked here forever. He helps me with the gardening or whatever else needs doing. Why?"

"I thought of having a word with him. Anyone who's been around the joint that long might have seen a thing or two. I think I'll wave him down," I said, suiting action to word.

I shot him a friendly sign but didn't get the reaction I was expecting. Startled ain't the word for what he was. He looked like someone had given him the hotfoot. I made as if to head in his direction, and he fled like all the hounds of Hell was after him.

CHAPTER TWENTY-SEVEN

"That's strange," Victoria said. "Maybe he didn't realize you wanted to talk to him."

"More likely, he didn't like the look of my face. That's okay," I said, trying to pass it off. "He wouldn't be the first."

"It's not so bad," she said. "I think it's the kind of face that grows on you the more you see it."

I might have blushed if she'd been looking in my direction, but she was still kinda fascinated with watching Hooper hightail it. "Tom can be eccentric, but he and Mr. Wynter were always thick as thieves, and there's nothing he doesn't know about the cemetery. Maybe you'll get another chance to speak to him. I can put in a good word for you, if you like."

"That would be aces," I said appreciatively. "There's another someone I'd like a chance to jaw with and that's Mr. Cressley. Any chance of my sneaking up on him when Liv ain't around?"

"I can often find him in his office this time of day if I need him. It's a room just off the kitchen. If you go to the back door of the house, and rap on the window just to the right of it, you might be able to get his attention."

"Thanks for the tip. I feel like I still gotta lot to learn about what's going on around here and how it all ties back to Wally."

"Well, please be careful, Mr. Malhaven. Curiosity killed the cat, you know." She gave me the hint of a smile and wafted away from me like a dream.

That gave me something to chew on. Was it meant as friendly advice? Or a not-so-friendly warning? I wished I knew whether she was up to something. It made it hard to know how to play it when we met. She'd let me in on a few of her secrets, but I still didn't know if I could trust her or not. It was impossible to know where you stood with a dame like that. It made me feel like I was always being pushed off my balance, swaying this way and that according to her whims, not mine.

I took her advice about Cressley, and that, anyway, turned out to be solid info. A short tap at the window, and the curtain was pushed aside to show him gazing out at me. He held up a hand which I took to mean hang on, and sure enough, the kitchen door popped open, and he waved me through.

He took his role as host seriously, setting me down at the big kitchen table and pouring me a hot cup of joe from a pot he had simmering on the stove. He shoved a plate full of doughnuts in my direction to complete the refreshments. The coffee was nice and strong, and the doughnuts weren't too sweet. This was way more in my line than tea and cake in the parlor.

"This is the stuff. It's kindly of you to entertain me like this on such short notice," I thanked him.

He shrugged to indicate it was no trouble at all, then raised one bushy eyebrow, which I took to mean, *now, whataya want?*

"You strike me as a man of great discernment, Mr. Cressley. I'll be the first to admit I'm out to sea with this Wally business. You been around the family a long time. Won't you let me in on what you make of it all?"

He examined me closely. I got the idea he was sizing me up, trying to figure out how sincere I was. I tried my best to look earnest and frank which ain't so easy for me. Something about that scar makes me look like a crook no matter how I try to arrange my features.

Cressley seemed satisfied with whatever he saw, though, 'cause he pulled a notebook out of his pocket and a fountain pen that was a real beauty. To my untrained eye it looked like genuine 24-karat gold with the initials "C.C." engraved on the barrel. Of course, that set me off immediately into some pretty wild speculation as to Cressley's first name. It gave me a kick to think maybe it was something exotic. Carlos? Cyrus? Claude? Constantine? The mind boggled.

And where did he get hold of a classy writing tool like that? Maybe this butlering was a better racket than I'd of thought, but I set those minor concerns aside as Cressley started scrolling the nib across the paper. He had first-class handwriting, and he was quick at it, too. I guess he got a lot of practice. He pushed the pad over to me so I could read what he'd written.

Miss Bernadette and Miss Ernestine find great pleasure in the story.

"You got that right. What about Miss Livinia, though? It seems to get right up her nose."

Miss Livinia only wants what is best for her sisters.

I managed to stifle the snort that almost shot out my nose at that. It seemed to me Liv was all about what was best for Liv, but I didn't want to upset him. It made me curious, though, as to his true feelings about his boss.

"Miss Livinia seems like a very determined lady. Might not be so easy sometimes working for someone who's so determined as that. I got a lot of admiration for you."

There was a long pause. I got the feeling I'd strayed into some dangerous territory. The answer to my observation when it came was short and sweet.

Miss Livinia Wynter is a true lady.

Guess that told me where Cressley's loyalties were at. I didn't blame him. It can't have been easy keeping a job when you can't speak. That started me off thinking about how long he'd been a mute, and what happened to him. An accident. Isn't that what Liv had said?

But that could cover a lot of ground. I thought about inquiring—asking questions is my job, after all—but staring into that dignified, solemn face, I lost my nerve.

I decided to throw out a different observation and see how it landed. "Someone seems like they're out to get me since I started asking questions around here."

Maybe you should stop asking questions.

That was a stumper. If I couldn't ask any more questions, what did we have to talk about? I decided to ignore the hint in the interest of keeping the conversation humming along.

"Do you remember anything about this Hornschmidt murder? It must have been front page news at one time."

I never read the newspapers.

That hurt. No newshound likes to meet up with a mug that don't want to keep in the know. How you gonna understand what's going on in the world without us? That's what we like to think anyhow.

"What about Mr. William Wynter? I heard he was quite the guy. Big man during Prohibition and all that."

Mr. Wynter had a somewhat colorful past.

This seemed more promising. "That's what I hear. Running booze, stashing cash and gold around the place. I even heard there's some tucked away in that marble joint where he's enjoying his final sleep."

Mr. Wynter was an interesting man.

I ain't no dope. I could see where this was going and that was absolutely nowhere. I decided to throw one more out there anyway, purely for kicks.

"I don't guess you'd tell me if you knew about anything that was going on around here right this minute? It could be perilous times for some of the current inmates if it turns out they're up to no good."

All times have their perils.

I had to throw up my hands at that one.

"Okay, Mr. Cressley. I get the picture. I hope they appreciate you around here. You're one of the best. Steadfast, hardworking, and discreet. I'd tip my hat to you if I still had one."

That set him off one last time.

I am very sorry about your hat. Both of them.

Inscrutable, I thought. Was it a genuine expression of simple compassion for a man mourning the loss of his headpiece? Or was he apologizing for some kind of involvement in their destruction? Mikey had said he thought the goop with the gun was an old guy, and Cressley qualified for that, white hair and all. He supposedly had the night off during the séance. Had he crept back to the house to try and warn me off?

If so, who was he working for? Victoria seemed to feel a certain amount of affection for him, and she was quite a woman. It took no stretch of the imagination at all to see him lured into doing her dirty work. And, of course, there was Liv. He was making no secret of the fact that he would stick up for her through thick and thin.

I heaved a gentle sigh. Everywhere I turned, things got more cloudy instead of clearing themselves up. If someone was trying to leave me baffled and confused, it was a job well done. I could have sat there exchanging witticisms with Cressley for the rest of the afternoon, but I know when I'm licked. I shook his hand just the same. I can appreciate someone who knows how to keep his trap shut, mute or not.

Frustrated, I barreled out the kitchen door full speed and ran over an innocent passerby. Unbalanced, we both tipped over, and it took more than a minute to get ourselves untangled. When we could both sit up, I looked over to apologize only to stop dead in satisfaction. Maybe things were gonna look up for me after all. The mug sitting opposite me was none other than Santa himself, Mr. Tom Hooper.

CHAPTER TWENTY-EIGHT

"What did I ever do to you?" was his first reaction. His second was a look of terror when he seen who it was that bowled him over like a pin. Lucky for me, he was no spring chicken, so I was able to get up and grab ahold of him before he had a chance to leg it again.

"What's the big deal?" I asked. "You keep trying to give me the cold shoulder. What, you never seen a face like mine before?"

"Seen worse," he admitted, trying to butter me up. "Let me go, mister. I got things to do. Unlike some bums, I gotta do real work to earn a living."

"Funny guy, huh? Well, let me tell you, we're gonna have a discussion sooner or later, so you might as well make up your mind to that now and get it over with."

He scowled at me, but what was he gonna do? He might have had the Santa beard, but he was as skinny as a broomstick on a diet and couldn't have been more than five feet and a half in his stocking feet. He was wiry, I'll give him that, and he gave it the old college try, but I have a grip like iron, so I wasn't too worried about losing him.

"Let's take a load off," says I, steering him over to a nearby tomb that was a convenient height for parking ourselves comfortably. "You don't have to get so excited. I just heard you been around this joint a long time and wanted a little history lesson is all. Nothing to get yourself so worked up about."

I didn't want to be responsible for his arm turning black and blue—he must have had at least forty years on me, and I fell in with Q's viewpoint on respecting your elders—so I changed it up by draping one beefy arm over his shoulders as another way of keeping tabs on him. I probably ought not to have bothered as the spirit seemed to have left him, but I was taking no chances. It had been a long day, and I felt like I was striking out every time I got up to bat. The only useful thing I'd picked up was Mikey's observation about the hair. Well, Hooper had white hair, too. That was two suspects at least between him and Cressley. Then it occurred to me there was a third in the mix if I could imagine that slick-talking lawyer Monroe lurking in the bushes to wave a gat around.

I was bound and determined to get something out of my final witness of the day one way or another. I'd been around the block a few times and thought I knew a way to crack him open like an egg. "Everyone around here's been trying to tell me what a big deal this William Wallace Wynter was and how you sat at his right hand. It all sounds like so much hot air to me."

"That ain't so," he squealed. "Billy Wynter was the greatest man I ever knew!"

"Billy, huh? Kind of familiar, ain't you?"

"That's the way he was. He didn't put on no airs, not with me. We both grew up dirt poor not more than fifteen miles from here. Sweating it out in the fields all summer. Shivering in a one-room shack all winter. That was life for a lot of us boys. But Billy was different. He had smarts. He always said he was gonna make something of hisself and he did."

Old Tom had tears in his eyes and looked ready to tell me anything I wanted to know so long as he could champion his hero. I had a feeling I could get him going by pretending to doubt his idol, and it had worked a treat.

"I gotta admit that's something," I said. "Working your way up from less than nothing to owning a fancy house and a big property like this. Didn't it make you sore being nothing more than the gardener while your old friend ordered you around?"

"I tell you it wasn't like that. Billy never made a decision without talking to me first. He always said I was the only one he could trust 'cause I knew him when. And I got plenty out of it. He bought me a farm outside of town and enough money to pay for plenty of hands to run it. I never have to step one foot in them fields if I don't feel like it. And he bought me a new truck whenever I wanted," he finished like that was the capper no one could argue with.

"He didn't buy you that shiny new one I seen you riding around in," I said, indicating the Chevrolet sitting parked not so far from us.

"No," he said, looking sly. "But that ain't none of your business."

"If you say so. Billy's been gone a long time now. What makes you keep hanging around? Sounds like you got it pretty good. If I was you, I'd retire to that farm and put my feet up for a change. We all gotta end up in a place like this sooner or later, but why not escape it while you can?"

"I promised Billy I'd keep an eye on his daughters for him. He thought the world of them girls. And Mrs. Jankowski ain't so bad herself. She always lets me know how much she appreciates my help. There are some things too big for a woman to do all alone around here, you know. Besides, I worked all my life. What am I gonna do sitting on the porch with my feet stuck up in the air? I wouldn't last a day."

"I can appreciate the sentiment. It's the sign of a wise man to know that hard work is good for the soul," I said, trying to burnish him up a bit. "Sounds like Mr. Wynter must not have been afraid of hard work either, building up a solid business like this. What do you think gave him the idea anyhow? It's kind of an unusual line of work, ain't it? Operating a boneyard."

"Saw a need for it, I guess. There's some small graveyards in the city, mostly round the churches, but he had a vision for a nice place. Like a park. People like that when they come to visit their folks. Makes them feel better to think they're resting out here among the trees and such. And there's more cash in it than you'd think. He figured out it was better to lease the plots than sell them. Think about adding that up year after year."

"Huh. That's something. But what do you do if they don't pay their rent? Evict the poor saps?"

"We move them to the pauper's corner. They're stacked in deep there. Then you can lease their old digs to someone else."

"That does sound like a good racket. And he built himself the nicest digs of all. That's quite a tomb he's got there. Impressive."

"Yeah, it's a special place all right," Hooper agreed, before looking frightened like he didn't like the direction we was headed.

"That right?" I encouraged him, but he shut up like a clam on that topic. Made me wonder if there was more to that crypt than met the eye, but I agreeably dropped the subject since it seemed to give him the willies.

"I hear Mr. Wynter had his finger in more pies than just the cemetery?"

"Mebbe," Hooper conceded, looking shiftier yet.

"Prohibition's long over, and poor Billy has gone on to his greater reward now. Wouldn't do no harm to gab about it, would it?"

"I guess not. There was lots of guys back then who ran liquor. It was so common, it was kinda respectable really. Those abstinence nuts were the real criminals. Imagine asking a guy to give up his booze," he said, the old outrage back in full force. "We was doing everyone a service really. People would have gone crazy without us."

"So, you helped out with it, too, then?"

"Mebbe I did, mebbe I didn't," he said. "Like you said that's a long time ago now. What with the war and all, most people don't even remember them times."

"Still, it must have been pretty exciting. Bet you could tell a few stories about ducking and diving to outsmart them revenue goons. Can't have been so easy moving through that kind of merchandise without getting caught."

"We never worried about that. Billy had a system."

"He did, did he? Sounds like a smart guy. Or maybe he just got lucky."

"Luck had nothing to do with it!" Hooper argued, riled up again. "Billy planned out every bit of that operation until he knew it was foolproof. We never touched one bottle until we got every kink in the plan worked out and did all the hard labor we got to do."

"Hard labor? Whataya mean by that?"

"Oh… nothing. Just, you know, it's no walk in the park setting up a distribution system like that. The worst part was trying to find men we could trust. Me and Billy tried to do it all ourselves to start with, but it was way more than we could handle on our own."

"That right? So, what other kinda guys helped you out?" I asked, wondering about Cressley, if he'd been around back then, or that lawyer.

"Most of them were just mooks. Billy paid them twice what they could get anywhere else to keep 'em happy, so they'd keep their traps shut. That's the worst part of running an operation like that. Never knowing if someone's gonna have loose lips." Hooper gave a hoot of laughter that startled me, it was so loud. "He always said Cressley was our best man. Couldn't talk if he wanted to, you know," he crowed, hitting me in the chest with one scrawny arm to display his glee at this wisecrack.

I guess that answered part of my questions about Cressley. At least how long he'd been around and how long he'd been mute. Maybe I'd get up the nerve one day to ask him how it happened.

"Cressley can write up a storm, though," I objected. "I seen him do it. Didn't that cause you and Mr. Wynter any concern that he might spill the beans to the cops?"

"No," he replied, sobering up. "Cressley's a solid guy, and he owed Billy a lot. Would have done anything for him. No, Cressley's one that never gave us a minute of worry. Not like that Hornschmidt dope," he added, sounding bitter. "Guys like him are just too dumb to live."

CHAPTER TWENTY-NINE

*I*t took me a second to get what I was hearing, but Hooper knew what he'd let slip right away. He ducked out from under my arm, looking back with an expression that was telling me, *I said too much*, as clear as if he'd been hollering it in my face, before he set off at a run. I had to hand it to him—for an old geezer, he could still move. I got up to lumber after him, but what with my bum leg and the head start he got, I never stood a chance. He hopped into his truck and zoomed away down the gravel driveway leaving me standing there in a cloud of dust like a chump trying to puzzle out what I just learned.

I lit a cigarette and had a smoke to help me think. So, Wally was involved in Mr. Wynter's booze racket. I wondered how that came to be. According to the papers, Wally delivered milk, but maybe he delivered something more than just milk on his rounds. That would be one way of distributing the stuff. On the other hand, they must have been doing big volume was the impression I got. Didn't seem like one driver was gonna be able to take care of all that on his own, but maybe they'd recruited more than one deliveryman and more than one truck.

And what did it have to do with the murder and this so-called haunting? Hard to see how a guy going after his wife and kid like that fit in, but the sightings had started about a year after Wally's death. The booze operation would have been in full swing by then. I wondered if the ghost was just another part of Mr. Wynter's "foolproof" plan. He seemed like the type to cover all his bases. Starting up this rumor of a haunt running around might have been a way to scare people away from the cemetery or explain any unusual activity at night.

From what I was hearing about old Billy, it seemed like the kind of prank he'd have enjoyed. Putting one over on the local population 'cause he was so much smarter than the rest of us dupes. It would have been a cinch to stage a spectral presence at the gates and arrange for one of his daughters to lay eyes on it, although it seemed kinda rough to use your own flesh and blood that way.

To be fair, it hadn't seemed to do them much harm. Having their very own wraith provided them with some excitement, and I couldn't imagine they had much of that in their lives, particularly the two older ones. It was Livinia who got to take care of the business side of things. Seems like that left the other two wandering around at loose ends. No wonder they were ready, willing, and able to believe in Wally.

Couple of other things Hooper let slip gave me something to think about. That whole "too dumb to live" crack struck me as sinister. Wally'd hung himself in his jail cell before the trial started according to the paper, but could that have been staged? Maybe he'd become a threat and they had to get rid of him. Mug like that, about to go on trial for his life, don't have a lot to lose. There was a risk he might flap his jaws about the sauce operation. If so, this was starting to look serious. Rum-running back in the day was one thing, but offing guys that stood in your way was something else again.

I also recalled the way Hooper had acted when I brought up old man Wynter's tomb. I was just being friendly, thinking he'd appreciate me complimenting his boss's refined tastes, but he'd acted like that subject was strictly off the table. Which, of course, made me want to know all about it. What had Victoria told me? That he'd planned and built it way back in 1920, I thought. Could just be he was a forward-thinker and liked to get his ducks in a row.

But now I wondered if he built it for another purpose entirely. That'd be a smart place to stash the booze while they went about handing it out. Who's gonna have the nerve to knock down the door of a joint like that looking for contraband? It looked big from the outside, big enough to be a pretty good warehouse, and they could have dug down, too. Maybe it had a basement or something.

The more I thought it over, the more I started feeling downright curious about that tomb. Stomping out the butt of my smoke on the ground, I strolled over to give the place the onceover. It was just as impressive as I remembered. At least two or three times the size of any other thing like it in the whole cemetery. I'd thought it was just his conceit talking, wanting to make a splash and remind people what a big man he was even after he was gone, but now I had to wonder if there was more to it. I sure wished I could see inside. I was stooping down to examine the elaborate locks on the door when I was interrupted. Or caught out, more like it.

"Mr. Mal-*vern*, just what do you think you're doing?"

Liv's icy voice sent a creepy shiver down my spine. I already knew I wasn't in her good books. It seemed like a decent guess that catching me snooping around her father's grave wasn't doing anything to help my cause. I tried to pass it off. You got to make the best of these situations.

"Good afternoon, Miss Wynter. Just admiring your father's handiwork here. I heard he designed it himself. Quite something, ain't it?"

Guess she didn't buy it, 'cause she just screeched out, "Cressley!" at a volume that hurt my eardrums. The old guy popped up outta nowhere like some kind of genie from a bottle and came over and took me by the arm with a lot of verve. He shot me an apologetic look, but there was no mistaking that pressure on my appendage—I was being escorted off the property. I could have broke his hold easy, but I decided to give in gracefully. I could always sneak back after dark.

I went to tip my hat to Liv, aiming to be polite in the face of her discourtesy to show her how it was done, only to be reminded yet again that I was topless. It wasn't so easy breaking the habit of a lifetime. Made me wonder if Victoria was making any progress on the hat repair front. I was feeling unsettled enough as it was without the added burden of constantly reaching for something that wasn't there. It was starting to make me feel like a nut.

I shook Cressley's hand at the gates just to show there was no hard feelings and drove back into town. I decided to stop by the paper and fill Q in on my day. I'd been even less successful than I'd expected, but he was interested enough in what I'd picked up. He promised to do some research on the history of rum-running in the city to see if it shed any light on Wynter's mode of operation. I also filled him in on Victoria's time at the Sisters of Mercy and her memories of the boy named Kit, which reminded me to give him the lead on the nursing job for his sister.

"I'll be sure and let Marlene know, Mr. Malhaven. Thanks for the tip. It's too bad that Mrs. Jankowski didn't remember more or that you couldn't find out something about Peter while you were at the orphanage."

"Yeah. That Sister Honoria is no joke, that's for sure. I guess I could go back and try to talk her around, but she seems like a tough cookie. I'd give just about anything to see their file on little Peter Hornschmidt."

Q surprised me with his next suggestion. "We could break in."

"Break in? To the orphanage?"

"Why not? I imagine their security isn't very tight."

I pondered the thought. "I suppose I could give it a try. I can't pretend I never slipped in somewhere after hours trying to get a bead on a story. But I'll go it alone. No reason for more than one of us to run the risk, and someone like me has less to lose if we get caught than a fine upstanding citizen like yourself."

Q shook his head. "No, you need me. I'm the expert on filing systems. You can keep a lookout while I find the information we need."

We argued back and forth for a good bit, but Q got a determined look in his eye that made me think he might go with or without me and better that I went along. I agreed to meet up with him at the orphanage around midnight in the hopes it would be lights out by then for the nuns, me not thinking they kept very late hours at such a place.

After leaving the office, I tried to take stock of what I knew, although it seemed easier to list what I didn't know. I still didn't know where Peter was now, or what had caused his pop to go off on him and his ma like that. I didn't know if Wally had hung himself or been offed. I didn't know if the ghost was real or not, although I had a strong opinion about that one.

I also didn't know exactly how Wynter had distributed the booze. That last bit wouldn't have been so important since it was ancient history, except I had the beginnings of an idea that someone might have adopted his methods for a more up-to-date dope operation. And if that was the case, the biggest question of all was, who was running it?

Victoria and Liv seemed like the two obvious candidates, although I supposed someone else could be doing it under their noses. Tom Hooper, Mr. C. Cressley, even that lawyer fellow, Monroe. If they'd all been involved in Wynter's original operation, they'd have the know-how to set up and carry out the modern scheme. Prohibition might be long over, but there was plenty of other contraband out there on the streets and plenty of money to be made off it. On impulse, I stopped in at the precinct house and had a jaw with Flanagan.

"Glad to see you, Jimmy, my boy. I been keeping my eyes and ears open. Word on the street is there's been an uptick in the smack business lately. Market's being flooded, but no one knows where it's coming from. Very hush-hush. Somebody's running it with an iron fist. Can't get no one to crack, not even the lowest of the low two-bit dealers we pick up now and again."

"That is interesting. Sounds like someone has a get-rich-quick scheme in motion."

"Well, it'd be a fine idea for them to put the brakes on. The way they're putting it out there, the bottom of the market's gonna drop clear out. That's just supply and demand. Too much supply and the price is gonna sink. They're shooting themselves in the foot if they want to rake in the dough. Don't seem like good business to me."

"Maybe it's a fire sale," I suggested, thinking about the pressure my investigation might be putting on someone. "You know, they got a premonition their time is up, and they're dumping their inventory."

"I won't say you're not on to something there, but whatever they're up to, it's a fact that they've managed to attract plenty of attention, and not the kind they want, I shouldn't imagine. The Mayor and the Commissioner's calling a special meeting day after next to caucus on it. They'll probably give orders to throw everything we got at it, see if we can't shut it down. Last thing we need is a bunch more dopeheads passed out in the street 'cause they got access to cheap stuff. You find out anything yet that I could pass along to the top brass?"

"Maybe," I said, my stomach doing flip-flops at the possibility of throwing Victoria under the bus if it was her back of it after all. I decided to keep the tire tracks I'd found under wraps for now, do some more digging into that myself. "I got a few tips today that I gotta follow up. As soon as I got something concrete, I'll be back down here first thing to let you know."

"You do that, Jimmy. Best to let the professionals handle it if you get a real lead," Flanagan said with a serious look in his eye. "I got the feeling whoever's behind this is feeling the heat, and guys like that get desperate. I don't want to be picking you up off the street in some dark alley again."

"You and me both, pal," I agreed. "I'll sleep with one eye open until all's said and done. Not to worry. No more trouble for me, I swear." Just the kind of dopey promise you should never make, ain't it?

$\mathcal{I}$ spent the rest of my day revisiting that list of vans I'd made to see if I could find one with a patched tire but came up empty again. At least it gave me something to do to pass the time until my rendezvous with Q. Toward midnight, I pulled up into a parking space a block or so away from the Sisters of Mercy and hoofed it over there to find him waiting for me in a doorway across the street. I complimented him on his choice. It was the perfect spot for a touch of surveillance.

The orphanage was mostly dark, but there was one light shining through a window on the main floor that worried me. It seemed to me it might line up with about where I'd noticed Sister Honoria's name on an office door during our tour. The thought she might be working late crossed my mind. Q and I held a conference and decided to give it a little while to see if there were any developments. Finally, after about a half hour, the light went out. We gave it another twenty minutes or so to make sure she didn't change her mind then walked across the way and started checking the ground floor windows.

We found one that was unlocked all right, but tug as we might, it wouldn't open all the way. I stood fuming at the small gap in frustration. There was no way a big, beefy guy like me was gonna fit, but Q suddenly stooped and wriggled through before I could stop him. Now I was in a pickle. I didn't like the thought of Q roaming around on his own in there without a lookout to keep an eye peeled for trouble. I stepped back and looked up at the big double entrance doors, unsure what to do next, wishing one of those stone angels would come to life and offer me some advice.

While I was pondering, I saw the light go back on in what I thought was Sister Honoria's office. I didn't think it was Q being careless enough to turn on the bulb 'cause he had proudly shown me the flashlight he had stashed in his pocket for his midnight scouting adventure. As I recalled from the grand tour, the room with all the files wasn't too far from that very spot. Seemed to me Q was in danger of being caught and that would be the worst kind of news for him. I'd known the cops to come down extra hard on black folks, and I hated to think what his mother or sister would say to me if they found out I had led him into such a predicament as that.

Some kind of action was called for and without thinking it through as hard as I probably should have, I ran up the front steps and banged on the door. It was only after I knocked that I stopped to consider that I didn't have a very good excuse for showing up there past midnight, but it was too late for that 'cause the door was thrown open and Sister Honoria was standing there giving me the once over like I was one of her tiny charges who was being extra naughty.

She raised one delicate eyebrow in my direction by way of inquiry.

"Uh, hello," I said. Not the most brilliant line, but all I could think of.

"Mr. Malhaven? What on earth are you doing here this time of night?"

"Uh… hello there." Okay, not much of an improvement but you try to come up with something clever when a stunner in a habit is giving you the piercing look of a tiger about to pounce on a mouse.

She glowered at me another moment, then her expression softened a bit and she reached for my arm. "Mr. Malhaven, I do believe you've been drinking to excess. Now aren't you ashamed of yourself?"

"Why, yes, yes I am," I said, grasping at the lifeline she'd thrown me. "You'll have to excush… that is, excuse me, ma'am, if you can." I stumbled a bit for good measure to play it up.

"Of course, I can. God forgives all his creatures, and it is incumbent upon me to do no less. But you shouldn't be wandering around the streets this time of night in your condition. You might find yourself getting into trouble. Come in here and let me warm you up some coffee."

Thinking the longer I could spin this out, the more likely Q would find what he was looking for and get himself safely out of there, I decided to go along with her scheme. She led me inside and down the hallway to a big kitchen where she deposited me in a chair at a table while she busied herself around one of the stoves. I decided to close my eyes and prop my head on one hand to give the impression I was dead on my feet. The strong smell of java in front of me prompted me to open my eyes and take a sip of the boiling liquid while she sat down across from me to monitor my progress.

"Say, that's a good cup of joe," I said appreciatively, giving her a wink by way of keeping up the pretense of my being three sheets to the wind.

"I'm glad you're enjoying it," she said with a somewhat satirical tone. "Now, maybe you can tell me what brings you to our door at this hour?"

"You know how it is. I was just passing and thought I might drop in and ask you a few more questions. A reporter's job never shtoops, never shtops, never stops."

She was giving me the kind of eye such that I couldn't tell if she was buying it or not, but she was looking more indulgent, like she was feeling sorry for such a sad sack as I appeared to be. "I don't know what else I could tell you, Mr. Malhaven. As I said, we don't discuss our children."

"Yeah, yeah. It's just that I was chatting with Mrs. Victoria J up at the cemetery. You don't have to worry none—she volunteered that she sprouted up here, so you won't be breaking any confidensh… confidensh…"

"Confidences?"

"Egg-zackily."

She smiled at that, showing off a nice pair of dimples. "Mrs. Jankowski is a good friend and an example of how well many of our children do after they leave us."

"She's had a hard time, poor kid," I observed.

"Life has thrown her many challenges," Honoria agreed. "But she always meets them with faith and strength."

I wondered if that was as true as she thought. Maybe I wasn't the only person Victoria was hiding a secret life from.

"She was telling me about this fellow inmate she remembered, a friend of hers, a boy named Kit. She thought maybe he had had a pretty hard time himself. I hate to think of a little kid like that, just a helpless little tyke…" Under the table, I dug my fingers into the big scar on my leg so as to force tears into my eyes at the pain.

"Why, Mr. Malhaven, you're really just a big softy at heart, aren't you?"

"It would make anyone feel miserable hearing about a poor kid like that," I said, pulling out my handkerchief and dabbing at my eyes. "Just imagine what he went through before he ended up in your tender hands."

I thought maybe the tears would push her over, but she was too smart to fall for such a ruse. "As I've said, we cannot discuss our children. Whatever they've experienced, the best thing we can do for them is provide as welcoming and stable an environment as we can while they are under our care and pray for a loving family that will take them into their hearts and home."

"You're quite the pip, Sister Honoria," I said, with a bit of a smirk.

Guess I'd taken the drunk act too far. Rising up and crossing her arms in front of her, she looked down at me in a way that made me think she would like to rap me across the knuckles with a ruler. "You seem to have recovered sufficiently, Mr. Malhaven, to make your way home. I'd be happy to telephone for a taxicab for you."

The way she said it left no room for argument. I figured my time was up and just had to hope Q had hopped it by then. "No need, ma'am. A brisk walk in the fresh air will do me a whole world of good."

At least this time I remembered I didn't have a hat to tip and satisfied my sense of propriety by giving her a sweeping bow instead, keeping in character as a confirmed alcoholic, you know. The return of those dimples on her face as she escorted me to the front door told me she had a good sense of humor hiding in there somewhere. We parted on reasonably good terms given that she thought I'd turned up drunk as a skunk at her door after midnight and been fresh with her to boot.

It was a relief to find Q waiting for me back across the road. I was a lot more shaken up than he was. He was just anxious to fill me in on what he'd found out.

"I was able to find a ledger listing out all the adoptions during the twenties. Peter's was listed in 1926 to a family called Bellingham from Chicago. They seem to keep files on all the adoptive families, but I couldn't find the one for Bellingham so that's all the information I had time to get. I heard you talking with someone in the hallway and decided I better get out of there. I'm sorry."

"Hey, don't apologize! That took a whole lot of gumption. You're a good partner," I said, punching him in the side as light as a feather to demonstrate my approval. "At least we got a name now. Shouldn't be too hard to track down these Bellinghams. That's not the most common handle, is it? Let me drop you off home so you can get some shuteye and get back to your world-class detective work in the morning."

I suited action to word, then sat in the Champ smoking and thinking over my own next moves. My talk earlier with Flanagan had rattled me. I knew the kinda heat commissioners and mayors start to take from the voting citizenry when situations like this dope epidemic got out of control. And I'd seen them take extreme measures to stomp on whoever was at the center of it. Could I stand by and let the chips fall where they may? Take a chance that Victoria wouldn't be swept away in the mayhem?

Standing on the sidelines wasn't my style. Whether it spelled the slammer for Victoria or not, I just had to know what was what. And now I knew from Flanagan that the clock was ticking, there was only one place to go where I could find the answers I needed most. Back to the boneyard for me.

CHAPTER THIRTY-ONE

I stashed the Studebaker and myself behind the big stand of trees across from the gates and waited to see if there was anything doing. A cold drizzle of rain had started up which made me lament my lack of head covering all over again. I told myself to toughen up and kept my eyes peeled over the way to see what I could see. I was in luck for a change. Before too long, the dark van drove up, and a guy dressed all in white jumped out and took a hard look around before unlocking the gates. I waited for him to enter before crossing the road and slipping in behind him. I learned a thing or two in the war about moving stealthy, so it was no problem shadowing with him none the wiser.

Wasn't too surprised to discover he was making direct for Wynter's vault. What did surprise me was when he trotted past the big front door and disappeared around the side. Nosiness overcoming my common sense, I dashed forward to see what he was up to. Peeking around the corner, I was astonished to see he had vanished into thin air. I scanned the graves in every direction, but there was nowhere close he could be hiding. He had to have gone inside.

I ran my mitts over the cool, damp wall of the crypt. All I could figure was there was some kind of secret door which meant there must be a way of triggering it. It was dark, and I hadn't been smart enough to think of packing a flashlight myself or borrowing Q's. I tried lighting some matches and feeling around for a while but hadn't experienced any success when I heard a voice.

"What are you doing?"

Same question as Livinia asked earlier, more or less, but this wasn't Liv. I looked up to find Victoria staring at me in fascination. She had her wool coat on with something floaty and yellow sticking out below and a bright scarf, all over pictures of birds of every kind, protecting her honeyed hair from the misty rain.

"Are you looking for something?" She came over and started running her own delicate hands over the same spots I'd been exploring.

I didn't know what to say. If she was the crime boss I'd been suspecting, then she already knew what I was looking for, and I was in danger. If she was innocent, I didn't want to get her involved in something that might put her in danger.

Flummoxed, I said the first thing that shot into my brain. "I like the feel of it. The marble. So smooth and… and cool, you know?" I finished weakly. This just wasn't my night for thinking quick on my feet. First, Sister Honoria and now this but, like I said, I was flustered.

"I see," she said, looking and sounding pretty cool herself. "You came all the way out here and broke into a cemetery at this time of night just to touch some cool stone. I'm sorry, but isn't that rather odd?"

"I didn't break in, the gates were open," I blurted out. What can I say? I was disconcerted.

"They are? They shouldn't be. I should go check on them," she said.

"Good idea," I said, not sure if it was or it wasn't, but there didn't seem to be any way I could stop her. "I'll come with. It might not be safe around here."

"Why? There might be some strange characters running around?" she asked, cocking me an amused look.

"Exactly. You can't be too careful."

I was nervous. This was yet another pickle I found myself in. I felt like either I was being led into danger, or I might inadvertently be leading Victoria into danger. Without knowing which was which, I didn't know what best to do. Gotta admit I was shillyshallying, and I'm not one what does that. Just goes to show the kind of effect she had on me.

Before I could make up my mind how to handle the situation, we'd made it all the way back out to the gates. Imagine what a jolt it was to me when we found them locked up nice and tight with the van nowhere to be seen. Victoria turned to me with a look, those eyes of hers as dark and wide as I'd ever seen them.

"It was open before, I swear," I assured her. "Whoever did it must have come back out and locked 'em up again," I suggested, my mind going a million miles an hour trying to figure out how the galoot in the white outfit had made it past us without being seen.

"Uh-huh," she said in a way that told me she wasn't buying it.

There was an awkward intermission while we sized each other up. I decided to level with her, at least a little.

"Look, Victoria. I think you and me both know there's something going on around here. Are you sure there's nothing you wanna tell me? I'm not such a bad guy. I might even could help you out."

She looked troubled at that which made me worry, but she wasn't ready to confess. "I don't know any more than I've told you."

I knew it wasn't the right thing to do, but she looked so sad and defenseless there in the bit of moonlight from a break in the clouds, I felt like I just had to give her a heads-up on the trouble that might be headed her way.

"I'm not the only one who thinks something stinks around here. I got a pal on the force, and they're getting plenty interested, too. They could make things awful hot for somebody, if you know what I mean."

At that, she looked plain scared which scared me plenty, but she had guts and seemed anxious to prove it to me even if it hurt my feelings some. "I don't know what you're trying to suggest, but I'm sure no one here has anything to hide. You'd be doing your friends a favor to let them know that so they don't waste their time on us. It's beginning to sound to me like you've read too many detective novels.

Maybe you're under the impression that you're the hero of your own private-eye adventure, instead of just a two-bit reporter who covers the human-interest beat."

My heart sank down into the soles of my feet. This wasn't Victoria of the daylight, spilling her innocent little secrets to me like she trusted me to hold them close like the precious things they were. This was the Victoria of the night. The one who was secretive, who drank, or worse, to quash her sad memories, and as a consequence, couldn't be bothered overmuch about other people's feelings. And I guess I had really hit a nerve and spooked her 'cause she wasn't done with laying into me yet.

"If anything, it seems to me that any trouble we've experienced came in these gates with you, riding on your coattails. Maybe if you'd go away and leave us alone, trouble would, too. Since you managed to find a way in, I'll assume you can find your own way out. Goodbye, Mr. Malhaven."

And with that, she was gone again, leaving me feeling almost as bad as I did the night that punk sliced open my face. And worse than that, I felt none the wiser about whether she was standing in line for the stormy weather to come from the cops or not. Why did I still care after what she'd said, you ask? Was I a sucker for punishment? Nope, but I couldn't help but think about those sweeter times with Victoria. Did they make up for moments like this? That was the million-dollar question, wasn't it?

So, there I was, stuck on the inside of the gates, feeling about as low as I ever had in my life. What to do? It struck me that Victoria might have had a point. I seemed to be the focus of a lot of the trouble. It was my head, my hat—make that *hats*—that had taken the brunt of the violence. Somebody wanted me to walk away, and so far, I'd been too pigheaded to do it.

But what was I hoping for? Victoria had it right. I was just a stringer for a small-time paper. I wasn't exactly saving the world. I guess you could argue I might be doing it a favor by helping the cops get some of that poison off the streets. I'd seen the damage it could do. But I also seen enough to know that as soon as one supply line was cut, two more would spring up in its place. There was a lot of misery in the world, and always plenty of crooks waiting around to make a buck off of it.

What else kept me going? Was it that I couldn't get rid of the hunger I had to solve all of Victoria's problems for her? Did I really think I could be the kind of man that helped her live in the sunlight all the time, so that she never had to visit that dark place she went to in the night ever again? I knew in my heart I wasn't. That "goodbye" she'd thrown at me just then had sounded too final. But did you ever want something bad enough that it felt like cutting off an arm to walk away from even the dream of it?

When did you turn into such a sap? I asked myself, standing there in the dark, staring at those locked gates. Should I haul myself up and over them and disappear into the night for good? Or should I stick it out, stand my ground until I finally found out what was going on?

Flanagan had given me a deadline. The day after tomorrow things was gonna start to simmer with the cops whether I solved the puzzle or not. I couldn't shake that picture in my mind. Victoria surrounded by a sea of boys in blue, her lovely hands chained, being led away and looking back at me with those big gray-blue eyes overflowing with tears.

I debated about half a second more before I decided. I might not be the most ambitious guy in the world, but no one ever called Jim Malhaven a quitter. Whether I liked what I found out or not, it was time to stop burying the lead and blow up this ghost story once and for all.

Or die trying.

CHAPTER THIRTY-TWO

Once I made up my mind, I did some more scouting around the vault, but the clouds had come back to hide the sliver of light the moon had briefly been offering, and it started in to spitting rain again. I decided the best thing I could do was find myself some shelter and wait for the dawn. Once the sun was on its way up, I could get a better look at Wynter's crypt before anyone else was out and about. That place felt like the key to the whole thing. If I could just get inside, maybe everything would fall into place.

I found another tomb in a far-off corner of the grounds. Not as grand as Wynter's final abode, but it had a welcoming front porch with a bench for folks to sit and ponder on under a marble overhang big enough to protect me from the worst of the elements. I resolved to stay awake this time. No more snoozing on the job.

There'd been worse nights on watch duty during the war and way worse berths, but it's still not what I'd recommend, hunkering down in a graveyard in the dark and bone-chilling cold of a rainy autumn night. You couldn't help but think about your own bitter end to come, sitting there in the middle of that vast, silent company with no one lively enough to sit up and jaw with you to help pass the time.

I'd come close to ending up six feet under myself the night I got cut. The doc told me it was a miracle I hadn't bled to death from that big wound on my thigh. I remembered thinking when I heard him say it that it was a wakeup call for me. A push to stop drifting through life and make something of myself. I think that resolution lasted all of two days before I got discouraged and fell back into my old routines. Made me wonder what it would take to really get me fired up if that hadn't done it.

It was a relief when that first glimmer of dawn appeared in the eastern sky. Too much soul-searching ain't good for you, not in my opinion. I stood up, easing my creaking bones this way and that to work the kinks out, before setting off again to visit Mr. Billy Wynter. I kept a watchful eye out, but all seemed peaceful, so I gave the vault a thorough onceover, running my fingers along all the nooks and crannies of the fancy design and moldings on the back wall.

"Bingo!" I'd been at it a while and was on the verge of giving up, so I couldn't help but celebrate when one of the pieces of decoration finally gave way under my hand. A door that had been invisible sprung open just enough to be able to see it was there. All excited, I was gonna push on through the gap when I heard the sound of a loud motor headed my way. That plus the thought that had just occurred to me that I didn't have a light in case it was pitch black in there decided me to close the door and wait for another opportunity. Maybe come after dark again when no one was around, and after I had a chance to outfit myself better for the expedition.

I walked away casually from the joint, aiming to look like I was just out for a pleasant early morning stroll in case I got caught. Sure enough, I turned the corner and ran into old Tom Hooper, just hopping down from his truck. He looked about as rattled to see me as I felt at almost being caught at Wynter's grave. There was no doubt in my mind that he knew all about that hidden entrance, but I wasn't ready to let on that I knew about it, too, whatever suspicions he might be entertaining.

"Morning, Mr. Hooper. You're out bright and early."

"I might say the same to you," he growled. "How'd you get in here? I just opened up the gates."

"Secret of the journalistic trade," I said.

"Trespassing more like it. Breaking and entering. Miss Livinia won't approve of that. She might want me to set the law on you," he said.

I could see he hadn't warmed up to me since the day before. He was probably even less happy to see me in case he had reason to worry about what he'd let slip.

"Miss Wynter might enjoy that, but is inviting the heat around really what you want?" I asked, giving him what I hoped was a knowing look, but which might have just looked like I was scrunching up my face 'cause I was about to let loose with a sneeze for all I knew, but it did seem to make him reconsider his position.

"Well, it don't have to come to that. Not if you take a hike. *Off* the premises, not on," he clarified for my benefit. "I guess I could let it go this once."

"That seems fair enough. You're a good man, Mr. Hooper," I lied. I found it never hurt to lay the butter on thick. Doesn't always work, but it works often enough to make it worth a fling.

At least it didn't seem to make him mad. In fact, he surprised me by reaching into the cab of his trunk and bringing out a parcel all tied up with string.

"Your hat," he grunted.

"My hat?" I asked, looking at the package with a wary eye. The last time I'd been the recipient of a parcel wrapped up like that it hadn't been good news for the hat. "What are *you* doing with it?"

"Mrs. Jankowski asked me to drive into town and fetch it from Klein's this morning on my way in to work. Had to roust him out of bed. Guess hat makers don't keep early hours. Mrs. Jankowski goes way back with Klein's daughter, so he promised to do a rush job on it for her. She seemed to think you was missing it. So, here, take it, why dontcha? You need an engraved invitation or something?"

I took the offering and tore it open, and there was the fedora in all its glory. I eyed it up and down, inside and out and couldn't see a sign of those holes. Guess that Klein knew his business. Settled it on my noggin and felt whole again. My spirits, which had been dragging along the ground, picked up.

We might have parted with suspicion on both sides and harsh words on hers, but here was proof that Victoria still thought enough of me to make haste with getting the hat—her late husband's, no less—back to me, knowing I felt like a dunce without it. I tried tipping it to Hooper, just as a practice run, and boy, it felt fine. A day that started out that good couldn't possibly go bad, could it?

He just gave my polite gesture the evil eye, spitting out, "Now you got it back, you can scram out of here, can't you?"

Some people just don't appreciate good manners, but I was feeling so swell that it bounced right off me. "Sure thing, now that I got what I come for."

That gave him something to puzzle over as I sauntered away. My step felt lighter as I went. The more I thought about it, the more it seemed like Victoria couldn't hate me, not and go to all that trouble to give me Lukasz's hat not just once, but twice.

I waited until I was out of sight of old Tom and snuck over to her cottage—it seemed only polite to thank her after all. I tapped lightly on the door in case she was still asleep, but it opened at once, and she peeked out cautiously. I could see she'd been weeping, and not just a little. Those gorgeous eyes were red and swollen from quite a jag. It knocked the wind right outta me again.

"Your hat," she murmured. "I see Mr. Hooper found you."

"I found him, I guess. It sure was a nice thing you did after all the trouble I been to you, getting it fixed up so fast."

"The Kleins are old friends of ours. Jakob remembered the hat right away—making it for Lukasz, I mean." She gave out with a small hiccup at that, and I couldn't stand it no more.

"Victoria," I said, as soft and sweet as I knew how. "I gotta ask you just one more time. Won't you let me help you out? Anyone could see you got troubles, and... well... anyone with eyes could see I'd do anything for you."

She turned pink at that but made as if to close the door. "It's nothing, Mr. Malhaven. Don't worry about me. I've learned to take care of myself. I have to go. Really," she added, seeing I was ready to argue until I was blue in the face. "Trust me. I'll be fine."

She did shut the door on me then. I spread one meaty paw and leant my weight against the wood, concentrating as though I could will her to change her mind and let me in, like some kind of magic spell or something, but it didn't work. Short of busting in and giving her a good shaking until she told me what was going on, which is no way to treat any kind of a dame, there didn't seem to be much I could do.

It made me feel lower than the dirt beneath my feet to know she didn't believe in me enough to let me help her, but it's not like she knew me so well. And she knew my job was all about spilling secrets, not keeping them. She'd confided a few she knew weren't newsworthy, small things about her daughter and her husband, but she couldn't trust me with something big. Something that might tempt me to call up Morty and tell him to hold the presses.

I shuffled off home, more determined than ever to come back that night to explore Wynter's crypt and see if I couldn't get to the bottom of it, with or without her help. Maybe if it all came out, whatever it was, she'd let me throw her a lifeline then.

It had been a long twenty-four hours, so I spent the day grabbing some shuteye before setting out again late in the evening armed with a flashlight this time and a heavy lead sap. I'd had my fill of firearms during the war, but that didn't mean I was willing to walk into a dicey situation without some kind of assistance in my pocket. I had decided against dropping by the paper and checking in on Q's progress. I was afraid he would worm it out of me what I was up to, and I didn't want to drag him into any more danger, him being a young man with his whole future still in front of him.

The gates were closed tight, with no sign of fishy activity underway, so I clambered over them and hoofed it over to Wynter's tomb. There was a surprise waiting for me. The secret entrance was standing wide open. Was it a trap? I didn't care. I wanted to get this over with once and for all. I got that feeling I used to get before we rushed those beaches in the Pacific. Like it was time to do or die, and I didn't feel like dying.

Before I knew it, I was inside, shining my light around to get my bearings. There was a fancy stone coffin standing in the middle. Wynter, I guessed. Of more interest to me was an opening in the floor with steps leading down out of sight.

I barreled down them, readying myself for a fight of some kind, but all I found was another room about the size of the one above. This one was empty except for some trash on the ground here and there, but it had two doors in it—one open, one closed. Deciding that open was my best bet if I wanted to catch someone red-handed in the act, I went through the door on the left and started creeping along a hallway that I figured out was a tunnel carved from the earth.

It was damp and clammy, with water dripping from the roof, and places here and there where the walls or ceiling had given way some. Those piles of fallen earth on the ground didn't give me a good feeling, but there was something worse to come. Much worse.

The beam from the flashlight played over it first. From a distance, it looked like a bundle of clothes someone had left lying on the floor. Then I caught a glimpse of it in the light. That honey-blonde hair of a shade I'd have known anytime, anywhere. I don't remember walking up closer after that. All I remember was standing over her and staring down into those eyes, wide-open and slate blue like a stormy sea, staring right back at me.

Only the thing is, they didn't see me. They wouldn't be seeing anything ever again.

CHAPTER THIRTY-THREE

Staring at the neat hole right in the middle of that lovely white forehead and just visible below the funny little fringe of hair she wore, my vision faded to black, then to red. I heard people spout that saying, *my blood was boiling*, a million times, but I never understood it 'til that moment. It felt like every part of my body had been doused with gasoline and lit on fire, and I could've bust right out of my own skin if I only knew a way to do it.

I wanted to bellow like a bull, howl like a banshee, bawl like a baby, but some corner of my brain must have still been working 'cause I knew I had to keep it quiet, keep it together, if I wanted to catch the human cockroach who had done that to the woman I loved. Standing there, watching her so still and silent on the ground, I knew that I would never know another minute's rest until I found out who done this and why. And then I knew I'd never know another minute's rest even after that.

Sinking to my knees, I reached out to cradle her cheek in my palm. She was cold—she'd been there a while. Maybe even since not that long after the last time I spoke with her. What had she said to me? *Trust me. I'll be fine.*

"You lied to me, you lied to me," I whispered over and over, folding myself in two so I could put my lips down close to her ear.

I couldn't help myself. All I could think was that if I had bust into her house the way I wanted, if I had grabbed her and held her close and never let her go, she wouldn't have come to be lying here like this, deep in the earth, cold and alone. Shivering like a newborn and feeling about as weak, I lay myself down beside her there in the dirt. Lay on my back, not even touching her, just staring up at that ceiling like I wanted to know what the last thing she might have seen before the light faded was. Lock it away in my own memory.

Couldn't begin to tell you how long I stayed there beside her, eyeing the earth above us. You can't stop time, but sometimes it don't mean much. I do remember hearing a loud noise, harsh and ragged in the quiet, only to come to realize it was me, breathing as heavy as if I'd run a hundred miles. Nope, I can't give you an exact time—it could have been five minutes or a thousand years—I can only tell you I lay there long enough to where the roaring in my brain started to die down enough for me to think again.

I wanted so much to curl up in a ball right there beside her and never get up again, but a thought kept jiggling around in my brain, annoying me. The thought was, what kind of a monster could look into those lovely eyes and pull a trigger, knowing it would put an end to them forever? Whoever it was, I looked forward to meeting them so I could snap their head off at the neck with my own two hands.

I forced myself to cogitate. Did this calamity mean Livinia Wynter was now suspect number one? I realized I had no problem imagining her doing the deed. And if not her, one of her lackeys. Maybe Victoria had stumbled into something she shouldn't have, and so she had to go. Or—and I hated myself for even thinking it—was it some kind of falling out among thieves? Had Victoria been up to her neck in some kinda swindle, and one of her cronies had turned on her?

And then—worst thought of all—was it because of me? Had I stuck my nose in too far and made someone nervous? Had they seen me and Victoria together, gotten worried that we were getting too close, that she was gonna let me in on the secret? It took my breath away to imagine for even a minute that if it hadn't been for me, she might still be walking around. How's a guy supposed to live with a thought like that lodged in his brain?

I reached over to touch her cheek one last time. It was too late for me to help her now. The only thing I could do for her was to track down her killer and put an end to him. Or her. I didn't care too much what happened to me after that, but I knew I had to at least do that much before they buried me in a cold, dark room of my own.

Heaving myself to my feet, I was still so shook up, I had to reach out a hand to steady myself against the wall. Some of the dirt gave way when I touched it. I swung my flashlight to and fro, noticing more than one weak spot. If these tunnels had been dug around the time the tomb was built, they were nearly thirty years old. That seemed like a long time. Made me wonder if they had an expiration date.

It was a wrench to walk away from her. Made me understand what she'd said about not wanting to leave her daughter's grave. Even though I knew Victoria was gone, that there was just an empty shell left lying on the floor, it still felt disloyal to abandon her. Advising myself to pull it together, I explored farther down the tunnel. Didn't get far before I ran into a steel door with a padlock as big as my hand. I'd need something like a crowbar, or maybe a stick of dynamite, to break open a lock like that.

I felt so downhearted and tired, it was hard to think, but it finally dawned on me that there had been another door back at the start of the tunnel. The smart thing would probably be to go check it out. Of course, that meant walking past her again. I forced myself to keep my eyes up, aware enough of her to skirt around her, but not looking down. I was afraid if I saw her face again, I'd lose my resolve to keep going, and I had to keep going for her sake. It's one of the hardest things I ever done, leaving her like that, but I promised her I'd be back, and soon.

I returned to the room beneath the tomb and tried the closed door on the right. It swung open to reveal another tunnel looking just like the first but leading off in a different direction. Praying it would lead me direct to the killer, so I could put them out of their misery, and maybe me out of mine, I walked along, bouncing the light here and there. This tunnel didn't look in no better shape than the first. It crossed my mind it wouldn't take much to bring it down. Maybe that would be the smart move if I found the hound who'd done for Victoria —collapse the tunnel on us both. I sure didn't have much to live for.

I kept going, wondering if I was just gonna run into another dead-end of a locked door. Sure enough, there was a steel door just like in the first tunnel, but this one was standing open. I walked in prepared to put up a fight, but all I seen was boxes stacked high to the ceiling. I pulled one off a pile and opened it up. Lots of little wax paper packets. I didn't need more than one guess to know what they contained before I even opened one. White powder.

I was no expert, but I figured I'd stumbled on the source of all that smack Flanagan and company were so eager to track down. It also didn't take a genius to know those boxes represented a heck of a lot of moolah. Someone had decided to go all in, but I had to side with Flanagan's point of view. It's just bad business to flood the market. Made me wonder just what kind of an amateur operation we were dealing with.

Seeing the tunnel continued on past the stockroom, I decided to keep exploring. It was chancy going. Someone had made an effort to prop up the walls and the ceiling here and there, rough braces made of two-by-fours and ten-penny nails, but the whole setup made me uneasy. Reminded me of some caves I'd been trapped in once on an island, surrounded by the enemy and no way out. That had been an unpleasant feeling, to say the least, and it was one that came back at me now like a rocket.

My nerves started to kick in, so I don't guess you'll blame me none when I report I jumped about three feet in the air when I heard a moaning noise just up ahead. For some reason, Wally popped into my head. I didn't think I believed in ghosts, but that was the most eerie sound I ever heard in my life. It was all getting to me. Finding Victoria like that. Feeling trapped deep below the surface. And now this weird sound.

Not ashamed to admit I thought seriously about turning tail and abandoning the whole idea. I'd found the drugs. The girl I cared about was gone beyond any earthly punishment even if she was involved. What was to prevent me getting out and calling for Flanagan and his boys to take over? This was their line more than mine. The only thing that stopped me was the idea I might get robbed of the chance of coming face to face with whoever had ripped my heart out of my chest and stomped on it. I wanted someone to pay for what I'd found in the other tunnel, and I wanted it to be personal.

I stiffened my spine up and walked on. Shone my light ahead as the wailing got louder and louder. Came around a corner and found out what was making all that racket.

Definitely not a ghost.

CHAPTER THIRTY-FOUR

First thing I noticed was Cressley squinting into the light I was shining. It was him making that crazy din, but he shut up when I lowered the flashlight enough so he could see it was me. He was kneeling on the ground clutching something to his chest. I came nearer warily, and he showed me what it was—Livinia Wynter, and she didn't look so good. My fury rose at the sight of the pair of them. For all I knew, Victoria's killer was in my sights right then. But there was something about Cressley's face that made me stop and think. His looked the way I felt. Like his heart had been wrenched out and stomped on, too.

"What's the story?" I said.

He made that weird moaning again, like he was trying to talk, and showed me one of his hands. It was covered with blood. Then he pointed to Liv. She was dressed all in black, but I could still make out that her dress was wet all across one shoulder and down onto her chest. I eased over cautiously, keeping an eye on them both. If this was a trap, it was a pretty neat one. Neither one of them looked like they cared one bit whether I lived or died, like they had a lot more important things to occupy their minds.

I reached out and pulled back Liv's dress a bit to get a look. She'd been shot. Looked like Cressley had torn up some of her petticoats and was trying to use them to slow down the bleeding, but she looked about as pale as you could be and still have an address in the land of the living. She opened her eyes a bit when I touched her but didn't seem to know me. She looked over to Cressley, however, and lifted one limp hand to caress his face while breathing out a softly sighing, "Cornelius, my love."

He grabbed her hand and gave it about as passionate a kiss as I ever witnessed. It would have made me blush if I wasn't so busy rearranging my ideas. If I ever seen a pair of sweethearts, that was it. It went a long way toward explaining Cressley's loyalty, but it upended a lot of my notions.

I wondered if Victoria had found out about it along the way. I remembered how cagey she'd been when I'd commented on how bad Cressley had it working for Liv. And, having a suspicious nature, I wondered if Liv's monthly visits to spend the night with an old school chum which happened to coincide with Cressley's monthly night off were just a cover for an old-fashioned lovers' meet-up.

Forcing myself to set aside the riddle of the butler and his lady, I thought "Who dunnit?" was the next most logical question, so I asked it.

Cressley went into a weird pantomime. He kept pointing at Liv then holding up two fingers to me.

"There was two of them?" I asked.

He nodded, looking frustrated, then pointed at Liv, who'd drifted away from us again.

"Did you know them? Can you write it down for me?"

He shook his head, reaching into his pockets and pulling out the linings to show me he didn't have nothing to write on or with, and neither did I for a change. He started the pantomime again, two fingers, then the point at Liv, before getting a frantic look in his eye and making as if he was gonna try and lift up Liv and carry her away in his own skinny arms. Given that the top of his head barely reached her shoulder, that didn't seem like a legitimate scheme to me.

I reached out and grabbed his quivering chin, turning his head to face me so he had to look me in the eye. "This is the most important question you ever been asked. Did either one of you hurt Victoria Jankowski?" I growled at him, making a face that I hoped would scare the truth out of him. He did such a good job of looking thoroughly confused by the question as he shook his head back and forth like a madman that I decided to believe him.

"Okay. Give way," I said. Pushing him to the side, I hefted old Liv over my shoulder. It's not the most dignified position for a lady, but I figured since she was out for the count, what she didn't know wouldn't hurt her, and she might be running out of time.

"You take the light and lead on," I ordered Cressley, handing over the flashlight to him. He was looking at me with such a pathetic look of gratitude it made me want to kick him in the seat of the pants for some reason, but I restrained the impulse and trotted along after him as best I could.

It was tricky going back through the tunnel. The ceiling wasn't so high, and I had to lean over in an awkward, crouching run that soon had my bad leg feeling like someone was attacking it with a chainsaw. Lucky for me, it wasn't too great a distance back to the room below the crypt, but then there was a struggle to get her up the narrow steps. We ended up with Cressley at the top, pulling his hardest, while I gave her a hefty push on her bottom, thinking all the time how much she'd hate that if she knew anything about it.

When we got her up, I asked Cressley another question. "The bad guys—up or down?"

He pointed back down the stairs which I took to mean I'd have to retreat underground again to catch up with the criminal element I was so desperately eager to meet.

"Okay," I told him, "You sprint for that Caddy fast as you can and we'll load up Liv here. Then you drive like a bat escaping from hell for town. Get her to the hospital, then if you have a spare moment, see if you can rally some troops for me. Ambulance, fire, police, dog catchers. You name it. Anything and anybody you can get here to help. I don't think she's got too long, so leg it," I added, giving him a push when he seemed reluctant to get going.

He got a martial look in his eye, like, *anything for my Liv*, and exited stage left at a run. I stripped off my trench coat and lay it over Livinia to try and keep the cold off her. I wasn't exactly feeling all warm and loving toward her all of a sudden but finding out about the secret romance between the butler and the lady of the house softened my heart a little. I imagined her pride had kept them from carrying on openly, even tying the knot, but that just made it more pitiful somehow.

Maybe it's because I was aching all over from my own personal nightmare, but I found myself hoping she'd pull through, so they could still have a chance to make a go of it. I didn't want to be around to see the look on that poor man's face if he had to see her all cold and stiff the way I'd found Victoria.

I was impatient to carry on with my search, but I made myself cool my heels the few minutes it took for Cressley to get back with the car so I could load Liv in. He screeched away with a squeal of tires. I headed back inside the crypt, grabbing my flashlight and plunging down the stairs again. I knew there was a locked steel door down the one corridor, so it only made sense to go back down the one we'd just come up. See if there was anything beyond where I'd come across those two lovebirds. I proceeded more cautiously once I got past the point where I'd found them.

A little ways ahead, I reached a dilemma—the tunnel split off in two. I have a rule to always take the right hand whenever there's a choice. It's not a very good rule, but I stuck with it just the same. This time it didn't work out. I hadn't gone more than a few hundred yards when I hit a cave-in that blocked the way ahead. I shone my flashlight over it just for kicks, figuring I'd need to turn around and try the other way, when I caught the glint of something. It was a shiny, black shoe that looked like it had spent some time at the shoeshine stand recently. Then I noticed it wasn't just a shoe. There was a foot in it. That seemed worth investigating.

I couldn't find anything so convenient as a shovel to dig with, so I knelt down and started using my mitts to push the dirt aside. It was soft and loose. Made me think the slide had happened not so long ago. The earth hadn't had a chance to settle and pack down. It made the work easier anyways, and before long there was a couple of legs exposed to reward me for the effort. There was an uncomfortable moment when a bunch more earth rained down from the ceiling onto my head, but my fedora deflected most of it. I keep telling you there's nothing so practical as a good hat.

I found some discarded two-by-fours and did an impromptu reinforcement job that looked like it might hold it up for all of another five minutes and kept digging. Got as far this time as a hand. A hand clutching a pistol. Now this was getting really interesting. The gun looked just the small caliber to have made those neat little holes in Victoria and in Liv. It made me furious thinking I'd missed the chance to wreak my own kind of vengeance, and in frustration, I stood up and gave the body a swift kick. Big mistake. That started off a rumbling that I knew was no good.

A light bulb went off in my head. I patted down the guy's pants quick, fishing a wallet out of a back pocket just as the earth started giving way. Threw myself back and scrambled away like a crab as the whole thing crashed, undoing all my hard work, but at least I hadn't found myself buried beside the stiff.

Time to find out who he was. I retrieved my flashlight and flipped open the wallet, looking for some kind of identification. And there it was. The name of the monster was… Harold Monroe, Esquire, Attorney-at-Law.

CHAPTER THIRTY-FIVE

*J*should've been celebrating at that point. Here was the name of the no-good animal who took from me the only thing I ever cared about, and he'd already got his just reward. But two things stopped me from throwing a party on the spot.

The first was thinking back to my meeting with Monroe at Morty's office. I was having a hard time believing that fussy man was an efficient and cold-blooded killer. Call it instinct or just hard-won experience, but I was pretty sure this wasn't the answer I'd been seeking all wrapped up in a neat little package for me when it came to who was to blame for Victoria's death. The second thing was remembering Cressley had indicated there was two guys involved. Two of them. Cressley had been emphatic about that. If this was one, where was the other? Buried deeper in that pile of rubble? Or still on the loose? I wasn't gonna rest until I found out.

If Monroe was one of them, who did that leave as likely candidate for Villain Number Two? Tom Hooper sprang into my brain. He'd worked right alongside old man Wynter, raking in money by the barrelful during Prohibition days. I wondered how he'd fared since his good friend Billy's death. Was Livinia as generous to him as her father had been? Or had the well dried up since Wynter's passing? That could be reason enough to tempt Hooper into starting up a new racket. He'd know all about the tunnels. I had a pretty good notion at this point that they might run all the way into the city somewhere. What better way to shift that kind of merchandise than underground? It took a lot of the risk of being caught in the act of moving it right out of the equation.

Hooper seemed like a wily old bird. Sly and secret, he'd made it clear he wasn't interested in helping me out with my investigation. Made sense he'd try to avoid the company of a top-notch reporter like myself if he had something big to hide. And let's not forget that nice shiny new truck he was tooling around in. I didn't think many farmers could afford that kind of transportation. It would also explain why he'd kept on at the cemetery all these years. Had to stick close to his center of operations.

The more I thought it over, the more likely it seemed, and the more motivated I became to track down Mr. Thomas Hooper if he was still hanging around. Things was all done in the tunnel I was in unless I could round up some heavy earthmoving equipment or fifty guys with shovels and pickaxes, so I thought I might as well backtrack and see where that left-hand tunnel got to.

This one was more promising. Fewer cave-ins for one thing, as in none that I could see, and the tunnel was all lit up with a string of bare bulbs. Made me think someone had been that way if they'd left the lights burning.

I set off confident, not too worried about who or what I was gonna run into. I didn't have a whole lot left to lose. It seemed like I walked a long way but that could just be 'cause my leg was giving me hell and every step I took felt like I'd taken twenty, but I didn't even think about giving up now. No doubt the boys in blue would be on their way as soon as Cressley got a chance to drum up some help, and I still had an idea I might get my own personal revenge in on somebody before they caught up with us.

I was limping along, feeling grimmer by the minute, when I heard it. Sounded like a gunshot, and I'd heard a few thousand of those in my life, though this didn't sound as loud as a rifle or a machine gun, and it didn't sound that far away. I lumbered into the best imitation of a trot I could manage. It wasn't long before I came upon quite a sight. It was the other two Wynter sisters, Bernie and Ernie, bending over something that bore a close resemblance to a corpse.

Bernie said something I couldn't hear, but I heard her sister's query clear as day. "Is he dead?"

"That's just what I was wondering," I said.

My sudden appearance on the scene seemed to give them an unpleasant start. The neat one, Bernie, shone me a gimlet eye that reminded me for a second of her younger sister, Liv, but she caught up fast with my unexpected arrival on the scene.

"If it isn't Mr. Malhaven! How fortuitous! We have just been through the most appalling ordeal."

"Is that right?" I said, trying to figure out who the galoot stretched out in front of them might be.

"Why, yes. This man kidnapped us and attempted to force us down this awful tunnel to who knows where or for what evil purpose," she added, pulling the collar of her coat together with one hand modestly like she'd been on the verge of the worst shame a maiden lady could conjure up in her imagination.

Keeping one eye on them two, I prodded the stiff on the ground with one of my hoofs and rolled him over so I could get a better look. It was old Tom Hooper, looking more serene than he had in life except for that neat hole, right in the middle of his forehead.

It felt for a minute like my brain run amuck. That wasn't the first hole like that I'd seen that day. I'd had time to start to get used to the idea that Victoria was gone, but it all came flooding back at me now a thousand times as bad as before. Her sweet face, so pale and beautiful and still. That dark well of grief and rage that I knew would never leave me. Every nerve in my body stood to attention as I lifted my eyes to those two.

Those two. It came back to me now, that gesture Cressley kept making, holding up two fingers and pointing at Livinia, over and over again. Liv's two sisters. That's what he was trying to tell me. I knew it deep down in my bones, but gazing at those two old dears, both watching me wide-eyed and innocent, like butter wouldn't melt on their tongues, I found it hard to take in. I tried to gather my thoughts and calm the river of wrath that was surging through my veins.

"Looks like our Mr. Hooper has met with an unfortunate accident," I commented through gritted teeth. "What gives?"

It was Bernie doing all the talking now, her sister cowering behind her the same way she used to do with Liv.

"Isn't it dreadful? He had a pistol, you know, and was threatening us with it, but I managed to wrest it away from him," Bernie said, showing me that very thing in her hand which was still wrapped casually around the grip with her finger on the trigger, I couldn't help but notice. "But I know so little about such things. I'm afraid it went off accidentally, and just look at what has happened. I was so horribly afraid that I simply couldn't help it. Do you think I'll be in terrible trouble with the police, Mr. Malhaven?"

"You know," I said, trying hard to keep my cool, "I shouldn't be a bit surprised."

Ernie jumped in at that, all twittery like a hungry sparrow. "Oh, how can you say that? My sister was only defending our honor and our lives. Who knows what he might have done? And the gun just went off —anyone would call that an accident, wouldn't they?"

"I suppose you could argue it that way, though that's quite a shot for someone who don't know what they're doing. Square between the eyes. Don't know if I could do it myself. Not that neatly. Guess you got lucky. Beginner's luck, don't they say," I suggested, trying for the light touch. I didn't like the look on Bernie's face, or the fact that she still had that gun in her hand, and I didn't want to end up like old Tom, not until I'd made them pay.

"Why, Mr. Malhaven," Bernie said, sweet as my ma's banana cream pie, "if I didn't know better, I might almost think you didn't believe us."

I hastened to smooth down their ruffled feathers, anxious to buy time while I thought over what to do. "Now why would you say that?

We always get along, don't we? Ain't I been Johnny-on-the-spot with this whole Wally yarn? Talking it up, helping you make a name for yourselves and your boneyard here? And what about that séance? That was a good time, wasn't it? At least until that bullet took a tour through my topper. I'm sure you ladies will be glad to see it's all better," I said, pulling it down off my skull to show them. "Mrs. Jankowski did me quite a favor there, getting it all fixed up good as new. She's thoughtful that way, ain't she?"

I watched them close when I brought up Victoria. I guess I expected to see one of them flinch, but they held their ground. I was starting to have a whole new respect for those birds. Goes to show I was just as guilty as anybody of dismissing them as a couple of old maids with more hair than smarts.

"Oh, yes, and we're so glad you weren't hurt," Ernie piped up, looking like she'd had a brainstorm. "Wasn't that a terrible thing, someone shooting at you like that? You know, now I'm wondering if it might not have been Mr. Hooper since we know he owns a weapon?"

"Could be, I suppose," I said, setting the fedora back on my cranium and fingering my chin like I was considering the whole mystery deeply. "Or it could have been that lawyer, Monroe, I suppose. Maybe they was working some kind of scam together. I say that because I'm sorry to have to inform you, knowing how he was an old friend of the family and all, but I believe the honorable Mr. Monroe may be lying dead in one of these other tunnels. I didn't see enough of him to notice if he also has a hole in the head, but as he's buried under a couple of tons of dirt, it don't seem too important."

"Mr. Monroe!" cried our lady Bernadette. "I can't believe it! And to think, he and Mr. Hooper, men my father knew and trusted, should have been up to such devilry. It almost makes you lose faith in the human race, doesn't it, Mr. Malhaven?"

"Lose faith in the human race? Yeah, you might say that. You might say that. Absolutely," I agreed with my whole heart. I was approving so keenly of her sentiment 'cause I had just that moment noticed something tied around Ernie's neck. It was bright and colorful and covered all over with birds, one of every kind, and I remembered exactly where I'd last seen it. I knew I shouldn't tip my hand to them, but a kind of madness came over me at the sight of it, worn so casually like that.

"That's a nice-looking scarf you got there, Miss Ernie. May I inquire exactly where you picked that up?"

CHAPTER THIRTY-SIX

"This old thing? Why, I've had it for so long, I can't even begin to remember," Ernie said right back at me, lying straight to my face as one bony hand played with the filmy material I'd last seen embracing the honey-blonde hair of my one and only love. I thought I might have to step up and slap her across the mouth just then, but her sister marched in before I could do such an ungentlemanly thing.

"Give it a rest, Ernie. I do believe Mr. Malhaven is on to us, isn't that right?" Bernie asked me with a grin so wicked that it shut down any last grain of doubt I might have been entertaining that those two charming ladies could possibly be behind such evil doings. "I told you to leave that scarf alone, but you would take it."

"But Bernie, it's genuine Hermès! A work of art. It would have been a crime to leave it down here to rot!"

"Which one of you shot her?" I interrupted their tiff, trying hard to control the quaking that threatened to take over every part of my body. "Which one of you did that thing?"

Bernie gave me a look I would have described as sympathetic if it'd been anyone human shooting it in my direction. "I believe you were quite taken with her, weren't you? She was very lovely. It was regrettable we had to do that, but it was really her own fault, you know."

"How's that?" I muttered, I think, since I hardly knew what I was saying as I stared into that unrepentant mug with more hatred than I ever knew it was possible for one man to feel.

"She tried to blackmail us, I'm afraid. You look surprised, Mr. Malhaven. It was quite a surprise to us as well. We've known Mrs. Jankowski such a long time. I would never have thought it of her, but then, how well do any of us really know one another, wouldn't you agree?" she said archly.

"You got that about right. What did she have on you?"

"I suppose there's no harm telling you now since you won't be walking out of here, no more than Hooper, Monroe, or Victoria will. She somehow discovered the tunnels and our operation and followed us down here and started making such wild demands. It was really very foolish of her, but then I suppose she underestimated us. We find that people do, but it quite works to our advantage, so we don't mind, do we, Ernie?"

"Not at all," her sister chimed in with a girlish titter that raised the hair on the back of my neck. "You'd be surprised what you can get away with, Mr. Malhaven, when you're just a pair of spinsters."

My mind rebelled at the idea of Victoria involved in a blackmail plot, but what did it matter anymore? Whatever she'd done, whatever she'd been, she was beyond the reach of all of us now. The only thing that seemed to matter was wiping that expression of smug self-satisfaction from those two faces in front of me.

"I guess that's right," I said, catching sight of some more two-by-fours on the floor near my feet. I got a kind of an idea but wanted to keep them talking while I turned it over in my brain. Figured the more they bragged, the more relaxed and in charge they'd feel, and the more likely I'd be able to get the drop on them. "Was that the deal with Hooper and Monroe, too? Were they putting the screws on you?"

"Oh, no. They were part of our operations. They'd helped Father run his empire, so they knew exactly how to set up the distribution system again when we decided to go into business," Bernie said.

"And why was that?" I asked. "I got the idea your pop left you girls pretty well off. What made you think of taking up a fiddle like this?"

"There's plenty of money in the estate, of course, but it's Livinia who holds the purse strings. We could never spend a penny without going hat in hand to her like we were beggars instead of her sisters," Bernie explained with a bitterness that stuck out a mile.

"It's so unfair!" Ernie cried. "I don't know what Father could have been thinking, except he made no secret of the fact that the baby of the family was always his favorite. Bernie's the eldest. She should have been left in charge by rights. She's so much cleverer than Livinia. And bolder, too. Livinia would never have had the nerve to do the things you've done, would she, Bernie?"

"No, Livinia lacks for imagination, that can't be denied. But she is our sister, so we must forgive her for her trespasses against us."

"Trespasses against you? What about what you done? I'd have said putting a bullet through her shoulder ain't the friendliest thing to do," I objected.

"Why, Mr. Malhaven, what you must think of us! We'd never harm our own sister," Bernie protested. "I'm afraid that was Mr. Monroe. Livinia had gotten suspicious, partly due to your impertinent investigations," she said, giving me the eye like wasn't I quite the roguish so-and-so before continuing.

"She and Cressley followed us down here. We've been wrapping up our business dealings lately anyway since we knew the heat was on, as I believe you'd say. Dumping our inventory and cashing out as much as we could. We have plenty of funds put away to live comfortably far from this dreadful place. The only thing we asked Monroe to do was keep Livinia and Cressley covered while we packed up the rest of the money and what does the fool do but shoot her. To be fair, he was shaking so hard, I believe the gun went off by accident, just as it did during the séance, but still, I can't abide that kind of incompetence, so he had to be punished."

"I see. Like Mr. Hooper here had to be punished?"

"No, that was just tidying up loose ends. The worst mistake one can make is not eliminating all witnesses, you know," she said, giving me the eye in a way that was bound to make me feel uncomfortable.

"I'm surprised you'd leave Cressley and Liv alive then, sister or no sister," I said, genuinely curious.

It was Ernie who rushed in to give me the scoop on that one.

"We honestly do hope Liv will be all right. We know she'd never turn us in. She's far too proud to let the world know that her sisters are criminals *and* that we did it all right under her very nose. And Cressley is too loyal to the family to utter a single word." Ernie tittered at her joke at the poor guy's expense. "Father saved his life, you know. He was suspected as an informer by a rival rumrunner. They were cutting out his tongue when Father and his men happened upon the scene. I believe there was quite a set-to, but Father's men came out victorious. He felt rather sorry for Mr. Cressley for suffering such a terrible injury and gave him a job, and he never regretted it. You'll not meet a more faithful retainer than he, and he knows how to hold his tongue as well." She giggled again.

Her rotten sense of humor was getting on my nerves, but I tried to keep it together. I decided to lay it on thick. Nothing sets people more at their ease than a touch of the old soft soap.

"You two are something, ain't you!" I said admiringly, with as straight a face as I ever had in my life. "I always had a feeling there was more to you than meets the eye. I bet it was you that set up that whole Wally gag to begin with, wasn't it?" I hit a sour note there, 'cause Ernie looked daggers at me.

Bernie explained my mistake. "That was Father's idea to begin with. He thought it might help provide cover for his activities. I'm afraid Ernie fell for the ruse, at least at first."

"You don't have to rub it in, Bernie. I *was* rather vexed at Father when I found out it was all a hoax. But it's served us as well as it did him back in the day. At least it did until you became too nosy about it," Ernie amended, looking more than a little vexed with me.

"I thought that's what you wanted?" I defended myself. "Publicity to scare off the riffraff. Didn't I fall in with your plans?"

"Some publicity is a good thing," Bernie agreed. "But then we couldn't get rid of you. We had one of our delivery drivers give you a tap on the head as discouragement, and Ernie went to quite a lot of trouble to cut up your hat. I would have thought either of those was quite sufficient a hint for you to drop the whole matter."

"Some people got hard heads," I observed sourly. "But then what was the big idea of inviting me to the séance? Didn't you think that would just add fuel to the fire?"

"We'd arranged for some more surprises to frighten you, concluding with Monroe shooting into the room above everybody's head, although as it turns out he couldn't even manage that correctly. However, things did not all go according to our plan," she said, looking uncertain for the first time. "First, someone got up to some funny business with the planchette, and then that terrible child interfering with Mr. Monroe. It was absolutely infuriating. You'll never know how maddening it felt to have to act like doting old aunts when we could have gladly pinched the heads off that silly fainting girl and that horrid little boy."

"Oh, I think I can imagine how you felt."

"At any rate," she continued, ignoring my witticism, "it became obvious to us that you were one of those *dogged* types, you know. That we could not depend on you to become discouraged from delving deeper into the past, especially when it was clear that you had developed an ulterior motive."

"Oh, I had, had I?"

"Yes, of course. Those puppy dog looks of adoration you were sending to Mrs. Jankowski were impossible to miss."

I don't think the look on my face just then could be described as puppy dog or adoring, more like a Doberman slobbering against its leash. I'd had about enough of hearing them bandy about Victoria's name and my sentiments for her like they were nothing but a joke. I decided then to go for a dodge that would never have worked on a real crook, but for all their tough talk, those ladies weren't the hardened wise guys they liked to think they were. I thought it just might work if I could sell it hard enough.

"You know, I'm not so sure I don't believe in ghosts after all. Did you hear all that weird wailing earlier?" Rolling my eyes in fright, I whispered hoarsely, *"I think there's something down here with us."*

The ladies giggled nervously at that, but the uneasy look they exchanged told me all I needed to know. It might run counter to their cool pose and even their common sense, but it's not possible to remain for long in a narrow, damp corridor deep under the ground, knowing there's a sea of coffins floating over your head, without feeling at least a touch superstitious.

"Oh, geez!" I suddenly screamed, bugging out my eyes and pointing behind them. "What the hell is THAT?"

CHAPTER THIRTY-SEVEN

I could hardly believe my luck, but it got 'em. Both gray heads swiveled around to look where I was pointing just long enough for me to grab a two-by-four from at my feet and smash it into the ceiling raking through the dirt with all the pent-up frustration, hurt, and anger I had in me, and that was quite a lot. The loose soil started to rain down with all the noise and fury of a thunderstorm as I backed away, but it wasn't coming down quite fast enough.

Bernie got the picture first and turned back to face me, swinging her hand up as she came. I heard the shot almost the same time I felt it. A tearing pain through my good leg. Letting out a few choice words I won't repeat here, I fell back as she readjusted her aim to squeeze off another round. Lucky for me that extra time was enough. The avalanche of earth cut them off, but not before I seen their beady eyes staring at me with pure loathing.

I seem to have started something bigger than I intended 'cause a loud rumbling started up as the ceiling above me shimmied like the underbelly of a snake. I considered just lying there and letting it eat me up, but it's funny how your body takes over in those situations and knocks you into another gear. Survival mode, I think they call it, whether you got anything you want to survive for or not. Before I knew I'd made any such decision, I was up and running, if you care to dignify it with that name.

If you never seen a man with two gimpy legs try to sprint, I'm here to tell you it ain't a pretty sight. I felt like I had two little imps, one hanging onto each leg and stabbing me with a shard of glass every step I tried to take. It took everything I had to make it back out to the steps, but I was too slow. The ceiling there was coming down, too, blocking the way out. There didn't seem no choice but to head back down the tunnel where I'd found Victoria. I knew there was nothing but a locked door and the woman I loved lying dead at the end of it, but that seemed as good a place as any to wait out whatever was left of my time on the planet.

At least the roof here was holding up better. I had a chance to slow down and try and catch my breath. I almost sat down and gave up then I was in so much pain, but I wanted to keep my promise to Victoria. I told her I'd be back, that I wouldn't leave her alone there in the dark for too long. That was the only thought I had as I limped down that corridor. The next thing after that, every thought I ever had in my life left my head completely. I just couldn't take in what I was seeing. I stared and stared for what seemed the longest time, and then everything faded to black.

"Mr. Malhaven? Jim? Jim, are you okay?"

I heard it, but I didn't want to open my eyes. What if what I thought might be there wasn't? I knew I wouldn't be able to take it if I was wrong.

There was a small sobbing sigh close by me. "At least your hat looks okay."

That did it. I had to open my eyes then. Open them to stare up into a pair of stormy eyes filled with tears and looking at me with a lot of worry and a hint of some other emotion that would have stopped my breath if it hadn't already been kicked out of me by the sight that had greeted me down that hallway: Victoria, kneeling beside her own dead body.

"Urgha," I finally ventured, when I got some air into my lungs again.

"Jim? Are you trying to say something?" she said, bending close and laying a hand on my chest.

"Are you a ghost?" was all I could think to ask.

"No, I'm real."

I reached out a hand to touch her cheek. It was smooth and warm, gloriously warm, like the sunlight striking your face on a cold winter day. She caught my hand in her own and held it close. We can pause here for an interlude, and you can skip ahead if you like. I wouldn't wanna burden you with the image of a big lummox like me, ugly scar and all, blubbering uncontrollably like an infant. We'll just take that as read.

I tried to pull myself together for her sake, but the best I could come out with was the less than astute observation, "But you're dead."

"No, I'm not," she assured me. "But… oh, Jim… I'm afraid poor Janice is."

"Janice?"

"My sister."

It hit me like a truckload of cement then. I felt like the dumbest mug that had ever been born. "There's two of you, ain't there?"

"Yes," she agreed. "We are… that is," she corrected herself, looking torn up, "we *were* twins."

The second she said it, everything fell into place. Victoria of the day and Victoria of the night had been two different women all along. How could I have been such a fool? It's funny how the mind plays tricks on you, makes you believe what you been told, even when the evidence starts stacking up trying to tell you something different. They'd passed themselves off as the same person, and I'd gone along with it, even scratching my head to come up with any reason I could think of to explain the two different characters I'd seen with my own eyes. Any reason except the right one.

"Twins. That explains it," I muttered, feeling dim-witted from the shock and, in my defense, a certain amount of blood loss as well. "Victoria of the sunlight and Victoria of the moonlight. I couldn't understand how the woman I loved could be both them things."

She looked troubled at that. "How can you say whether you were drawn to me or to her? You never knew who you were talking to all that time."

"Oh, I can tell you exactly who I was talking to each and every time now that I know the truth."

I brought her hand up to my lips, and the look in her eyes told me there was a chance that the dream I had once thought was hopeless might work out for me after all if I didn't try to rush things. That was more than good enough for me. Best news I ever had in my life.

"I don't mean to insult your sister," I said. "But you don't seem anything alike aside from your looks. Were you close?"

"No, not at all," Victoria said. "In fact, I'd never met her in my life until a few weeks ago. Didn't even know she existed."

"How's that?"

"We don't know anything other than that I was left at the orphanage in Carsworth City, and Janice was dropped off at the orphanage in Farrelburg. Just twenty or so miles from each other," she said sadly, "but there might as well have been an ocean between us."

"Split up, huh? I wonder why."

"I don't know. Maybe the woman… our mother… felt like it would be easier to trace her if it was known she'd given birth to twins. Anyway, Janice was luckier than me. She was adopted by a family from Chicago."

"So, what brought her here? If you didn't know about her, how'd she find out about you?"

"I'm afraid that may remain a mystery now. She refused to tell me. Just showed up on my doorstep one evening. You can imagine my shock. I was delighted at first, of course, to find out I not only had a sister but a twin at that, but…" she hesitated. "I guess you saw what she was like. It didn't take me long to find it out either. Janice told me she'd had a fight with her family and needed some time away, but she seemed to have some secret agenda that I couldn't figure out. Refused my offer of putting her up in town, insisted on staying with me even though the sisters strictly forbid me from having overnight visitors of any kind."

Victoria put one hand up to her forehead in a graceful gesture I enjoyed watching. That smooth brow furrowed, but as it wasn't spoiled by a bullet hole, I didn't mind.

She continued her tale. "That's when she came up with this scheme of hers. She'd stick close to the cottage during the day, and then we'd switch places at dusk. It seemed to me like I got the better end of the bargain, but I think she liked the nighttime best and was happy to sleep the day away. There didn't seem too much harm in it. The only people who see me regularly enough to know me well are the sisters and Tom, and none of them would be roaming around the cemetery at night. But then…"

"But then, a nosy reporter showed up and wouldn't leave the two of you alone," I finished up for her.

"That's right," she agreed, looking down at me with a lovely grin. "I tried to discourage him at first, but, well, he has one of those types of faces that you get kind of used to seeing around after a while."

After that, there's no telling how long we might have stayed on there, exchanging goofy looks, if I hadn't noticed something. A very distinctive smell. She must have noticed it, too, because we exchanged another kind of look altogether before both blurting out the same thought.

"Fire!"

CHAPTER THIRTY-EIGHT

I could imagine what might have happened. Some of those cave-ins had broken open a lightbulb or two and an incandescent spark had caught some of the ancient timber meant to hold it all up alight. Or maybe it'd been set on purpose. I didn't know if that wicked pair of sisters had survived having the better part of the tunnel raining down on their heads or not, but if they had, I wouldn't put it past them to set the whole thing ablaze to try and cover up any evidence of their dirty tricks.

Victoria and I had been jawing away like we had all the time in the world now that we'd found each other again, but that wasn't so. And the fire wasn't the only thing we had to contend with. I sat up and winced in pain as both my legs cramped up in agony.

"Jim! Your leg! I tried to bind it up as best I could, but I think it's still bleeding. We have to get you out of here."

I gazed on that beautiful face and couldn't find the nerve to tell her we were trapped. What with the cave-in back at the entrance and that door with the padlock in front of us, we were caught like rats scrambling around in the hold of a doomed ship while the waters rose. A half an hour earlier, I wouldn't have given a damn, but now I had everything to live for, not least of which was making sure Victoria made it out of there alive. I'd thought I lost her once already that day. There was no way while I still had one breath left in my body that I'd go through that torture again.

Glancing around, I was struck by the fact that the tunnel was all lit up with bulbs like the other one had been. I'd been so preoccupied since I'd arrived, I hadn't noticed it earlier.

"Hey," I asked her, "were the lights on when you got down here? And now that I'm starting to be able to think sensible again, what brought you down here in the first place?"

"I was worried about Janice. She never came home last night. She'd never done that before, and… well… this will sound rather strange."

"It can't be any stranger than anything else I seen and heard today. Lay it on me."

"This horrible sensation came over me early this morning. It woke me up, like a nightmare. I felt like I just knew… I just knew that something had happened to Janice. It was like a light had gone out in my mind. A light I didn't even know was there. That sounds crazy, I know."

"I dunno. I heard somewhere that twins have a special connection. Maybe you and Janice had one, only you never had cause to know about it before."

"Maybe so. That's why I'd been crying when you came to see me this morning. I was so sure something was terribly wrong, but I didn't know what she'd been up to or where to start looking for her. I regret now that I didn't tell you about her right then and ask for your help. I guess I felt like it wasn't my secret to tell."

I patted her hand a bit at that to buck her up, and she confessed the rest of the story. "I spent all day searching for her off and on, trying to look like I wasn't searching for someone who had no business being at the cemetery to begin with. I had no luck at all until I saw Tom sneaking into the back of Mr. Wynter's vault. I couldn't believe my eyes. All these years and I never knew any of this was here. I slipped down the steps and into this tunnel after him. He flipped a switch and turned on the lights, so I had to fall back so he wouldn't see me as I followed him. And then… then… I found her."

I had to wince in sympathy at the shock in her voice what with remembering that awful moment of stumbling across what I'd thought was Victoria. Even knowing that it hadn't been her after all, it still gave me a chill to think back to that black despair. Something else struck me, too.

"Where'd you find a place to hide in here when Tom came back by you so he wouldn't see you?"

Victoria looked at me, puzzled. "But he didn't. No one came by until you did."

"He didn't come back this way?" I said, feeling a bit of optimism for our future for the first time. "That means there's another way out of here."

"Well, of course, there is. There's an open door just down the way," she said, pointing off in the direction where I'd seen the door, only it had been locked up tight then. "I explored a bit after finding Janice, but I didn't like to leave her alone… like… like that, not for long."

"I know exactly what you mean," I said. "Well, that's a different bag of tricks. Let's see if we can get me upright. I don't like the smell of that smoke. I was gonna suggest we wait for the big dig out by some guys I hope are on the scene right about now, but we may not have time to linger around here for that."

It was a struggle getting me up off the floor. Like I'd discovered the time Victoria found me stretched out in the road, she had some muscle on her from all that gardening and such, but I was feeling weaker than I wanted to let on, and now I had not just one bum leg, but two. Once I was standing, my gams started protesting louder than ever before. The pain nearly took my breath away, but I was bound and determined not to let her down.

We staggered along the tunnel but couldn't help but pause when we reached Janice's body. It was one of the eeriest things I ever experienced, staring down at that familiar face again, but this time, knowing that it didn't spell the end of all things for me like I'd thought. Janice may not have been anything like her sister except in looks, but I still felt for her. No one deserved to end up that way.

Well, almost no one. There were a couple of other sisters I could think of that I wouldn't mind seeing in the same position, but I had something more important to accomplish just then, and that was making sure Victoria made it safe above ground. I knew she was upset about abandoning her twin. It seemed wrong somehow, leaving Janice staring up like that, vulnerable and alone.

On an impulse, I took off my hat and lay it gently over her face. I'm not the most sentimental guy, but it felt like leaving her a blessing, so she knew somebody cared. Victoria seemed to get what I meant anyway. She gave my arm a squeeze like she approved though she was too torn up to say so.

There being nothing else we could do for poor Janice, we soldiered on. Sure enough, the door was standing open this time. Relief don't begin to describe what I felt at the sight. If Tom had ended up dead at the Wynter sisters' feet in the other tunnel after Victoria had seen him come down here, then that meant there were connections somewhere, connections that might lead to a way out. We just had to find them.

I was praying there'd be a simple path out of there, but it seemed like nothing that day was gonna be easy. We found ourselves at a crossroad of sorts where the tunnel split off into three different directions. I felt all used up. It had been a hell of a day, and I was beat down in body and mind. The shock of finding Victoria alive and well after the gut-wrenching blow of thinking I'd lost her for good was playing tricks on me, too. I guess I must have started losing it about then because I started asking her stupid questions, like, "Are you sure you're alive?" and "Are you really here?" over and over like a dope.

She was patient with me in that sweet way she had, but I could tell I had her worried. I knew I wasn't making so much sense myself, but I couldn't seem to help it. And on top of it all, we now had to make a decision about which way to go. We could still smell the smoke, and we were farther than ever from the tomb, where I assumed some kind of rescue effort might be starting up. That meant it was up to us to save ourselves.

"Which way? Which way?" I heard her debating softly with herself.

"Always go to the right," I started mumbling in between checking in with Victoria that she was still among the living. And in this particular case, that didn't seem like such a bad idea. If one of the tunnels hooked up with the one where I'd seen the sisters, it made sense to me it would be the one to the right. Looking back, it should have occurred to me that the other tunnel had suffered a pretty good cave-in courtesy of yours truly, so maybe that wasn't the best destination to aim for, but it turned out it didn't matter anyway because Victoria suddenly shushed my ramblings by laying a firm finger over my lips.

"Hush. Listen," she whispered.

I was feeling more than foggy, but I got the idea she wanted me to shut it. We stopped short and kept our ears open. This next part you probably won't believe, and I don't blame you none. I don't really believe it either, although I was so out of it at that point, I might have seen or heard anything, but Victoria believes it, so I'll report it. That's what I do. Report things. I always leave it up to the reader to decide what to think about it.

There's no doubt at all there was some kind of weird noise going on down there. I could hear it just as well as she could. The difference was I thought it was a breeze, whistling through some opening somewhere that we couldn't see yet. Victoria had another idea. She says it was a person doing the whistling. And she swears she knows the song they was whistling.

"*Daisy, Daisy, give me your answer do,*" she sang softly, then started pulling me toward the center tunnel. I tried to resist, tell her to go to the right like I wanted, but a tiredness like I'd never known come over me just then. I decided whatever she wanted to do was all right by me so long as we stayed together.

The lights were out in this new tunnel, and we couldn't find a switch, but we kept hearing whatever that sound was just ahead, guiding us as we felt our way along. I should say, to be fair, Victoria felt her way—I just stumbled along behind her like a broken-down ox. It felt to me like I knew three things and three things only: the feel of my hand in hers, the piercing agony in both my legs, and how I was so tired, I would have given the world to lay down right where we were and sleep for a thousand years.

But Victoria was having none of that, tugging and coaxing me whenever she felt me lagging. It seemed like quite a march, but she tells me it was no time at all before we found ourselves standing at the bottom of a staircase leading up to an open door and a bright light that did us both good to see.

"Well, ain't that something?" I remarked, just before I hit the dirt with my face.

CHAPTER THIRTY-NINE

*N*ext thing I knew, my old buddy Joey Flanagan was observing me with a satirical look in his eye. "You never pay attention to sage advice from those that are prettier and wiser than you, do you, Jimmy? Didn't I warn you that I had not the slightest interest in an encore performance of scraping you up off the ground after you stuck your nose in where it did not belong? And here we are," he said, shaking his head to express his grave disappointment in me.

"Where is here?" I croaked out, staring up and seeing what looked like that same bright light that was the last thing I'd seen before I was seeing nothing at all.

"We're just below a kind of a storeroom, I guess we'll call it, at the back of that stately mansion the Wynter sisters refer to as home, sweet home. We set men to digging out the crypt looking for you on account of a rumor we heard of your being underground. Some of the rest of us decided to pass the time by coming on up here to see what we could see, and what do I find? My old friend Jimmy stretched out on the floor with a lovely lady crying her eyes out over his pathetic carcass. Something tells me it ain't been all bad luck with you since last we met," he said with a smirk that would have earned any other guy a swift sock on the jaw from me. If I'd had the strength to lift my arm just then, that is.

"Victoria?" I asked, looking around. "Is she okay? She is alive, ain't she?" I added, suddenly struck with the uncanny notion that the whole last part of my adventure underground had been nothing but a hallucination.

"Is she alive? I should say so and then some. Don't worry your silly little head so much. I asked her to clear out and give us some room, but she's waiting for you just above. The ambulance men are fetching a stretcher, and then we'll get you out of here. I don't know if you're aware of it, but you ain't in the best shape just at the moment. It's the hospital for you, old son, but you stay with me in the meantime, do you hear, Jimmy? Jimmy?"

That was the last thing I heard for quite a while.

The next time I come around, I swear the first thought that jumped into my brain was I'd have to give that Margo Cummings girl a break on her whole fainting routine. I'd thought it was an awfully weak gag until I started performing more dives myself than a prizefighter on the take. It was getting to be downright mortifying.

I quickly deduced I was in the hospital, but I was surprised to see I had a room all to myself. Chumps like me with no dough to spare usually got stashed in a bed in an open ward with at least a dozen other saps in a similar predicament. I was not surprised to see Flanagan standing guard over me like a watchdog over a junkyard. For all that he liked to get up my nose whenever he could, he was a loyal pal. The best a guy like me could hope for.

"Ah, you're awake finally, are you?" he said, leaning over from the chair he'd pulled up beside the bed. "That's an immense relief to me. It's not as entertaining as you might suppose spending hours on end watching an ugly kisser like yours for signs of life."

"Who asked you to?" I growled back. That's just the way it is with fellas like us. Always with the wisecracks, but we understood each other plain enough.

"If it comes to that," he shot back at me, "it was because of a promise I made to a certain young lady to keep an eye on you until you either quit the sleeping beauty act or she come in to visit with you again."

"Really?" I asked, in earnest this time.

"Really," he said, softening up his own hard guy patter.

The thought of seeing Victoria again was quite the distraction, but I tried to gather my thoughts and pump Flanagan for some info before he got away from me.

"Give me the scoop," I demanded. "What's been happening from your point of view?"

"Where do we start? I guess with that old guy Cressley. We were summoned to the hospital and found him nearly beside himself, and Livinia Wynter with her toes turned up to the ceiling."

I must have turned pale at that, 'cause he held up a hand to calm my nerves.

"Excuse the unfortunate choice of words. She's still in the world so far as I know, getting private, round-the-clock nursing back at the Wynter place. It was touch and go at first, but last I heard, she was picking up steam. Anyway, Cressley started scrawling lines on a pad with a pencil when we showed up. He was tearing off pages and flinging them at us so fast, we all took a turn reading a page until we got the idea that something big was doing out at the cemetery."

"And rushed to the rescue?" I guessed.

"And rushed to your rescue. *Again*," he agreed, with a resigned look like it was an everyday occurrence with me. "Miss Livinia Wynter and that butler fella seem to think an awful lot of you. They coughed up the spare change to get you into this swanky joint," he said, pointing a thumb at the private room. "You must have made quite an impression on them. It don't come cheap."

"That is something, ain't it?" I said, appreciating the generous spirit behind such a gesture. Maybe I'd finally won old Liv over with my rescue attempt. I already knew Cressley treasured it, recalling that look of slavish devotion on his face when I'd hefted Liv to safety. I had an idea I'd won a friend for life with that little effort. "What about the others? Those tunnels was rotten with suspects, alive and dead."

"You said it. It took a few days…"

"Days? How long I been out?"

"Like I said, days. You came within an angel's whisper of meeting up with your maker in the great city in the sky, you know. And now you got two bum legs to show for it." He couldn't help getting another dig in. "I did try to warn you, didn't I?"

"That's enough of that," I said. "What's done is done. Will I be able to get up and take a stroll?"

"You'll be able to limp around alright, but you probably won't be doing any jigs. You got lucky this time, though I was surprised myself at how long you been out. The doc says it takes people that way sometimes, especially if they've been under some kind of a mental stress. Did you have a shock or something? Other than being shot and nearly buried alive, that is."

"You could say so," I conceded, not ready to confide in him that I'd had the worst shock a man could have followed by the very best. "I guess I'm not as tough as I like to think."

"We're getting old, Jimmy," he said, shaking his head in commiseration. "Anyway, as I was about to tell you, the fire brigade was able to squash the fire quick enough, but it took a few days and a lot of men to dig out all that dirt. We had to go slow in case we started another collapse. Didn't want to lose one of our guys who's still alive and kicking just to extricate some stiffs that was only gonna get thrown back under the ground anyway."

You may have noticed Flanagan ain't always the most sensitive. Maybe it comes from being a cop for so many years. Makes a man kinda cynical seeing the worst of the worst day after day.

"Did you find them all? Monroe, Hooper…"

"…and that spitting image of your lady friend? Yeah, we got them all out, and one more besides. Miss Bernadette Wynter."

"Bernie, huh? Crushed by the tunnel?" I asked, not remorseful one bit if I'd been the cause of her departure from the scene.

"Partially, but that ain't what killed her. What killed her was a bullet through the head."

"Can you repeat that?" I said, not sure I heard him right.

"I said she had a bullet through her head. Right between the eyes, just like those others we found. You gotta give someone high scores for marksmanship."

"I don't get it. You said she was trapped in the rubble. Why would someone waste a bullet on her?"

"Well, I got two different theories on that. One theory is someone saw she was a goner anyway and didn't want her to suffer so they decided to put her out of her misery. The other theory is someone didn't want her to survive long enough to blab to us any interesting details of their wrongdoings."

"Someone?" I asked, with a sinking kind of feeling in the pit of my stomach.

"Someone such as her very own sister."

"Ernie? You think she'd do a thing like that? She's the most shy and retiring of the whole bunch. Always seemed to be under the spell of either Liv or Bernie, whichever she was in the room with."

"It's the quiet ones you gotta watch. Ain't you learned that yet?"

He had a point there.

"So, where's Ernie now?"

"Jimmy, my boy, you've hit upon the very question that's dancing upon everyone's lips. Just where is our Miss Ernestine Wynter, and what kind of shenanigans is she gonna get up to next?"

ow that I was awake and showing no signs of kicking off any time soon, Flanagan had to leg it back to the precinct to catch up on the search for the missing sister. He had men watching the cemetery and all the local bus stops, train stations, and even the county airport, but there was nothing to have stopped Ernie from lifting a car and driving herself away to anywhere in the country. Once, the mind would have boggled at that sweet old lady pinching some poor sap's jalopy, but no more.

It was quiet in that room without Flanagan's big personality, but I wasn't lonely for long. Q and his sister, Marlene, showed up at my door. I waved them on in.

"Ain't this fine?" I said. "I been wondering how you been getting along."

"Better than you have it would seem," Q said. "I'm afraid you've had quite an adventure since last we met, Mr. Malhaven. And not a very pleasant one."

"Oh, it wasn't all bad," I said, thinking back to that moment when Victoria had been restored to me. "But I'll admit, it's kinda boring around here. Entertain me with some news."

"That's why we came," Q said, his eyes bright with excitement. "I found out all about that family that adopted Peter Hornschmidt from the orphanage—the Bellinghams, you know."

"Is that right?" I said appreciatively. "I never doubted for a minute you'd come up with the goods. What can you tell me?"

"They live in Chicago. I have a contact in the research department at the Tribune who was very helpful. She sent me everything she could find on them. The family was quite wealthy at one time but lost everything in the stock market crash of '29. Only the one child, whom they rechristened Bryant Nicholas Bellingham after they adopted him. They have been living in what one might call reduced circumstances, but things were looking up for them. Bryant was engaged to marry the heiress to a large fortune, a Janice Newell."

"Janice?" I said, the image of Victoria's poor sister as I'd last seen her springing to my mind. "Say, is that a coincidence or what?"

"Not at all. The police have identified the woman they found murdered in the tunnel as Janice Newell. She disappeared from Chicago a few weeks ago. The rumor was her family objected to her marriage on the grounds that they knew nothing about Bryant's real background since he was adopted. They were threatening to disinherit her if she went through with it."

"Seems like they have a lot of nerve to demand his pedigree when their own daughter was an orphan herself."

"Apparently, they had been assured by the orphanage when they adopted Janice that the mother of the baby was from a very respected and well-to-do local family whose daughter had found herself in trouble. I guess that was good enough for them."

"That sounds like the orphanage was laying it on thick then. Both Victoria and her sister were left on their respective doorsteps with no explanation so far as I know."

Marlene jumped in. "Mr. Leonard at the Sisters of Mercy was telling me how much institutions like theirs depend on the patronage of wealthy donors and that adoptive parents often show their appreciation by writing out a check year after year. Perhaps someone at the orphanage in Farrelburg was anxious to impress the Newells. They would be very valuable patrons to have if they're as rich as they say."

"Say, does that mean you got that job with the nuns, then?" I asked Marlene.

"Yes, I did. I love taking care of the children, and Sam—that is, Mr. Leonard and… and everyone there has been wonderful to work with." Something about the way she stumbled over Leonard's name gave me a thought or two, but I decided not to give her any grief about it.

"What about having Sister Honoria as a boss? She's one that doesn't stand for any nonsense it seems to me."

"I don't intend to get up to any 'nonsense,' Mr. Malhaven," she replied smartly, giving me a grin to take the sting out.

"Sounds like a good plan," I said.

I thought over what Q had found out about these Bellingham and Newell families, trying to see how it all might fit together.

"So, maybe it's not such a coincidence that Janice came to visit Carsworth City then," I ventured. "If she knew Bryant was adopted from the Sisters of Mercy, maybe she thought she could find out more about his background and appease the parents. She struck me as someone who was used to money and lots of it. The notion of losing out on the family fortune just so she could marry the man of her dreams probably did not hold much appeal for her. We know Q managed to get a look at the records. Wonder if she could have gotten the same chance?"

Marlene nodded. "There are certainly times during the day when that part of the building is more or less deserted when everyone is in class or on the playground. If someone was bold enough and got the right opportunity, I think it's possible they could walk in and look up someone's file without being noticed."

"Bold enough, or cool enough," I observed, thinking that the woman I now knew as Janice was just the type to attempt a stunt like that.

"You think Miss Newell found her fiancé's record?" Q asked.

"Didn't you say you couldn't find that Bellingham file where you expected when you snuck in? If Janice found it first and took it away with her, it might explain one or two things. Say that the file just has the name of the parents. Maybe the murder was so infamous at the time, the nuns didn't feel the need to note it in the records, or maybe they want to protect the child by throwing a veil over that part of his history. But say Janice gets the name of the father, Walter Christopher Hornschmidt. Now she has to find out more about him, but that's not so easy for her. She's mostly just going out at night, so far as her sister knows anyway. Not so easy to stop in at the library, or even to consult our helpful morgue attendant," I said, with a nod at Q, "at the local newspaper."

I tapped my forehead with one finger to try and help the old brain along some. "She must have been feeling pretty frustrated until our fearless reporter lets slip with the very name she wanted to know more about so bad, but it sure wasn't what she wanted to hear. That Walter Hornschmidt was a nut who offed his wife and tried to do the same to his young son and was currently rumored to be an apparition haunting the local cemetery. Hardly the type of in-laws her parents would welcome into the family even after the fact. It was strange the way she reacted when I told her that name, but now it makes sense if it meant something to her after all."

"But once she found out what she wanted to know," Marlene asked, "wouldn't she have returned home to Chicago?"

"Maybe," I said. "Only by then, she might have been getting wise to the fact that there was something going on at the Wynter's place. She spent a lot of time roaming around at night. She might have seen a thing or two. And she now knows that her hoity-toity parents will never approve of the marriage even though Bryant, a.k.a. Peter, is the innocent victim of a crime. They're probably the kind to think his blood might be tainted from his father's madness. And, while we're supposing, let's just suppose she really loved this mug, Bryant Nicholas Bellingham, and was determined to marry him anyway. That means losing her money and he don't have none, so where's it gonna come from? Maybe that explains the blackmailing scheme she dreamed up."

"Blackmail?" Q and Marlene both came out with together.

"I guess that part wasn't in the papers," I said, grimacing at the thought of Victoria's sister stooping so low. "According to the Wynter sisters when I ran into them, Janice had found out about their operation and was putting the squeeze on them, only they thought it was her twin, Victoria, doing the squeezing. That's why they had to silence her."

Marlene made a quiet noise of sympathy like a dove. "Isn't it sad? It wasn't right, of course, for Miss Newell to do what you're saying, but to think of someone young and beautiful like that dying in such a way. It's too awful."

I could only agree with that sentiment. Janice had come across as a hard case, but they say a woman in love will do almost anything. I couldn't help but regret she'd come to such an end if for no other reason than she was the sister of the woman who was all in all to me.

Q must have had about the same thought. "The person I feel sorry for is Victoria Jankowski," he started to say.

We'd gotten so carried away with our "what if this" and "supposing that" we hadn't noticed the door had opened until we heard a soft voice.

"Why should you feel sorry for me?"

CHAPTER FORTY-ONE

My heart gave a flutter to see her face again. I knew I'd never get tired of staring at it, not in a million years, but Q and Marlene were looking mortified at being caught out gossiping about her, so I pulled myself together to smooth over the waters.

"Victoria, this is Marquis Sutherland, otherwise known as Q. I thought I introduced you once before, on the night of the séance," I said, remembering how riled up I'd been when I thought she was giving him the cold shoulder, "but that turns out to have been your sister instead, I believe."

Victoria set aside a package she'd brought in with her and gave Q one of her best smiles, shaking his hand firmly before agreeing with my guess. "I made the mistake of telling Janice about the séance, and she insisted on going. I didn't know how to stop her. She was a very strong-willed person," she added unhappily.

Q cleared his throat and ventured an explanation. "I was just trying to say how sorry I was, Mrs. Jankowski, how sorry we all are, I'm sure, that you lost your sister in such terrible circumstances."

She lay a hand on his arm by way of appreciation for his concern. "Thank you, Mr. Sutherland. That's very kind of you. And I remember your sister, Marlene, of course. You were such a help nursing Mr. Malhaven when he was so ill. He's very lucky to have such good friends."

Brother and sister seemed to guess that Victoria and me might have some catching up to do, so they made their excuses, leaving the two of us all alone.

"Hey," she said to me, coming over all shy.

"Hey," I said, feeling none too bold myself and wondering what to say next, but then she came over and took my hand, and it seemed we didn't need to say anything else at all. Not for a while anyway.

I could have sat like that forever, but maybe she was getting bored with it 'cause she asked me what we'd been talking about before she came in. I filled her in on Q's discoveries. I wouldn't of thought she could look any sadder, but when I got to the part about Janice's black-mail plot, she looked like she'd reached bottom.

"I wish she'd confided in me. I might have been able to help her somehow. Stop her from sinking to such a low ploy and putting herself in danger like that."

I nipped that in the bud. "You can't blame yourself for her ways. She was a cool customer all the way around. That's no way to go through life. People like that come to a bad end of some kind more often than not."

"I hate to confess it, but I didn't like her very much," she admitted. "Isn't that terrible? My own sister, my twin. It makes it almost worse to lose her knowing that I couldn't love her like I wanted to."

"Being made of the same flesh and blood is no guarantee of getting along. Look at them Wynter sisters."

"That's certainly true. When Mr. Flanagan and Mr. Cressley sketched out for me what Bernie and Ernie had been up to, you could have pushed me over with a feather. I guess I can take some comfort in the fact that I wasn't the only one they fooled so thoroughly. Poor Livinia. I was just visiting with her earlier. She has been truly humbled. All these years she thought she knew best and was doing the best for her sisters only to find out how much they resented her and that they had constructed an entire criminal enterprise right under her nose."

"And it's such a long nose, too." I couldn't help myself, but she gave me a playful slap on the arm just the same.

"You wouldn't have said that if you'd known I come with a generous invitation from her. Cressley is waiting downstairs to drive us home."

"Home?" I said, taken aback.

"Well, temporary home for you, I suppose. Livinia wants you to come stay at the house until you're fully recuperated. I believe she feels responsible for your plight because of her sisters, and also grateful to you because you saved her life apparently. You failed to mention that to me when we were underground."

"We had a lot of other things to talk about," I reminded her. "That's big of Liv, but I don't feel right crashing in like that."

"I think you'd be doing her a favor. I guess you've heard Ernie is still unaccounted for. I think it's making Livinia very nervous. Having a big, strong man about the place would be reassuring."

"A big, strong man with two bum legs," I reminded her. "Are they ready to let me loose from this joint?"

"Yes. I ran into the nurse in the hallway. She was just on her way to see if she could find you some crutches or a cane. The doctor says it's fine for you to walk some, as long as you take it easy on that leg. I hope you'll accept Livinia's offer. She's not the only one who wouldn't mind having a big, strong man about the place."

What guy in their right mind would keep protesting after that?

"And here," she said, jumping up to fetch and unwrap the package she'd brought in. "I had your clothes cleaned. And this," she added, drawing Lukasz' fedora out and offering it to me.

I took it gingerly, remembering where I'd left it, down in the tunnels below as a kind of benediction. "I'm beginning to wonder about this hat," I said. "I thought at first I was the luckiest guy in the world when you gave it to me, but bad luck seems to be following it around."

"Oh," she cried, looking tearful, "don't say that!"

I patted her on the arm. "Don't listen to me. You know I'm always making wise. It's a most excellent hat. It's not its fault the mook wearing it can't seem to stay out of trouble for more than two minutes at a time."

She smiled at that and pulled my old gray suit and trench coat and other such things out of the package, laying them out neat on the bed for me.

"And before I forget," she said, pulling something out of her purse, "this was tucked into the pocket of your coat. I wasn't sure what it was, but I brought it along in case it's important."

She handed me my lead sap, looking at me expectantly.

I laughed. "That's just my insurance policy. If you don't like the way someone's treating you, you can give them a tap on the noggin with it to remind them to mend their ways. Didn't do me much good down below, but we've been through a few things together, so I'm just as glad to have it back," I said, slipping it into the pocket of my suit.

I fingered the hat again. It reminded me of Janice, laid out so cold and still. Victoria must have had the same thing in her mind.

"They've taken her away," she said quietly. "Her parents. Back to Chicago. Given the circumstances of her death, they plan to have a private internment. I wasn't invited."

"That seems cold. Weren't they even glad to know she had a sister? Could be you could make it up to them a little for losing her."

"That's a good way to describe them. Cold, like ice. Meeting them helped me to understand Janice better. I was envious at first when I found out she'd been adopted, but now I wonder if I wasn't the lucky one after all."

"Those nuns raised you right, that's for sure."

"I wish we'd been kept together as children. That would have been nice, having a sister. It seems unfair we were split up like that, only to find each other for just a few weeks. I'll never even know now how she tracked me down."

"I have a kind of an idea about that. You never told me your maiden name, the one the nuns gave you."

She smiled like at a happy memory. "The nuns said the bells were ringing for Christmas Eve mass when they found me on the doorstep, like their very own babe in the manger, so they named me Bell. Victoria Daisy Bell. It's quite a name, isn't it? Why do you ask?"

"Her fiancé's name was Bellingham. We think maybe she got into the filing cabinets there at the orphanage and grabbed his file. Assuming the nuns know their ABC's, seems likely your file was right next to his. Maybe she grabbed the wrong file by mistake at first and happened to notice you'd been left on a doorstep the exact same night as she was. Might have got her to thinking. Maybe she was just curious to meet a fellow orphan who'd been abandoned under similar mysterious circumstances. Maybe she thought there was more to it than that. Either way, it must have been quite a shock when she came face to face with you, like she was looking in a mirror."

"For both of us," Victoria agreed, looking downhearted for a moment before bucking herself up. "No more crying for me. Not today, anyway. We have things to celebrate, like you getting out of here. I'll run downstairs and let Cressley know to bring the car around while you get yourself dressed."

"Aw, no help this time?" I asked.

She let loose with that thrilling laugh I loved to hear. "You look like you can manage on your own. Hurry up. We'll be waiting for you."

"Like the wind," I promised, but it wasn't anything like that fast. The pain was bearable, but I was shaky on my feet. I got everything in the right place, though, and even tied my tie in a respectable-looking knot, before slapping the fedora on my head telling myself not to be a superstitious fool about it. I heard the door open and was relieved that nurse must be back with some kind of stick to help me limp around, but when I turned it wasn't the kind of nurse I was expecting.

Not at all.

CHAPTER FORTY-TWO

"Why, Mr. Malhaven. Fancy us meeting again like this."

It was Ernie, dressed up as a nurse, starched cap and all, with a syringe clutched in one hand and a wild look in her eye that boded nothing but evil times ahead for me.

"Miss Ernestine Wynter," I said, stalling for time, "what a pleasure to see you again. What have you been up to? You've been missed by more than a few people. Won't they be glad to know you've turned up."

"I do admire your coolness under duress, Mr. Malhaven. It must have stood you in good stead during the war. I have the greatest admiration for all our valiant men who fought so hard to defend our country, but I'm afraid I can't let that stop me from doing what I must do."

"What must you do?" I asked. A little nonsensical, I know, but I'd like to see you stare down a lunatic on the warpath with the largest needle I ever seen in my life with as much aplomb.

"Why follow through on Bernie's plan and get rid of all the witnesses, of course. We've taken care of Monroe, Hooper, Victoria. Now you're the only one left, except Liv and Cressley, of course, and they don't count. They'll be loyal to the end, I'm sure."

It occurred to me wherever she'd been, she'd missed out on seeing the papers or she'd have known that "Victoria" was not Victoria at all, but I decided it wasn't the best time to try and set her straight. She obviously wasn't in her right mind and trying to reason with someone like that gets you exactly nowhere. Besides, best she didn't find out Victoria was still alive. Who knew what wild ideas that might give her?

"You're forgetting another witness," I said. "You took care of Bernie, too. Right between the eyes, didn't you?"

I found out fast that wasn't the smartest thing I ever come out with. Her beady eyes lit up with hatred, and she ran at me like a bull galloping toward a man in a funny suit waving a red cape over his head. In my defense, I was fresh out of bed and on my feet for the first time in days and balancing on a pair of gams that were none the best. That's the only excuse I can offer for how I found myself flat on the floor with a needle poking into my neck.

I'll never forget the feel of that cold steel. I didn't know what she had that syringe loaded up with, but I knew if she pushed the plunger, it was gonna be bad news for me. Panic leant me some pep as I fished my sap out of my pocket and swung it up at her arm with as much gusto as I could. I felt my skin tear as her hand slipped and the needle took a slice out of my neck, but at least I was free. She was scrambling around on the floor, trying to get her hands on her weapon of choice or mine, the sap I'd dropped after swatting her. I was doing my best to dampen her spirits by attempting to wrap her in a bear hug when the door swung open to reveal a startled-looking nurse holding a wooden cane in one hand.

"What on earth is going on?" was her entirely reasonable question.

Ernie squealed out a note of intense annoyance as other gawkers in the hallway started to gather round to catch a glimpse of the show. I'd finally got a hold on her, but she dug one boney claw into that fresh wound on my thigh making me see stars. Breaking loose, she lowered her head like the aforementioned bull and barreled out the door with a speed I would not have credited to a lady of her advanced years. By the time I'd recovered enough to try and make anyone understand what had happened, she had vanished again.

I had to cool my heels until the doc took another look at my leg, slapped a bandage on my neck, and Joey reappeared on the scene to take a statement. His men took the syringe away for testing, but we already knew it was probably chock full of the smack the sisters had been selling, more than enough of it to put even a big ox like me away for good. I finally limped through the hospital doors sporting my new cane, looking quite distinguished, I hoped, to find Victoria and Cressley waiting patiently out front with the big Caddy, having been filled in on the latest developments by Flanagan.

It occurred to me that with Ernie still on the loose and having a bee stuck under her bonnet about putting a period to my time among the living, heading out to the cemetery might not be the brightest idea. Taking a train across the country and leaving Carsworth City far behind, at least until the authorities caught up with her, would be the safest move. But then I thought about leaving Livinia, Cressley, and Victoria, especially Victoria, in the lurch like that. How could I relax on a beach somewhere, knowing they might be in danger? I'd always looked out for the men in my platoon as best I could during the war, and I figured this wasn't any different.

I wasn't surprised when we got out to the house to find I'd been assigned my old room in the servants' quarters. Old Liv might be feeling softer toward me, but everything has its place, don't it? Cressley looked apologetic, but I seen he'd been busy fixing it up, moving in a big double bed with a soft mattress and a plush armchair in one corner. It was nicer than my digs by a mile, so I didn't mind what part of the house I was assigned to. It was close to the kitchen, too. That's always convenient for a guy with an appetite like mine.

Liv granted me an audience where she managed to express her gratitude at my assistance with extricating her from the tunnel as well as her continued disdain for my profession, and perhaps my character as well, with a nimble combination of graciousness and condescension that you couldn't help but admire. I noticed Cressley stuck close to her, and she seemed kinder toward him than ever before, but she kept up the formal pose, at least when I was around.

Looking death in the kisser like that should have made her think twice, in my opinion, about her snobbish sense of family pride.

Daughter to a bootlegger and who knows what else, sister to a pair of drug-runners and murderers. In my opinion, it was Cressley who'd be coming down in the world if they made a go of it, but it was none of my business. I figured I only had one line of business to justify staying in that house. And that was keeping Victoria safe.

I didn't know where Ernie was or if she'd ever found out her mistake about the identity of the corpse she'd nicked that scarf from back in the tunnel, but I was worried if she found out Victoria was still alive and kicking, she might be tempted to address the situation. She and her dearly departed sister seemed to have a mania for tidying up loose ends that was downright unhealthy for the rest of us.

The first day there, after the excitement at the hospital and the feel of that needle jammed in my neck, I just sat in the sun and enjoyed the sensation of being alive. We were having one of those warm-ups you get sometimes in the fall right before winter arrives with a vengeance to kick you in the teeth. Victoria bustled around, bringing me treats and warm drinks she'd made with her own two hands and tucking in a blanket over my legs like I was an invalid. I thought I'd never enjoyed anything so much in my life. Worth getting a bullet through the leg any day of the week.

The second day, Cressley drove me into the city so I could check in at the paper. Didn't want Morty to get the idea he could make do without me on a permanent basis. They'd already spilled a lot of ink on the whole sorry tale, but I quickly typed out one of those "And I Was There" yarns for him. Figured I owed him that much for giving me the go ahead on the story that had changed my life. I left out a few details here and there in consideration of Victoria's privacy, and my own, but he still looked across the newsroom and gave me the nod when he read it. A nod from Morty is the equivalent of winning one of those Pulitzer things in our corner of the world.

Stopped in to jaw a bit with Q and then it was back to the bone-yard. I didn't like to leave them unsupervised too long lest something happen without me. Cressley dropped me off at the house, and I limped on down to the cottage to sit on the bench nearby which was my favorite spot. It wasn't long before my favorite person came out to join me.

"How were things at the paper?" she asked.

"They're lost without me, naturally," I said. "Maybe the cops will figure out what happened to Ernie soon, so I can get back to working full-time."

"I know you feel like you have to keep watch over me, but I can take care of myself. I'm the one that got you out of that tunnel, you know. Me and Lukasz, of course."

This was a mild difference of opinion we'd been having off and on —she insisting she'd heard that certain song and only Lukasz could have been whistling it, me saying it was just the wind.

"Is this the same dame that wouldn't dream of attending a séance because ghosts are all so much hooey?" I teased her, but she looked serious.

"I've been thinking about that, too. What if Lukasz was there? At the séance. It sounds to me from what you describe that the sisters were making up that stuff about Wally, working up to putting something over on you. But then a real spirit arrived. The one that asked that question. I don't think that was the sisters."

"Why not?" I protested. "You said yourself that they knew he called you Daisy."

"Yes. But think about what the spirit asked: '*Where's* Daisy?' Like it was looking for me and somehow knew Janice wasn't who they were looking for. The sisters didn't know about Janice. Why would they have phrased a question that way?"

"I think you're reading too much into it. Sure, Ernie and Bernie might be smarter than we gave them credit for, but that don't mean they're geniuses. Maybe it was the best line they could come up with."

"What about the way the planchette shot across the room and the table rose up from the floor? You said you couldn't figure out how they did that."

"That's only because I never got a chance to investigate. My hat got murdered," I said, fingering the brim of that same topper, "and Margo fainted away again, and that Mikey character was on the loose, and then I went down for the count with a fever. That gave the sisters more than enough time to do away with any evidence of funny business, and I can think of lots of ways to fiddle something like that."

She pulled away from where she'd been sitting close beside me and gave me a hurt look that made me sorry I'd ever said a single word. "Does it really bother you so much if I want to believe Lukasz has been watching over me?"

"Well," I said, pulling at my collar, which suddenly felt way too tight for my neck. "I guess I don't know that I like the idea of him hovering around over our heads while I try to get to know his wife a little better. I don't know if you noticed, but he ain't the only one who's sweet on you."

"I noticed," she said, settling back in. "But you don't have to worry. I have a feeling he was only around because he felt that I still needed him. That I wasn't ready to let him go. I think he was staying until he saw that there was someone else to watch over me."

"Someone like me?"

"Unless you know anyone else with cool gray eyes, a rakish scar, and a heart as soft and squishy as a marshmallow?"

If I admit I blushed at that description, dear readers, you won't razz me about it too much, will you?

She looked out to where the sun was starting to dip in the sky, turning it every color you could imagine, before speaking low and sweet. "It's all right, Lukasz, my love. Go home. Go home to Karolina. I'll be fine now."

That got to me but good. I reached up and took off the hat that had been his and laid it over my heart. "You're a good man, Lukasz Jankowski," I said solemnly. "Rest in peace."

Her hand stole into mine as we sat there together, watching the sun disappear.

CHAPTER FORTY-THREE

The next couple of days were about the same. Cressley ran me into town in the mornings so I could play at being a reporter for a few hours, then home, or at least what was starting to feel more and more like home, where I'd wander around and see what Victoria was up to. I was taking it easy on the leg, but there was still some things I could do to help her out seeing as how she was short-handed now that Hooper had gone on to his greater reward.

I got to be an expert at raking up leaves for one thing. You might even call it my specialty. I found it kind of soothing. I was a city boy, born and bred, and never experienced being out in nature like that before. Watching the leaves shift colors before they dived gracefully to the ground. Discovering some late-flowering bloom tucked in here and there among the gravestones. Even the silence of the place, a quiet such as I'd never known back in the city. It all stole over me, and I started to feel a kind of peace I realized I'd ever known before.

The only fly in the ointment was Liv. We could tell she was feeling better 'cause she started to assert herself again. Sending a stream of orders out to Victoria. Treating Cressley like the paid help again instead of the man of her dreams. And she didn't leave me out, although her biggest complaint to me was that I was eating her out of house and home. And what could I say to that? I'm a big guy. It takes more than the average to keep someone like me stoked up.

It got to where I ate like a bird at dinnertime, when me and Victoria were invited to attend Liv in the formal dining room while Cressley served us like the pro he was, towel draped over his arm and everything. Then late at night, I'd sneak into the kitchen and fix up a snack to tide me over to the morning, sitting at the head of the big table they had there for any informal meals, should there ever be such a thing in that house.

I enjoyed those midnight raids. Made me feel like a kid again, up to something he knew he shouldn't be when all the grownups were fast asleep. So, you can imagine my surprise one night when I was caught out, feeling like a very naughty boy indeed.

"If it isn't Mr. Malhaven. We do keep meeting in the oddest places."

It was her, in the flesh. Ernie. She seated herself at the other end of the long table and rested one hand on top of it. A hand wrapped around a gun. Surprisingly, she didn't seem in as big a hurry to use the gun as I would have expected, but I soon found out why.

"I've been coming down here to get a snack when no one is around, but, you know," she said, looking at me with eyes that looked about three times as big as normal, "it's been terribly lonely without Bernie. We were never apart a single day in our lives before now. I don't think I've ever felt so alone. I suddenly thought if I couldn't talk to someone tonight, I might just die."

I didn't know what her plan was, but I certainly didn't count on her having gotten over the idea of tidying me away like a clump of dust with a broom. If she felt more like talking than shooting, however, I didn't mind humoring her, but I wasn't gonna pretend we were making small talk at some kind of fancy cocktail party either.

"It's too bad you didn't think ahead to what you'd do without Bernie," I said, "before you shot her in the head."

I thought it would rile her up again like it did at the hospital, but she just gazed at me dreamily. It got through to me then that she'd broken into some of her own inventory and wasn't quite of the world at the moment.

She smiled in my general direction in a vague sort of a way. "I only did what Bernie asked me to do, you know. Her poor body was crushed by that terrible avalanche. You caused that, didn't you?" she asked, not angry, just like she was musing over the fateful sequence of events. "She knew she was dying by inches, and she didn't want to go that way, so she asked me to shoot her. I always shoot whoever Bernie tells me to."

"You do, do you?"

"Yes. Monroe, Hooper, even poor Victoria Jankowski. Bernie insisted we had no choice, and Bernie always knew best, but shooting Mrs. Jankowski was quite a shame. She'd always been so sweet to us up to then. So sympathetic about the way Livinia treated us and everything. I quite miss her, too."

"So," I asked, just to be clear. "It was always you that pulled the trigger, not Bernie?"

"It had to be me. Bernie was too vain to wear glasses, and she was just about as blind as a bat. Couldn't have hit the side of a whale, though she did manage to hit you, didn't she? Lucky shot?" Ernie tittered.

"Beginner's luck," I said, playing along. "It's just too bad for you that she missed the vital organs. I been expecting you to come back again to try and finish the job after that rumble at the hospital. Where you been all this time?"

"Hiding in the attic. There's a secret room up there where Bernie and I used to sneak away and play as children. Even Livinia never knew about it. We used to have great fun, but it's terribly lonely up there now."

"Maybe you should turn yourself in. You'd have plenty of company then."

"I suppose I would have some company, for a little while at least. Just until they get the electric chair ready for me. I will get the chair, don't you think? I've killed quite a few people, and who knows how many more are to come before all is said and done? They would've given poor Wally the chair, you know, only Father took care of him first."

"Is that right? How'd he do that?"

"Oh, I don't know. Paid somebody on the inside, or something. Father had people in his pocket everywhere back in those days. There wasn't anything he couldn't make happen if he wanted it to. Even framing Wally for killing his wife."

The dope takes people that way sometimes. Turns them into talkers. I got the feeling she'd had a lot on her mind lately and was anxious to share it with someone, anyone, and I just happened to be handy.

"Your pop framed Wally Hornschmidt for doing his wife? Why would he do a thing such as that?"

"To protect me of course, silly," she said, batting her eyelashes at me in a way that made my skin crawl.

"How's that?" I encouraged her.

"Because *I* killed her, of course. And tried to kill that brat, but I'm afraid he survived. I hadn't had so much practice at killing then. I'm sure I'd do a much better job of it now," she said brightly.

Feeling like I'd taken a blow to the head, it took me a minute before I could formulate another question. "Why? Why on earth would you attack Wally's wife and child? What were they to you?"

"They were nothing to me. They were just in my way. Wally loved me ardently, you know. He would have married me if he didn't already have a wife, so I decided it would be best to get rid of her. Father was rather angry with me when he found out what I'd done."

"I can imagine," I said, thinking that must be an understatement for what old man Wynter had felt to find out one of his precious girls was a killer. "So, are you telling me that you and Wally…"

"Were terribly in love? Yes. It's true I was a *bit* older than him, but he didn't care. He used to write me poetry. Isn't that romantic? I would have done anything for him, but I'm afraid it was his passion for me that brought him to grief in the end. I never imagined Father would try to blame his wife's death on him like that. I begged and pleaded with Father to spare Wally, to whisk him away somewhere safe. He could have done it if he wanted to, but Father was a hard man."

"Stern, was he?" I asked, trying to keep up with the revelations Ernie was throwing my way.

"He could be so very cruel. Making me believe Wally had come back to visit me from the spirit world when he knew how I'd felt about him. Isn't that a terrible thing for a father to do to his daughter? And, of course, it was he that forced me to give them up, you know. Bernie, and even Livinia, to her credit, tried their very hardest to talk him out of it."

"Them? Give who up?"

"My girls, of course. They say it runs in families, you know. Bernie and I were twins. Not identical, though people did say we looked very much alike, particularly when we were younger. So, I wasn't surprised at all when I had twins myself. And he just gave them away," she ended with a wail of grief that was the most heartfelt thing I'd heard from her yet. "My beautiful daughters, so perfect in every way."

<h1 style="text-align:center">CHAPTER FORTY-FOUR</h1>

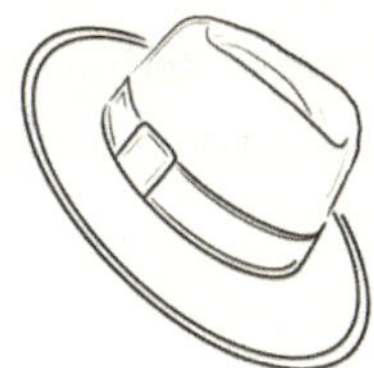

That did it. If my brain could have boiled over, it would have right about then. Wally and Ernie. Twin girls that were given away. It sent a shiver down my spine to even think my next thought, but I had to ask the question.

"When was that?"

"When? Well, Wally died in September, and our girls were born at the end of November. It took Father a while to make arrangements for them, so I had almost a whole month with them. The most wonderful, joyous month of my life. But that just made it all the harder when he found them a home. He came and took them away from me on Christmas Eve. Christmas Eve! Oh, how could he be so heartless as to rob a mother of her children on that night of all the nights in the year?"

Tears were rolling down her face. I felt like I was being pulled into a million pieces myself. To feel sorry for a killer, horrified for what was to come for her, I wouldn't have thought possible. But I had an inkling now of how she and her sisters had ended up so twisted. I'd thought my pops was no prize, but old Billy Wynter was making him look like a candidate for Father of the Year in comparison. What made a man so merciless and uncaring? Maybe his own harsh boyhood and desperate climb to success had left him that way, started a cycle of misery that was still playing out right before my eyes.

"He took them to the orphanages?" I said. "Split them up?"

"No," she said, looking startled. "He kept them together, of course. He placed them with a family far away in another state. So I would never have the heartbreak of seeing them from afar, you know, and not being able to claim them as my own."

"Did he?" I said, half to myself, not really thinking.

"Of course he did," she protested, looking at me with eyes that were growing wild. "That's what he told us. You can ask Livinia. It was the only way I could stand it, knowing they'd always have each other the way Bernie and I did."

I could see it now. A busy, impatient man with an empire to run, tired of having three women weeping and wailing over him, deciding it was easier to tell them what they wanted to hear. While all the time, he'd cold-bloodedly split the twin babies apart like some kind of judgment of Solomon and sent them on their different paths. I thought I could see now where Janice got that casually cruel streak from. I had a feeling she and Billy Wynter would have gotten along fine.

Whereas Victoria, she was as different as she could be. Maybe she took after Wally. He sounded like a soft-hearted sap. Victoria was no sap, but she had a softness and sweetness that seemed sorely lacking on the Wynter branches of the family tree.

Ernie was getting wound up now. "You don't understand what a comfort it's always been to me, knowing they're together. There's no bond like the one between twins, you know. Bernie and I could practically read each other's thoughts. There's a terrible silence there now in my mind where her voice used to be. I don't see how I can ever get used to it. I really don't," she said to me in a voice filled with despair.

I heard the kitchen door to the outside open behind me just then. I didn't have to turn around to see who it was. The look on Ernie's face told me everything I needed to know. I stood up to go and lend an arm to the woman I loved. There was a horrifying truth still to come for Ernie and for Victoria, and I didn't see any way to protect them from it.

Ernie rose to her feet, the gun trembling in her hand in a way that I couldn't help but be alarmed about as she pointed it at us.

"You're dead!" she screamed at Victoria.

"No," Victoria replied. I was proud of how calm and beautiful she looked standing there, facing down that gun like she hadn't a care in the world. "That was my sister, Janice."

"But… but… she said she was you. She looked just like you."

"Yes, we were twins. I'm sorry. We should never have played a trick like that on all of you to begin with, but I had no way of knowing it was going to lead to such terrible consequences."

"Twins?" Ernie blanched as white as white could be.

Victoria looked curiously at me, unsure of why, but aware there was a whole world of heartache behind the question. There seemed no getting around it. I thought it would be better to rip the bandage off the wound and get it over with. Looking Ernie square in the eye, I answered the plea for truth I read there.

"Yes, twins. Victoria and her sister, Janice, were separated as babies. Left on the doorsteps of two different orphanages. On Christmas Eve, 1922," I said, pulling Victoria close as though I could shield her from the things to come.

Ernie shrieked, an earsplitting noise such as I had never heard before and hope to never hear again, before collapsing back into her chair. She stared at Victoria, muttering, "My babies, my babies," over and over again. Her eyes glazed over, and I thought we'd lost her to some other world from which she'd never return, but suddenly her vision cleared as she looked at Victoria and seemed to really see her, see her and know her for her daughter for the first and last time.

"Why, aren't I a silly?" Ernie asked, in a high, girlish voice. "I really should have known. I should have known all along. You both have his eyes."

Ernie shifted her gaze to me then like a warning, so I knew what was to come just in time to turn away, pulling Victoria close to me so that she wouldn't see. The gunshot was loud in that quiet night, but Victoria's shocked cry was muffled by the fierce embrace I held her in. I pulled her out of the kitchen door as Cressley arrived on the scene from his room down the hall. I guess it didn't take him long to figure out what had happened because he followed us out into the night, his face long and full of the kind of sympathy that don't take words to express.

I handed Victoria off to him. "Take her to the cottage. Stay with her until I come."

He looked torn, and I knew he was thinking of Liv, but he turned and led Victoria away down the path, making a funny crooning noise that was his way of trying to comfort her. I stepped back in to gaze on what was left of Ernestine Wynter slumped on the table. Her marksmanship wasn't quite so spot on this time, but it was effective, nonetheless. I'd thought once that I would crow over the death of this woman, this vile monster, but now I felt only a deep sorrow at the waste of it all.

Her face was almost untouched. It looked smoothed out by death, almost like she was a girl again. I got a glimpse now of that other Ernestine, a woman pretty and charming enough to fool a man into risking his family and his life for love of her. Overcome with tiredness, I sat back down at the other end of the long table, like she and I were the hosts at a dinner party, but the guests were yet to arrive.

While I was musing on that, a guest did arrive—Livinia. I got the feeling she had taken the time to get dressed and do her hair, confident that whatever calamity was happening could wait until she was properly attired. She took one look at her sister, then came over and sat in a chair beside me.

"Did she discover the truth?" she asked me, looking rigidly ahead.

"The truth?" I repeated, too tired to play at guessing games.

"About Victoria and… and Janice."

"You knew? Since when?" I demanded.

She turned to look at me. "Since I found out that the woman who was killed in the tunnel was Mrs. Jankowski's twin sister, I've had a feeling of dread. I hoped I was wrong, but your face tells me I was right."

"I'm afraid so. The truth all come out just now, and it was too much for her to take," I said, looking down the table at the result.

"I suppose it's better this way," Liv said. "And not just for me," she hastened to add, as if she could tell what I was thinking. "Father might have been able to protect her once, but there would be no saving her from punishment now. I suppose he lied to us about keeping the babies together. Mrs. Jankowski never mentioned to us that she had a twin."

"Yeah, she never knew until a few weeks ago. Mr. Wynter split them up between two different orphanages, God knows why."

"Probably just because he could. That's the kind of man he was. It's why he let her have them for those few short weeks, just to make it even harder for her when he ripped them from her arms. I know you probably think my sisters were fiends. You may even think I am one," she said, giving me as piercing a look as I ever got. "But no one will ever know what we endured at that man's hands. Things no child should ever have to endure from a parent. Those things leave a mark that is impossible to erase."

What could I say to that? It was right along the very same lines I'd thought of myself.

"I wonder," she added, "if Mr. Monroe knew about the girls and kept track of them after Father took them away from Ernie. He was the one who insisted we hire Mr. Jankowski as caretaker. Maybe it was his way of trying to make it up to Victoria. He was a rather sentimental man at heart, but it seems little enough to have done for my niece. She was entitled to so much more."

Not sure of the proper etiquette for trying to encourage someone in her unfortunate position to buck up, I reached out and patted one of her elegant hands awkwardly with my big paw. She sniffed at that in her old Liv way, saying, "I'd better telephone for the police," as she got up. At the door, though, she turned back to look at me.

"Thank you, Mr. Mal-*haven*."

I had to grin. Hearing her say my name proper felt as good as a benediction from the Pope.

CHAPTER FORTY-FIVE

I filled in Flanagan on all the doings when he arrived with his boys. He was plenty satisfied. It was a lot less trouble for them the way things had turned out than if they'd had to stage a whole trial with the inevitable result. People weren't too keen on seeing a woman sitting in the electric chair, even if she was a killer, so I could tell he was happy to be able to skip the whole circus.

Escaping the kitchen as soon as I could, I headed to the cottage, worried about Victoria. Cressley looked relieved to see me and cut out to go comfort Liv, I assumed. I stood in the doorway, hesitating. I'd never been inside. It felt strange to stride right in like I had every right to be there, but then she looked up at me in such a way that I found myself sitting beside her and holding her close there on the little sofa that sat in the pretty sitting room she'd made for herself and Lukasz once upon a time.

She cried quietly. No sobbing, just a soft, gentle rain of tears that gradually wore themselves out. There don't seem to be nothing much to say in a situation like that, not that I knew of anyhow, so I just kept her company until she felt like talking.

"Is she gone?" she finally asked.

"Yes."

"I've been thinking over what she said. Does it mean what I think it means?"

"I'm afraid so, honey."

"She… she was my… *our* mother. Did… did she kill Janice?"

I answered that one with silence. There's some things too hard to say out loud, but she got the picture.

"I see. Poor thing. To find that out. She was sorry, wasn't she?"

"More than you'll ever know," I assured her.

"Why did she give us up, separate us like that? Didn't she want us?"

"She wanted you both more than anything on this earth. It was her father that wouldn't allow it and had a brainstorm to split you apart. I get the idea he was a nasty piece of work."

She shuddered. "He was. I was terribly frightened of him, actually. I didn't tell Lukasz, didn't want him to worry, but I wasn't sorry one bit when Mr. Wynter passed away. I would never have stayed on here if he'd still been alive. I suppose he was my grandfather, wasn't he? What a strange thought. And Bernie and Livinia are my aunts? I might have been better off when I was still an orphan," she choked out, with a gurgle of a laugh that held little enough of mirth in it.

"Hey," I said, "you're still you. It don't matter what you come from, it matters who you are now."

"I suppose so. I guess the next question, I'm almost afraid to ask. She said we had his eyes. Did she tell you who my father was?"

I didn't know how to answer that one. It seemed like too many blows for her to take one after another, but I don't have much of a poker face. She could tell I knew, and I knew she wouldn't rest until she got it out of me.

"Remember our old friend Wally the ghost?"

She did laugh out loud at that, tickled at the absurdity of it. "This gets better and better. Both my parents are murderers. You see who you've gotten yourself mixed up with."

I hastened to set her straight. "You're wrong there. Wally got a bum rap. The worst he's guilty of is being lured away from his wife by a fascinating older woman."

"But if he didn't… oh, don't tell me," she said. "I don't think I can take it. The jealous other woman?"

Again, I let my silence do the talking.

"Okay," she said. "So, Wally and Ernie were my parents, and Ernie killed Wally's wife and tried to kill his son. Wait—we've forgotten all about little Petey. Doesn't this make Peter Hornschmidt, now Bryant Bellingham, my half-brother?"

"I guess that's right," I said, not having considered that angle before. "What are the odds of Janice meeting and falling in love with her own half-brother? Guess it's just as well her parents wouldn't approve the marriage. That would be a hard thing for poor Petey to find out, wouldn't it?"

"It's hard to take it all in," she said, drawing a deep breath. "Is that it? Anything else I need to know about my loving family?"

"Only that it don't matter what any of them done. It's a terrible thing to have to think about, but it don't change who you are. They can't touch you. None of them can. I won't let them."

She smiled at that. At the folly of my thinking I held some kind of power over the dead, or the living for that matter.

"How was Livinia?" she asked.

"Liv was… Liv," I answered. "She don't waste her words, but she said enough for me to make out what was between the lines. Those girls must have gone through hell before their old man died. She said it left a mark, and I believe her. Makes me feel a little softer toward those two, Ernestine and Bernadette. They were twins. Did you know that?"

"No, they never said, but they were very alike, weren't they?"

"Maybe too much so. I think they created a world of their own. A world where they could justify anything they did so long as they did it together."

"I wonder what Janice and I would have been like if we'd grown up together. I feel like I've gained and lost a sister and a mother and a father all at once."

I hugged her close. "The good news is you won't get rid of me so easy."

"Oh, that's *good* news, is it?" she said with a bit of that old teasing manner I liked to see. It meant she might be down, but she wasn't out. Not by a long shot.

That's not to say she didn't have some bad times over those next weeks. There's not many that have had to take so many knocks, but Victoria was no quitter. I watched her fight back from her grief too many times to think that.

Ernie and Bernie were shoved into the family vault with their old man. That seemed cruel in its own way, that they should spend eternity locked up with him, but Livinia was a big believer in what's dead is dead and gone, so what did it matter? That's what she said, but I noticed that didn't stop her from picking out a nice double plot under an old oak tree for her and her hubby. No family vault for Liv.

And yeah, that's right, I said hubby. I guess after all the shame her family had brought upon the Wynter name, she decided marrying the butler would be the least of it. So, one Sunday morning, not too many weeks down the line, saw me standing up for Mr. Cressley in my crisp new gray suit courtesy of Q's mother while Victoria walked her aunt down the aisle. They ain't your average married couple, but they're happier in their way than many another I could name.

Livinia insisted that Victoria move into the main house. After all, she's in line for all that Wynter money now, and Liv is anxious to show her the ropes. That gave me a sinking feeling the first time I thought about it. I'd already felt like she was out of my league, and now she was an heiress to boot. I was ready to fall on my sword and make myself scarce, but she set me straight double-quick on that by threatening to break both my kneecaps if I tried to run, and my legs are bad enough as it is.

So, where does that leave yours truly?

You'll find me comfortably settled into that little cottage right there on the grounds of Wynter's Hill Cemetery. I still string along for the Crier whenever Morty has a scoop to throw my way, but I spend a lot of time now taking care of that self-same boneyard where it all started. It's the last place I expected to end up, and there's times when I ask myself if I shouldn't be more ambitious. Me and Victoria are taking things slow, but that's not to say I don't feel like I shouldn't hurry up and make something more of myself for her sake.

But then again, when I finish up my work and come to rest on my favorite bench there by the cottage at the end of the day, and a certain someone settles down beside me to keep me company, slipping her hand into mine as we watch the sun do a disappearing act that never gets old, I figure maybe the future can just take care of itself.

ABOUT THE AUTHOR

Helen Whistberry is an indie author and artist who took up writing after retiring from a long career working in libraries. She is the author of the Jim Malhaven Mysteries series, light noir novels with a cozy mystery feel and a touch of the paranormal that pay loving tribute to the wise guy detectives of the 1940s and '50s; and a Christmas-themed Gothic ghost tale as well as contributing short stories to numerous anthologies. When not writing or drawing, she enjoys exploring the natural world of the Southeastern United States and loves all animals, including her two cats and a rather silly six-pound Chihuahua. She also loves to read and review books by fellow indie authors. You can find out more about her books, art, and book reviews by visiting

www.helenwhistberry.com

Thank you so much for reading *The Weird Sisters*. I hope you enjoyed reading it as much as I enjoyed writing it!